Sweet Pea
The Chateau Series Book 2

EMMA SHARP

Copyright © 2019 EMMA SHARP

All rights reserved.

ISBN: 9798687638333

DEDICATION

To my Family.

Other Books by Emma Sharp

The Letter – Chateau trilogy book 1

Secrets and Surprises – Chateau trilogy book 3

Nellie, The Diary of a French Bulldog Puppy

Coming soon – Innocence in Provence

ACKNOWLEDGMENTS

Editor - Lynn Worton

Cover design - Sarah Jane Design

Web - www.emma-sharp-author.com

Email - info@emma-sharp-author.com

1

I wake the next morning in the middle of a big double bed; wrapped in a warm duvet. Alone. It's eerily quiet. Where's Enzo? No creaking doors, thudding in the attic or clanking pipes. Carefully, I untangle myself from the bedding and look out of the small window; the land is huddled under a blanket of fresh snow, at least a foot deep. How am I going to get home? Just as I start to look for my clothes, Enzo arrives with a breakfast tray.

"Hey, you should be in bed." He puts the tray down. Realising I'm only in my underwear, I take his advice and make a dash for the bed; my head instantly throbbing as it hits the pillow. Looking at me sympathetically he continues, "You need to take it easy for a few days, here, get this down you."

I look at him over my bowl of porridge. "I don't remember going to bed, in fact, there's quite a lot I don't remember."

"Well, I'm not surprised; you took a nasty knock on the head when you lost control in the snow, but the only thing that matters now is that you're here, safe."

Finishing my breakfast, I look up, "Where did you find Shadow?"

Taking the tray from me, he replies, "Well, I got a call from Xavier, he was worried that you'd set off and the forecast was bad; apparently he tried to talk you out of going but… Well, you went anyway and ended up in a ditch. I was on my way to look for you when I came across Shadow – running back towards the village. All's well that ends well."

I sigh and touch my head to feel a neat row of Steristrips above my eye, which feels swollen. Wincing, I ask, "Have I got a black eye?"

"You look like you've had a session with Rocky, but you'll live," he replies. His phone rings. Looking at me, he apologises and takes the call. "Sorry, I have to go, there's a horse down in the snow that can't get back up, it doesn't sound good, but I'll try my best. Don't do anything; I'll be back as soon as I can."

I climb out of bed and watch his Land Rover disappear behind the trees; I do hope he'll be okay. Locating the bathroom, I manage a quick shower. Not wanting to wear the same pants, I borrow a pair of Enzo's; too big but my jeans will hold them up. With Enzo absent, I examine his temporary home. I notice the cabin is small but snug, one open plan living-kitchen, with a bedroom and bathroom. Not much to explore, no photographs of family or friends, and very few personal effects. Glancing at my phone, I see I have several missed calls and texts from Xavier. I really don't fancy a lecture from him right now, so I send him a quick text.

Sorry to scare you, I'm safe and well at Enzo's, back soon.

"There, that's as much as he's getting!" I tell Shadow, who barks in agreement.

Flopping onto the sofa, I turn the TV on, but can't concentrate, pressing the off button I lean my head back and close my eyes. The last few months of my life are projected onto the inside of my eyelids like a film, starting with the letter from the solicitor; informing me that I'd inherited a Chateau in France. But they omitted some vital information – like its state of disrepair, and the secret staircase hiding treasures in the attic, the false wall concealing an old Bugatti, the hidden wine cellar, battling with red tape, and much more. The highs, making new friends, and the lows, as some people just want to be enemies.

Then there's Enzo, the Scottish vet with Italian ancestry, working in the south of France. I know I'm falling for him; but does he feel the same? He's going back to Glasgow in the summer to work at his local practice, while I've just committed to making a new life here in the Ardeche. Is there much point pursuing this burgeoning romance? A disturbing thought pops into my head – has he already got a girlfriend? He hasn't mentioned anyone, and I haven't found a photograph at the side of his bed. Surely, he wouldn't have let me kiss him if he were currently in a relationship. He doesn't seem like a player. Hey, what would I know? I have a poor track record when it comes to men.

I wish I could be more like my good friend Jenny, 'enjoy every day as if it's your last,' that's her motto; perhaps she's right. I've just had a lucky escape. This is my one and only life. It's not a practice. So, what if he goes back home? 'It's not the end of the world' as my gran so often used to say. She had so many funny sayings, 'take the bull by the horns'; 'make hay while the sun shines'; 'strike while the irons hot'; 'if the cap fits, wear it' among others. I do miss her words of wisdom. I'm brought back to the present by my phone, a text from Xavier.

Stay where you are, for now, ze electricity supply is off, zey are trying to fix it, will let you know when it's back on.

What am I supposed to do now? I can't stay here, there's only one bed for a start. I can manage without electricity for a day or two, can't I? I've got oil and logs. I won't tell Enzo; I'll just ask him to take me home when he returns.

I'm woken by a kiss on the top of my head. "How are you feeling? Sorry I was longer than I'd hoped; there's a tree down on the road, the power's out. You'll have to stay here until they get it back on."

Sighing, I ask, "How's the horse?" Enzo just shakes his head and walks over to feed the log burner. I know my protests will fall on deaf ears, but I'll try anyway. "I'll be fine at home; I've got logs and oil…"

"Non-negotiable. You're staying here, where I can keep an eye on you," he says, without looking in my direction.

Okay, I didn't think I'd win that battle. My phone rings, it's the insurance company asking where I want Dolly recovering to. I instruct them to take her to Jacques, he'll repair her for me.

"You need a 4x4, something like mine, I know you're attached to Dolly, but she's not practical; or very safe." Enzo lectures.

Nodding, I concede, "If this is a taste of winter here, then you're right, but I'm not getting rid of her." After supper, I know I need to address the elephant in the room, "I'll sleep on the sofa, it's quite comfortable…"

I don't manage to finish before Enzo interrupts, "I don't think so, not with a concussion; you use the bathroom first while I grab a pillow and blanket."

When I wake the following morning, Enzo is nowhere to be seen; just a note by the kettle, 'called out to an emergency, will ring'. After breakfast, I get another text from Xavier.

Ze power is back on.

I quickly reply.

Great, can you pick me up?

I feel bad bailing on Enzo, only leaving a note saying, 'Xavier called, and I scrounged a lift home', but I'm still confused and unsure of what to do about him. I never was particularly good at making the first move, and I've got so much to do; only a few days to Christmas. I'm making Christmas lunch at the Chateau for Alice, Gus, and Xavier; Enzo is on call but said he'd come if he's available. I've never liked Christmas since my parent's accident, gran always tried her very best, but it was never the same. I've worked for the last three Christmas days; always volunteered, it helps to keep busy. Stops me from dwelling on the past.

Xavier stares at me as I climb into his truck. "It looks worse than it feels," I say, as I fasten the seatbelt. Thankfully, he has the good grace to keep quiet on the journey home.

Alice is in the kitchen at the Chateau when I get back, with hot soup bubbling in a pan. She kisses me; then chastises me for going out alone in the snow. Before they leave, Alice announces that Christmas lunch will be at the farmhouse and that I'm to do nothing. I accept graciously, not really feeling up to cooking a goose and all the trimmings. The events of the last twenty-four hours are creeping up on me, and I know I ought to rest. Yes, practice what you preach, Laura.

2

I hear nothing from Enzo for the rest of the day; is he still out working? No, he would have rung or text to put my mind at rest, he's that sort of guy; trustworthy and dependable. I guess he must have arrived back at the cabin, seen my note, and be feeling hurt or let down. Should I have stayed? I'm just so confused. It's taken me months to come to the decision to relocate here and try to set up a business. I don't feel ready to throw a relationship into the mix right now, I need to concentrate and keep focused; it's hard enough dealing with Xavier. I don't need another man muddying the water. Yes, I need to keep my relationship with Enzo strictly in the 'friend zone'. Did I lead him on? I remember kissing his soft lips when I woke up. I can feign amnesia; after all, I did have a mild concussion. Yes, if he mentions it, I'll pretend I don't remember, but I really should text him and thank him for his help.

Xavier dropped in, so I scrounged a lift. I'm feeling much better now, thank you so much for all your help, and especially for finding Shadow. I hope your case wasn't too tricky. Change of plan, Christmas lunch is at the farmhouse now, instead of the Chateau. Hope you can make it.

Laura

I have an early supper and call it a day with no reply from Enzo. I know I've made the right decision; I really can't do with the anguish that romance seems to have as a side effect. Will he ring me? Should I text him? What shall I wear? How long do I wait before sleeping with him? So much insecurity; I just don't need it.

Shadow won't settle and insists on coming to bed with me, it's not like him. But I persist and eventually manage to get him to stay in his bed; just as I'm dropping off to sleep, I hear my bedroom door creak open. Blinking my eyes, I feel Shadow jump up onto the bottom of my bed; perhaps he's feeling a little shaken up too. The next thing I remember is waking up to find his head on the pillow next to me and someone banging on the door.

What time is it? Twenty past nine. I've slept for twelve hours! A quick glance at my phone reveals several missed calls from Sylvie and Alice, ooh, and a text from Enzo!

The banging starts again. Groggily, I drag myself over to the window to see Xavier's truck on the drive. I pull on a jumper over my fleece pyjamas and make my way downstairs before unlocking the big door.

"Mama sent me, she was worried," he says, pushing past me and placing a bowl of what looks like a stew on the table.

"I'm fine, I just needed to sleep, thank Alice for the… err… what is it by the way?"

He just shrugs in his usual manner and replies, "Food." Then carries on and relights the fires in the kitchen and small sitting room, before joining me for coffee. I pretend not noticing as his eyes keep straying to my shiner. Trying to carry on in business mode, I mention that I'm going to need a more suitable vehicle for winter.

"You need ze truck – like mine."

"No, it's too big, just a small 4x4 will be fine, I think I'll ring Jacques…" as usual he doesn't let me finish.

"I will call my cousin Bert, 'e will know of one going cheap." I smile and thank him for his generous offer but tell him that I would prefer to ask Jacques. "Where is ze dog?" he asks, then whistles. Shadow responds and bounds down the stairs into the kitchen. "I will take 'im 'unting today,"

"No way! He is still a little shocked after the accident, he needs to rest too. He's going nowhere."

"You are making 'im soft…"

I stand and gesture towards the door, telling him to take Beau out hunting instead. I close it firmly behind him as he takes the hint. Oh, the text from Enzo, at least he's still talking to me; I open it with trepidation and read.

I must go back home; my grandfather has had a heart attack. If you feel up to driving, you could come with me to the airport, then borrow the Land Rover until I get back. My flight is booked for six this evening. Let me know. x

Oh no, poor Enzo!

I'm so sorry to hear that. Yes, I'm fine now, sounds like a good idea, thank you.

Am I insured to drive it? A quick call to my insurance company sorts that problem. Next, what should I wear? So it begins!

I ring Sylvie and thank her for her concern, informing her that I'm fine now and invite her and her parents' round for Christmas drinks tomorrow evening. Something to look forward to. Trying to fill my time, I search for a suitable vehicle online, as well as catching up with emails from the building contractors that I've chosen to do the ground works for the caravan site. Typically, they are now on holiday for the festive season, so won't respond to my queries for at least a couple of weeks. The weather won't help either, the ground will be too hard now and too wet when it thaws.

Looking up from my laptop I see Enzo's Land Rover coming down the drive. Why do I still feel like a nervous teenager, having parked him firmly in my 'friend zone'? As I open the door, he leans in for a kiss. I manage to turn my cheek towards him just in time to avoid the kiss landing on my lips. Undeterred, he smiles and announces that my swelling is going down nicely. I try to keep the conversation on him, "How is your grandfather?"

"He's eighty-four and already quite frail, so I'm expecting the worst." He replies solemnly.

Thankfully, the roads have been cleared.
Enzo talks me through all the controls as
drives to the airport. He insists I have a
practice drive in the carpark before he leaves
to catch his flight. I don't hang about and
offer him my unbruised cheek for a quick
peck before he grabs his luggage and enters
the airport building.

Once he's out of sight, I sigh and sag back
into the seat. This car really is agricultural; the
gear change takes some getting used to, but as
Enzo said, if you can drive a 2CV, then you
can drive anything. The roads are quiet and
being high up gives me a clear view. Shadow
sits in the passenger seat glancing in my
direction regularly. I hope the accident hasn't
frightened him; I really must get him a
restraining harness.

I find myself comparing my surroundings
with home; very few of the properties are
decorated with flashing lights or have
exuberant Christmas decorations festooning
their windows and doors. Some villages, like

ours, have a tree in the square, but it's far more understated and less commercialised than home. The notion of sending everyone you know a tacky Christmas card doesn't seem to be the norm either. I have, of course, sent and received said cards to my housemates – previous housemates I should say; having already given the landlord my notice. I wonder who the next occupant in my old, tiny bedroom will be? I'm sure Jenny will keep me informed.

I park the Land Rover outside the Chateau and mentally cross it off my list as too agricultural. I'm sure I can do better. More comfort required I think, but nothing flash, I need to be frugal – back to my internet search.

3

Just before I fall asleep, I receive a text; its Enzo.

Arrived safely. I hope you had a pleasant journey home. What do you think of the Land Rover? Xx

How should I answer? The truth, I think. Should I put kisses?

Thanks for letting me know, I hope your grandfather is as comfortable as possible. Thanks for the loan of the Land Rover, it's practical but a bit too agricultural for me, I think.

I'm not going to overthink this; no kisses, I don't want to encourage him. Shadow is once again in bed with me. I can't be bothered to wrangle with him tonight, but tomorrow I'll bring his bed and put it in the corner of my room, he can sleep there.

I wake feeling better, the dull ache behind my eye has at last gone, the swelling has just about resolved itself too. I'll leave the Steristrips on for a couple of days, I don't want to risk disturbing my wound, not on Christmas Eve. I have guests coming and need to prepare; drinks and canapes will suffice, nothing formal. The shops in the village will close at lunchtime for at least three days, so that's my first job.

I'm surprised to find the small village almost deserted. Back home, the shops will be manic, with people frantically rushing to buy last minute presents and food, but it's quite different in rural France. It seems to be about spending time with family and close friends, and, of course, celebrating the religious festival, rather than focusing on the commercial side of things. People in the countryside seem to be more self-sufficient and share their surplus with each other, so they have less need to purchase food. Which gets me thinking about the walled garden; I need to research what to grow and when to plant it. I can't keep accepting produce from Sylvie. Xavier will have to help me, perhaps we need a rotavator, I'll ask him; it will give us something to talk about tomorrow. It's going to be a long day.

The afternoon brings leaden skies and heavy rain, at least it will help to get rid of the snow. I busy myself making canapes with various toppings, many containing chevre, mixed with local produce, including almonds, olives, smoked trout, figs, different grilled vegetables and of course truffles! Luckily, I went to the supermarket just before my accident, so have plenty of drinks in.

My phone rings just as it starts to get dark; its Xavier, what does he want?

"Ze pond is going to flood, we need to open ze sluice; come and watch so you can do it yourself in case of ze emergency."

I start to reply but realise he's gone. Where is the sluice? I suppose it must be at the pond.

Dragging on a big coat and wellies, I head in the general direction with my torch. I can hear the stream before I see it, the snow has thawed quickly, and the heavy rain has turned it into a cascade.

I can make out a figure in the distance holding a large lamp, it must be Xavier. As I get nearer, I can see he's at the far side of the pond. The stream is too full and fast flowing, coming right over the top of the small wooden bridge. The only way across would be to go right back behind the Chateau to the farmyard area, where there's a more substantial stone bridge, or down the drive to the road and back up the other side of the farmhouse. Neither option appeals, so I stay where I am and ring him.

He agrees and says, "It's too dangerous to cross ze stream, drive to ze road and walk up from ze farmhouse." When I arrive, dripping and cold, I'm too late to witness the spectacle; he has already lifted the sluice gate to allow the water to escape into the storm drain and down to the small river across the road. Water is running in tiny rivulets down his face, which doesn't seem to bother him, and he says, "I could not wait any longer, ze pond would 'ave flooded ze fields and spoilt ze vines, and zen flooded ze farmhouse. Ze trout would 'ave escaped too! I will leave it wide open tonight and come back in ze morning to close it again."

"I'll come with you in the morning," I say and leave to go and get ready for my guests.

I'm showered and changed with just minutes to spare as Sylvie, and her parents arrive. They find it quite amusing that the last time they visited for the evening, there was a big thunderstorm, and once again it's pouring with rain. Pedro has also put his 2CV away for the winter and arrived in an old 4x4. He has a few ideas for suitable vehicles for the winter for me to consider, a Suzuki Jimny is one of them.

My canapes are well received, and Rose discusses other toppings and various recipes that could be used at future functions. The rain has eased off, but Rose is anxious to leave as she explains that the road often floods after a thaw, as the meltwater runs down off the hills. "The gorges where we bathed in the summer will now be a raging torrent, quite spectacular, a visit for another day," says Sylvie.

The first thought as I open my eyes on Christmas morning is Enzo, quickly followed by a sense of guilt; shouldn't I be thinking about my parents or gran? I send him a quick text.

Merry Christmas, hope you manage to enjoy some of the festivities.

Should I have enquired after his grandfather? Perhaps not, what if he's already dead? I peer over to see Shadow has stayed in his bed in the corner, good boy. I wander over to him lazily and scratch his head in his favourite place and wish him, Joyeux Noel, before going in search of breakfast, toast with honey. Lunch isn't until three this afternoon. I've agreed to go over at two; Alice is going to church this morning with Gus. Apparently, Xavier refuses to attend. That reminds me, the sluice gate! Pulling on warm clothes and wellies I make my way over to the pond with Shadow to find Xavier waiting for me.

"Glad you managed to make ze appearance," he says, wearing his usual camouflage jacket. No Santa jumpers in sight.

"It is only just after nine… and happy Christmas to you too!"

He just scoffs and proceeds to educate me on the operation of the sluice gate; it's not that difficult, only a handle to turn which opens or closes a wooden board to regulate the water level in the pond. The stream has now calmed down and the danger has passed. Xavier suggests we leave it slightly open in case there is more torrential rain. Back at the Chateau, I text the girls in England, who are probably working anyway; the NHS doesn't stop just because it's Christmas. I don't have a reply from Enzo, perhaps he's with his grandfather.

I arrive at the farmhouse with my few gifts. Alice is thrilled with the amethyst pendant I chose for her and Gus is pleased with his gift voucher, but Xavier just shrugs as I hand him a bottle of cognac; which I happen to know he's partial to. Alice offers me her neatly wrapped parcel. Opening it reveals a beautifully knitted scarf. She beams with delight as I admire it, and I'm acutely aware that it's more than just a scarf; it's a symbol of just how much she's recovered from being able to create such a thing. "Oh, Alice, it's beautiful, thank you. I will treasure it."

I help to serve dinner, which consists of roast goose with stuffing, gravy, and seasonal vegetables, not unlike the traditional British fayre. Pudding is plum and cinnamon crumble with crème anglaise, flavoured, of course, with truffles; a French twist to an English classic, and it's perfect. I insist on helping with the dishes while the boys watch TV, something I've never witnessed Xavier doing previously, always too busy, I suppose. I make my excuses and leave just after six, another Christmas day dispatched!

Boxing day dawns bright and crisp, an improvement on the dark skies of late, which helps to lift my mood. I spend the morning looking at gardening websites to gain more information about some of the crops Xavier suggested yesterday, then, in the afternoon, I walk over to inspect the walled garden. I'm surprised to find it cleared of all the dead and overgrown vegetation, I know John made a start, but Xavier has obviously finished the job. I just need to wait a few weeks for the soil to dry out and warm up a little, but I have a greenhouse, so could start sowing seeds indoors soon.

I desperately want to get started on the campsite but know I have a while to wait yet. Feeling a little bored, I sit and work out which fruit and vegetables to grow next season with the help of the internet and order the seeds online. Xavier insists that we don't need any new machinery or tools, as he has already prepared the walled garden and can cultivate the land with the tractor, which I'd forgotten about.

4

The rest of the week passes by slowly; I busy myself trying to draw plans of how I'd like the rooms to look when I start taking paying guests, but I know that realistically it won't be this season, perhaps next year. I need the money from the sale of the Bugatti before I can start that project, and the auction isn't for a while yet. The campsite and possibly some functions, as well as selling produce, is enough for the first year. As soon as the holidays finish, I'll start sprucing up the main rooms downstairs. I'm sure I can manage to paint the walls and hang the pictures with help from Xavier, who is now officially my general manager. Just as I'm researching period colours online, my phone rings; its Enzo.

"Hello, how are you… and your family?" I ask tentatively.

After a short silence, he says, "My grandfather died peacefully yesterday with his family at his side."

"Oh, no; I'm so sorry."

"He's had a good life; at least I managed to see him again. I've decided to return to France tomorrow, there's nothing I can do here now. Can you collect me from the airport, please?"

We make our arrangements and hang up. I pity Enzo, what a sad way to spend Christmas.

It's another bright sunny day, and I enjoy the drive to the airport. As I'm sat waiting for Enzo to appear, it suddenly dawns on me that I won't have a vehicle for a while as Enzo will need his Land Rover back for work. I don't much fancy returning to pedal power but guess I'll have no choice until I find another car. I decide to text Jacques, but I doubt the garage will be open; probably closed for the festive season.

Season's greetings! How soon can you have Dolly back on the road for me, and have you had any luck locating a suitable winter vehicle? Sorry to be a nuisance. x

Looking up from my phone, I can see Enzo, his long legs striding swiftly across the car park towards me. Butterflies start to take off in my tummy as he opens the door with a big grin. I accept his kiss on my cheek and smile back as he says, "Wow! You look much better, just a neat scar and faded bruise; good as new I reckon… Do you want me to drive?"

"No, I'm fine thanks; you, on the other hand, must be exhausted, sit back and relax," I say, as he casually tosses his bag onto the back seat. He nods and smiles, leaning back into the uncomfortable front seat and soon his eyelids droop, and his head flops to one side. Poor Enzo, I think, and he's back at work tomorrow. Bumping down the track to his cabin wakes him from his slumber.

"I thought you'd want dropping at the Chateau first," he says, a little confused.

"Nope, first you need a decent meal, a shower and a rest. Xavier is going to pick me up in a couple of hours after we've had supper."

Looking surprised, he retrieves his luggage and helps to carry the food I've brought; I make toad in the hole followed by treacle tart, my gran's favourite, while Enzo has a shower.

"This is really good… I haven't had it since I was a kid," he says between mouthfuls.

"Well, it's a little different, made with wild boar sausage; it's all I could get I'm afraid, but it works quite well."

My phone pings with an incoming text notification, followed by another, Jacques, and Xavier.

I've been working on Dolly today. I've fitted a new window and knocked the dent out; I'd like to check her over in the morning then you can have her back. Can you get a lift over, late afternoon? I'll tell you about winter options when you arrive.

Well, that's excellent news. Xavier's text, as usual, is short and to the point. Perhaps he'll give me a lift over to collect Dolly tomorrow afternoon.

With you in 20 mins.

"Is everything okay?" Enzo asks, trying to read my face.

"Yes, good news. Dolly is mended, I can collect her late tomorrow afternoon."

"I finish at four, I'll come straight over and pick you up, but promise you won't go out in the snow," he says, concern etched on his tired face. Instinctively touching the small scar on my forehead, I grimace and agree.

Xavier is eager to get the business underway and arrives the following morning to help prepare the dining room for its makeover, heaving the large pieces of furniture into the middle of the room and covering them with old, faded bed linen. I show him the colour palette I've chosen, which he seems to like. There isn't a considerable amount to paint, as the walls are mainly clad in wood panels in need of a good clean, which we set about immediately. He fixes the secondary glazing units on the windows, which takes less time than anticipated, but hopefully will make a big difference.

I tell him that I want the chandeliers hung back in this room and the drawing room, but he suggests that we enlist some help. "I will ask Bert, 'e 'as a friend who knows someone who could do it for a small fee." I decline his offer and tell him that I will do an internet search for a professional, though I'm clueless as to know what to type into the search engine. Is there such a thing as a 'chandelier installer'? A few minutes later and I have my answer. Several companies offer such services, another job for after the festive season. Along with a joiner to refashion the doorway in the hall leading to the hidden stairs.

5

Just after four, headlights appear on the drive, Enzo. I've been feeling a mixture of nerves and excitement waiting for him to arrive. Why do I feel like this? It's ridiculous, I'm not a teenager with a crush. Opening the door, he steps inside wearing a bright orange padded jacket, with matching trousers, and a furry hat.

"It's freezing, minus ten, and almost dark. The roads are icy. I don't think we should collect Dolly this evening; can't you rearrange for tomorrow morning?" He asks, placing a cold kiss on my cheek.

"Well, yes, I'm free tomorrow, but aren't you working?"

"Not until four, then I'm on-call. It's been slow today, just a caesarean section on a little bulldog – mother and puppies all well," he says, with pride displayed on his face.

I hand him a mug of hot chocolate and show him the progress we've made with the dining room. "You could do with a bit more furniture in here, the few pieces you have here look a bit lost."

"Yes, I was thinking on the same lines, and I need some bits and bobs to display; nothing expensive, but in keeping with the period. I've sold most of the valuable items."

"Well, that's a coincidence," he says turning to face me, "One of my clients was telling me that he's going to a flea market tomorrow, about an hour's drive away… would you like to go?"

"Sounds like fun… but what about Dolly?"

"Mm, could we get her the day after? It might not be as cold by then."

"That's New Year's Eve, I don't think Jacques will be working. I'll text and ask him."

Ten minutes later and I have agreed to host a small party on New Year's Eve. Jacques is going to bring Dolly for me, along with some of his friends, and Enzo also has the night off. I'll invite Sylvie and of course Xavier, but I doubt he'll come along.

"Would you like to stay for supper?" I ask, hopefully.

"How can I say no to your cooking? You're amazing!" Enzo enthuses.

"Well, after several years on a student diet, anything is amazing."

Shadow decides it's time for a stroll outside, so we wrap up and accompany him. The night sky is stunning; inky black, punctuated by stars, dazzling like diamonds. We walk over to the pond, now frozen over, with the moon reflecting off its surface like a bare bulb in a bathroom mirror. Gone are the brightly coloured damsels and swooping swallows. The lively buzz replaced by a cold, eerie silence.

"It's difficult to believe we're stood in the same place; it feels like a different planet. Only a few days ago the stream was a torrent; now it's back to a gentle burble," I say as I begin to shiver.

Enzo pulls me in close and wraps his arms around me in a big hug. "Come on, let's go home; you're cold. You need some proper winter gear; we'll sort that out tomorrow as well."

"Yes, Dad… but not bright orange!" I say laughing.

Once back in the warmth, I open a bottle of our homemade red and make mulled wine, the dark red liquid is warming and soothing, and the evening passes quickly.

"I'll make a bed up for you, which room would you like?"

Lying in bed feels comforting, knowing Enzo is on the other side of the landing, and I fall asleep quickly. I wake to a noise downstairs, it's still dark. Shadow seems unconcerned, fast asleep in his bed. Pulling on a robe and slippers, I creep out onto the landing. Coffee: I can smell fresh coffee. Of course, Enzo. I must look a fright with bird's nest hair! Swiftly changing direction, I make it to the other side of the landing as he appears, climbing the stairs with a tray, loaded with goodies.

"Back in a minute," I say, disappearing into the bathroom.

On my return, I find him sat on my bed, pouring coffee. Trying to appear calm, I say, "Mm… smells good" and climb on beside him. A glance at my phone informs me it's just after seven.

"We need an early start; I thought we could collect the horse box on the way, in case you buy any large items."

Stepping outside takes my breath away; the trees are painted with frost, a ghostly apparition in the half-light. I stop to take several pictures, hoping one of them might be good enough for my new website, another work-in-progress.

The market is bustling, and it's an assault on the senses. It seems to stretch into the distance, blurring at the edges into the freezing mist. Following his nose, Enzo leads me to one of the many street vendors and purchases hot coffee and warm pain-au-chocolate, saying, "That should keep us going for a while."

We start to walk along the disorganised rows of the market, taking in the sights and sounds. There appears to be no order; bric-a-brac, alongside vintage clothes, furniture mixed in with old books and vinyl records. "I have no idea what I'm looking for," I say, peering around me for inspiration.

"That's the best way; keep an open mind and go with your gut instincts. You'll know when something catches your eye."

Continuing, we come across a stall selling ceramics. A large white jug decorated with scarlet poppies jumps out at me. "That's lovely; I can just see it full of wildflowers from the meadow, placed in the middle of the table, or on the piano."

Instantly Enzo is speaking to the vendor, bartering the price down. The process happens so fast that I'm not sure how much it cost. The vendor wraps it in newspaper and hands it to Enzo. "How much do I owe you?" I ask fishing in my oversized bag for my purse.

His face softens. "Housewarming gift," he says, placing a kiss on the top of my head. I can see I need to sharpen up, I don't want him spending any more on me; though I must admit, I probably wouldn't have had the confidence to barter like that.

By lunchtime, the mist has disappeared, giving me a chance to see the surrounding town. We're in a large market square, with a fountain at its heart, now still; the ice on the surface of the small pond shattered. Bars and restaurants, windows fogged with condensation, line the outside of the square, beckoning the hungry. Eager to try my hand at bartering, I push on to the areas we haven't yet seen. I stop by a small chair, Enzo looks at me puzzled, but I just beam back at him. "This will go beautifully with the little antique writing bureau I have… it's the same colour and just the right size."

A middle-aged man in a grey overcoat and fingerless gloves approaches us, putting on a fake smile. "A lovely chair for a lovely lady," he rattles off insincerely in French.

"How much?" I ask, trying to sound confident.

"For you, one hundred Euros," he says, stamping his feet and clapping his hands against the chill. Enzo steps forward, but I beat him to it.

"Really? There's one remarkably similar, around the corner for half the price," I say looking him in the eye.

"Mais Oui! It is in poor condition – wobbly, needs some attention… this one is much better." No doubt his usual repertoire.

I look at Enzo and wink then reply, "Perhaps so. I'll give you seventy-five."

"Eighty?" He replies without hesitation.

"Thank you for your time, I'll look…"

He doesn't let me finish. "For such a lovely lady seventy-five it is," he says, eagerly taking my cash from me.

Feeling pleased with myself, I try my hand at a few other stalls and come away with some lovely crockery, a colourful rug for the hall and nick-knacks for the bare shelves. Then head into the town for a jacket and salopettes. Enzo points out a lime green set, but I settle for baby blue.

6

On the way back, we stop at another street vendor and have pottage with warm bread and marrons chaud… roast chestnuts. They are so much nicer here than the scorched efforts that gran and I used to make at Christmas. The drive back passes in no time as we chat about our morning's work, and we're soon home. "Thank you so much for a wonderful morning," I say, as Enzo carries my purchases inside.

"Thank you for your hospitality. I had a wonderful evening, and I'm very much looking forward to the party tomorrow night. I'm on-call this evening and working until four tomorrow afternoon. I'll see you about six," he says, hugging me. I catch myself in time and offer him my cheek, instead of leaning further for a passionate kiss; he just looks at me and smiles, sensing that I'm holding back.

Back in the warmth, I unwrap my goods and wash the crockery and ornaments, putting them away in the cupboards. I don't want them on display for a party. Then I set about making up the spare rooms; I expect most people will be staying over, and I've no idea how many friends Jacques is bringing. A text from Sylvie confirms she will be coming and asks if she can bring a plus one; I wonder who that could be? A bang on the door makes me jump. Looking out of the dining room window, I see Xavier stood on the drive, looking grumpy.

"Are you alone now?"

"Yes, Enzo is on-call tonight, are you coming in?" I ask, stepping back into the hall.

I show him my purchases, but he seems disinterested and carries on walking over to Shadow, scratching him on the head. "I'm having a small party tomorrow evening about seven, you're all welcome," I say.

He shrugs in his usual way and walks towards the door, turning back abruptly, he asks, "Is Enzo coming?"

"Yes, and Sylvie, and Jacques, with a few of his friends; Gus enjoyed playing the piano with them last time."

Again, he only shrugs and leaves, saying, "Lock ze door behind me." What is his problem? Why did he come? That man gives me whiplash! I can't believe that he's jealous of Enzo.

New Year's Eve morning brings a stiff breeze chasing white clouds across the watery blue sky, and thankfully, it's not as cold. After breakfast, I take Shadow for a brisk walk over to see Alice. She's in the kitchen preparing food, her face looks red and puffy. "Alice, what's wrong?" I ask, putting an arm around her shoulder.

She shrugs me off using the onions as an excuse – but I know better; something is bothering her. I don't push, she'll tell me when she's ready. The boys seem to be out; hunting apparently, it's a tradition, no doubt Monsieur Le Maire will be with them. I invite Alice to the party, but she declines, saying she needs an early night. I have an uneasy feeling as I walk back home; something's wrong. Xavier seemed grumpy too, but I suppose that's not unusual. There's nothing like Christmas to bring emotions and family frictions to the surface.

I've had a productive day, the table is laden with food, and there's more in the oven. I make my way through the rooms, leaving clean towels in the bedrooms and putting more logs on the fires downstairs. What shall I wear? I wore a little black dress and heels to the last New Year's party I attended, but I would feel extremely underdressed looking like that here. Besides, I no longer possess anything like that. No, skinny jeans and a pretty top will have to do.

I'm about to feed Shadow when I see headlights coming down the drive; it's a little after four, it could be Enzo, and I'm not ready. He said he'd be here about six. As the car gets nearer, I can just about make out the shape – Dolly. It's Jacques; he's incredibly early, I didn't expect him until much later. The front door opens, and Jacques strides in with lots of luggage, then Jenny jumps from behind him.

"Surprise!" She shouts, rushing into the hall to give me a big hug.

"Oh, my God! When…? How…?"

"I've only got four days: but better than nothing. Oh, I've packed some more of your things," she says, pointing to a suitcase. "I can't believe how cold it is!"

"But I only Skyped you two days ago!"

"I know; Jacques told me about your accident. He said you were okay, but I wanted to see for myself," she says, walking over to Jacques side.

"I'm absolutely fine, that's why I didn't tell you, though I expect that it was a good excuse to get you off work." Glancing towards the stairs, I continue, "I don't know if there are enough rooms for everyone, how many people have you invited, Jacques?"

"Don't worry, we'll share, and the boys will crash anywhere. Where do you want these?" He replies, then carries the cases upstairs to the room I point out.

Two hours later, Enzo arrives with a crate of beer and some bubbly. After lugging them into the kitchen, he drops his small bag in the hall, before giving me a hug. Jenny pops her head over the galleried landing wearing very little and shouts, "Happy New Year!"

"Wow, Jenny! I didn't know you were coming," he says, looking at me quizzically.

"Spur of the moment decision," she replies before we hear Jacques voice calling her name. They obviously can't get enough of each other!

A short while later, the front door opens. "Oh, hello. Happy New Year!" I say to Xavier as he walks in with Gus.

"I will collect 'im at ten," he says curtly, then turns and leaves. Gus wanders into the drawing room and begins to play the piano, which brings Jacques downstairs.

"Hi, Gus, good to see you again; I've just had a text from the gang, they're on their way, let's go and practice." Messing up Gus's hair as he walks past.

Sylvie arrives next and introduces us to her colleague, Vince; her plus one. The boys appear soon after, and the party begins in earnest, with music and alcohol, and Jenny joining in, karaoke style.

Shortly before ten, Gus receives a text then walks over to me, "I'm going now, Dad's outside, thank you; it was cool."

I open the front door and beckon Xavier to come in and join us, but he shakes his head, and Gus climbs into the waiting truck. They drive off, and I return to the party.

"No Big-Ben I'm afraid; this will have to do," Enzo says, as he gets his phone out and counts down the seconds to midnight.

As it gets closer, we all begin counting, "Three... two... one... Happy New Year!"

The gang are all clapping each other on the back, Jenny and Jacques are locking lips in the corner, and Sylvie and her quiet friend raise a glass of bubbly followed by a peck on the cheek. Enzo strides over, and holds me at arm's length then says, "May I kiss you – properly?"

Time stands still, and everything blurs into the periphery. Tension crackles between us, I pause before leaning forwards, placing a gentle kiss on his lips; he pulls me closer, and deepens the kiss. There's no need for the fireworks that the boys brought, there are already little explosions going off in my body. In need of oxygen, I step back to find everyone looking at us then a cheer reverberates through the room. "About bloody time! Happy New Year!" Shouts Jenny, already tipsy.

Sylvie and her friend Vince, make their excuses and leave shortly after midnight, their relationship obviously in its infancy. I'll have to invite them here for supper when I get a chance.

"I'm just popping out with Shadow," I say, pulling on my coat and boots.

Enzo is behind me in a flash, doing the same. "I'm coming with you."

The wind has died down, leaving a still night, Shadow scampers off into the trees, no doubt following the scent of a rabbit. Enzo takes my hand, and we follow in silence. What should I say? Are we an item now? Or is this just a casual fling? But I remain silent. The screech of an owl cuts through the night air. Enzo stops and turns to me. "Don't over think this," he says, leaning in for a gentle kiss. "Let's just see where it goes."

"A bit of a commute; the Ardeche to Glasgow."

"A lot can happen in six months; don't let it come between us."

Sighing, I turn and continue to follow Shadow into the trees.

Back at the Chateau, the party seems to be over; Enzo helps me to pile glasses and plates on the kitchen table, then checks the doors and windows.

"Bedtime," he says, picking his bag up and heading upstairs.

"All the rooms are taken; you should have claimed one when you arrived."

"I'll crash on the sofa," he says, kissing me gently then turning to head back downstairs.

Standing like a statue, I watch him walk down the stairs, as a tingling sensation crawls down my spine. "He's a keeper," I hear myself whisper. "Wait!" I call in a loud whisper as I head after him. "We can share," I say quietly over the balcony.

Taking the steps back up two at a time, he's at my side in an instant. "Only if you're sure?"

Nodding, I take his hand and lead him into my room, feeling a little awkward once inside. Shadow lifts his head at the intrusion, then lowers it and closes his eyes; he obviously approves.

"The en-suite is a bit grim," I say, pointing to the small box in the corner, "I've got someone coming to give me an estimate…"

I don't get to finish. Enzo silences me with a passionate kiss, leading me over to the bed.

7

I'm woken with a gentle kiss. Forcing my eyes open, I peer up to see Enzo smiling down at me. Why does he look so good? My makeup must be smeared and my hair – well, I dread to think. "I'll make coffee," he says, jumping out. "Can I borrow your gown?" Helping himself to my pale green robe on the chair when I nod and heads to the kitchen.

I dash into the en-suite as soon as he leaves. My reflection looks back at me wearing a goofy grin. Did we really sleep together? What am I going to say when he returns? 'How was it for you?' It's been an age since I last had sex, I'm so out of practice, could he tell? After a quick spruce up, I grab my pyjamas and dive back into bed in time to hear dishes rattling as he comes back to the room. "Bit of a mess down there, I'll help you clear up after breakfast," he says, as he places the tray on my knee and joins me in bed. Not to be outdone, Shadow stretches and comes to greet us. "Good morning, boy, you really did land on your feet, didn't you?" Enzo says, scratching the dog behind his ears.

We munch our way through cereal, pain-au-chocolate and coffee, neither of us speaking. The rest of the Chateau remains silent; no one up yet after their drunken evening. I, on the other hand, didn't drink a lot, as I noticed Enzo hadn't too. Putting the tray to one side, he turns to look at me.

"No regrets?"

I smile back. "None, what about you?"

Leaning into me, he places a delicate kiss on my lips, tasting of coffee and chocolate. I respond passionately – the clearing up will have to wait.

Dirty glasses and dishes litter most of the surfaces in the kitchen. I really do need a dishwasher! What's left of the morning passes by in a fog; I feel like I'm floating. Enzo takes every opportunity to touch me as we set about clearing up. By midday, everything's back to normal – except me. I wonder if Enzo feels the same.

"Do you feel like taking a walk?" Enzo asks, interrupting my thoughts.

Shadow is the first to the door, waiting patiently while we pull on our outdoor gear. The weather is still and calm, quite the opposite of how I feel. Neither of us speaks as we follow Shadow through the farmyard.

The donkeys, huddled together in the field shelter, bray as we approach, but the goats continue grazing on a bale of hay. Xavier has obviously been earlier; I wonder how Alice is.

"I'm back on-call at four; can I see you tomorrow evening? Would you like to stay at mine?" Enzo asks as we make our way back home.

Trying not to grin, I turn and look at him, "That would be nice."

There are signs of life as we arrive back; Jacques is helping the gang to load their guitars into a small van. The boys thank me for hosting the party and bump their way up the drive. Jenny is in the kitchen, drinking strong, black coffee; when will she learn?

"Happy New Year!" Enzo says enthusiastically.

"Shh – ditto," Jenny replies, waving her hand in a quieting motion.

"That bad? Take a couple of paracetamols and drink a pint of water, it's the best cure for a hangover," he says, handing her a large glass. Turning back to me, he leans in and kisses me, slowly at first, then with more passion.

"Get a room," Jenny says jokingly, looking at me with questioning eyes.

"Duty calls; see you guys later," he waves and walks to the door, tugging me behind him. He pulls me in for a hug then whispers, "Can't wait 'til tomorrow evening; I'll pick you up at seven."

Ignoring Jenny, I float through the Chateau, changing bed linen and tidying up while Jacques and Jenny sprawl in the sitting room watching a film. Usually, that would have annoyed me, but today I don't care; nothing could upset me today, I feel invincible. It's early evening before Jenny and Jacques re-emerge, looking for food. Running low on provisions, we make do with poached eggs on toast before Jacques leaves; he's going back to work in the morning. The world, at last, returning to some sort of normality after the festivities.

"Well?" Jenny questions.

"Well, what?"

"Come on, I haven't seen you like this since we were students, and you were all over that physio bloke."

"You mean Nigel – that didn't last, and this might not either, don't get too excited," I say, knowing that it's me who's excited.

"He's besotted, can't keep his eyes off you; don't think he's going anywhere in a hurry," she says, just as I receive a text. "See!"

Thank you for the best New Year ever! See you tomorrow. Sleep well. x

Looking over to me she grins, "You've got it bad girl!"

"And you haven't; coming all this way just to see Jacques?"

"The difference between you and me is – I don't fall in love like you – I don't do exclusivity. Variety is the spice of life! Besides, I came to see you," she says piously, raising her eyebrows.

"Yeah – right," I reply, throwing a cushion at her.

The rest of the evening passes quickly, sharing news and gossip. I tell Jenny that I'm concerned about Alice, and she suggests we visit after breakfast.

8

Alice is pleased to see Jenny, and we take her down to the village for provisions, calling in to see Sylvie and her family on the way back. Alice looks tired and drawn but says very little, I wonder what's bothering her?

"I'm staying at Enzo's tonight; will you be okay? He could always come here instead," I say, feeling guilty.

"No, you go, I'll invite Jacques over; if that's okay with you?"

"Sure – then, let's spend your last two days together; no men." Agreeing, Jenny smiles, insisting we hit the sales; not that there's much in the way of shopping at our nearest town, and I don't fancy driving too far in Dolly in the winter.

My overnight bag is ready in the hall, and I'm preened and beautified, upon Jenny's insistence, of course. Enzo arrives on time, pulls me in for a teasing kiss and grabs my bag. Jenny pops her head out of the kitchen and winks. "Enjoy!" She shouts. Jacques' voice follows, echoing her sentiments.

Shadow jumps in the back, and we set off into the night. Filling the silence, I ask, "How was your day?"

His eyes sparkle, "It just got a whole lot better."

I'm amazed as I enter his cabin. Am I in the same place? Gone is his every-day clutter. The small table in the kitchen is set, embellished with a candle and a small bowl of roses. Where did he get them at this time of year? I look at him and smile. He grins sheepishly and takes my bag through to the bedroom, saying, "Make yourself at home."

I sit on the leather sofa listening to Fleetwood Mac singing in the background, while Shadow stretches out in front of the log-burner, as though it's a regular occurrence.

"Drink?" Enzo asks as he returns.

"Just juice, please; whatever you have in." I don't want to get drunk like Jenny. No, I want to savour this evening, commit every detail to memory. My memories of my first visit here are quite vague, that's what concussion does for you, but tonight is different.

He arrives back with two glasses of orange juice and sits next to me, just as my stomach rumbles. "Hungry?" I nod, smiling. "Good, I only have a small repertoire; Spaghetti Bolognese is on the list, I hope you like it."

"Mm, one of my favourites; smells good." He finishes his drink then excuses himself to cook the pasta.

"Can I help?"

"No, you're my guest, relax."

"This is delicious," I say later between mouthfuls, being careful not to dribble sauce down my chin.

"Glad you like it, I'm not the best cook," he says, looking back at me with an empty plate in front of him. Once I've finished, he briskly clears the pots off the table and returns with a dish from the freezer, placing it in the centre of the table. "It needs ten minutes to stand, would you like some wine?"

"No thanks, perhaps later," I reply, looking into the dish. "You made ice-cream! Of course, I remember you mentioning that you have a family business. What flavour?"

Grinning, he says, "Chocolate-chip, hope you like it."

"Love it. Tell me some more about yourself, I know very little," I say, feeling a little awkward.

"Well, there's not much to tell, I grew up in Glasgow, an only child, crazy about animals. It started when I was about eight with a baby thrush; I rescued it from a cat and nursed it back to health, then taught it to fly. Called it Chirpy; not very original, I know. Word got about, then friends and neighbours brought me any injured animals they found. Dad built me a shed in the garden; I ended up with quite a menagerie. It seemed to carry on from there," he says while dishing out the ice-cream.

"So, you weren't into football or rugby?"

"No, I didn't have much time, I was either tending to my animals or helping at the factory. When I left school, I went off to university – and here I am. What about you?"

"My life story isn't very conventional; my parents died when I was small, I went to live with Gran; when I left the sixth form I started nursing. Sadly, Gran died soon after, so I moved into a student house with Jenny and the girls. The rest, you know," I say, sitting back in my chair. "When's your grandfather's funeral?"

"Next week; but I'm not going, I can't take any more time off. My parents understand. I managed to spend the last day with him, he knew I was there."

Enzo won't let me help to clear the dishes. After stacking them in the dishwasher, he brings a pot of coffee through to the lounge. Sitting beside me, he asks, "Okay, so what's your favourite colour?"

"Oh, err, pastels; I like all of the pastel shades, what about you?"

Laughing, he says, "Orange, to match my hair. Music?"

"Mm, I like Abba and Cher; they remind me of my gran, but anything really, as long as it's not too loud or heavy," I respond, then look back at him.

"That's easy, I like U2, Crowded House, Deacon Blue, Fleetwood Mac. I'm not much into modern pop music."

The evening passes quickly with good-humoured banter until Shadow decides it's time to go out. He instantly starts scratching at the ground under the pine trees and locates several truffles, an activity I'm now used to. "I've seen the occasional wild boar down here, they're bigger than you think," he says, pulling me close.

"Don't tell Xavier, he'll be round with his gun; are they dangerous?"

"Well, I wouldn't want to come across one in the surgery, but generally if you leave them alone, they will leave you alone. Though, I am rather partial to wild boar sausage."

Back in the cabin, I feed Shadow and settle him down for the night.

"A night-cap. What's your poison?" Enzo asks.

"What have you got?"

"Brandy, whisky, Tia-Maria…"

"Yes, Tia-Maria," I interrupt.

Sipping the bittersweet liquid, I lean my head on his chest, and he strokes my hair, this feels so natural. Lifting my head, I offer him my lips, he doesn't hesitate; soon we're in a passionate embrace. "Let's take this to the bedroom," he whispers, picking me up and carrying me through.

I'm the first to wake, slowly turning to take in his sleeping body; gone are the fine lines around his eyes that crinkle when he smiles.

The creases of life erased by slumber. Carefully, I untangle myself from the covers while picking up his shirt from the floor; it will have to do. I slip it on and tiptoe over to the kitchen. No fancy coffee machine, like me he possesses a simple cafetière, perfectly adequate, and easy to operate. A soft touch on my waist makes me jump and bang my head on a cupboard door, halting my search for cereals.

"Sorry, are you okay?" He asks, taking my hand.

"I'll live; I don't think I need Steristrips this time – I wanted to bring you breakfast in bed." Turning, he creeps away back in the direction of his bedroom. Five minutes later, and I follow him with a tray, "Surprise!" As we dig into breakfast, I turn to look at him, "I hope you don't mind me leaving so early. Jacques will have gone to work now, and I promised Jenny we'd spend her last two days together."

"I completely understand. I've got the weekend off; we can do something then."

"Oh, it's the wine auction at the weekend; could we go?"

"Sounds fun; I'll research trains and hotels. Have a great time with Jenny."

"Will do, I've checked the forecast; no snow."

After a passionate kiss outside the Chateau, he drives off, tooting his horn up the drive. Its nine-forty, Jenny has probably gone back to bed; she's definitely an owl.

The local town has limited shopping possibilities, but it will have to suffice; I'm not in the mood for a road trip. "Let's go in here, there's a half-price sale," Jenny squeals, grabbing my hand and leading me into a small department store.

She makes a beeline for the fashion area while I mooch about amongst the household goods. Half-price Christmas table linens and decorations, crockery and glasses decorated with snowmen and Santa. An investment for next year; will I be ready to take paying guests by then? It's possible. Filling a trolley, I then amble over to Jenny, no jostling from fellow shoppers, so unlike home. She has several dresses laid over her arm, sporting more sequins than 'Strictly', grinning she disappears into a cubicle dragging me with her. Stripped to her underwear in no time, she shoehorns herself into the first garment.

"Well?" she asks while twirling in the mirror, turning like a glitterball.

"Err… a bit skimpy; where will you wear it?"

"Works Christmas party next week; I'm bound to pull."

"What about Jacques?"

"What about him? Holiday romance," she says, wiggling her eyebrows.

Dropping our bags in the car, she asks, "Where next?"

"Bricolage."

"Whatolage?"

"Bricolage – DIY; I need some paint and things."

We unload our goods and share a pizza and a bottle of wine while listening to each other's hopes and dreams for the coming year.

9

"Sorry it was a flying visit; I'll be back in the spring," Jenny says as Jacques loads her luggage into the back of a red car.

"Bye…"

"Hey, grab your coat and bag; you're driving," Jacques says.

"What? How do you mean… I see; you two want to smooch in the back!"

"No… but that sounds like a good idea. The car's just come in part-exchange; it's not even been valeted yet; I thought of you when I saw it."

"Oh, err, okay. Thanks," I say, grabbing my things and climbing into the driver's seat.

Thankfully, Jacques gets in the passenger seat next to me and runs through the controls, it seems simple enough. Apparently, it's a Yeti; I always thought that was some sort of mythical snowman, but no, apparently, it's a 4x4. I make steady progress down the drive. "Okay, stop; you've passed. I'll get in the back now," Jacques says with a cheeky grin.

I've never test-driven a car before; let alone bought one, I've no idea what to look for. A quick peep over my shoulder into the back tells me that Jacques probably doesn't want to discuss cars right now. Okay, time to take charge. Visibility is excellent, I can see well through the rear window; it's not too big, but not small either. Plenty of room for Shadow and provisions. Comfort: yes, it ticks that box, unlike Enzo's car. It has a radio, and a sat-nav, which is already on the screen. Air-con, somewhat useful, cup holder; it's the exact opposite of Dolly. It flies on the autoroute, with no flapping windows. Yes, I quite like it; but how much is it? I'll ask him on the way back.

"Do you want me to drive?" Jacques asks once Jenny is safely seen to the airport.

"No, I'll drive; you might want to wipe the orange lipstick off your face," I say, passing him a wipe and pulling out of the car park.

"What do you think?"

"Well, pink might suit you better." He laughs, and after the banter dies down, I ask him several questions then tell him I'll have the car: knocking five hundred Euros off the price. My bartering lesson from the flea market was obviously well learnt. Dropping me back home, he tells me that I can collect the Yeti in a few days. Well, that was a good mornings work!

Xavier is painting the dining room when I get back. "'ave you finished playing wiz your friends now?"

"I wasn't playing, that was a business trip; I've just bought a Yeti, and I'm going to Paris tomorrow for two nights for another business trip. I'll leave Shadow with you."

"Now I know you are crazy; do you know 'ow far zis is?" He snorts and carries on painting; I suppose I ought to help him.

Am I crazy? It was an impulsive decision, but I've been here over five months now; it's time to see some of this country. One of my colleagues took her bridesmaids to Paris for her hen do a couple of years ago. I remember her telling me all about it. It'll be fun, and I'll get to spend some time with Enzo. Of course! That's the problem – he's jealous. I'd almost forgotten his proposal! What a joke that was. Poor Xavier, he's so sombre and literal, he could do with getting out more. Perhaps I ought to suggest that he takes some holiday; if I remember correctly, he's entitled to holiday pay after three months. That would fall in the spring when the campsite is under construction; I'll need him then. I'll suggest he takes a week off while we're waiting for the weather to improve.

"What do I want wiv ze 'oliday? Who will do ze animals? 'Olidays are for tourists and children!"

Okay, that went down well, perhaps a word with Alice might help? We continue painting the dining room a pastel green colour. I'm pleased with our efforts, though Xavier has little to say, and I'm relieved when he leaves. I need to get to the bottom of this, he's never been charming, but he seems so much worse of late.

Next job, packing; what should I take? I need to travel light, just hand luggage. I remember lugging a suitcase with me on the way down here, not something I wish to repeat. Enzo will be here in a couple of hours, we need to be up and off at some silly time in the morning, it's a long drive to catch the TGV.

The café is heaving, so is the rest of the station, families struggling with pushchairs and luggage, couples leaning into one another on benches, groups of friends chatting animatedly. I can pick out Italian, German, English, and French conversation; as well as others I can't identify. Eclectic, multicultural. I'd forgotten what the real world was like and find it a little intimidating, I'm glad I'm not travelling alone. Enzo assures me that we are on the correct train as it glides away from the platform; too late now. I soon begin to relax and lean back into the comfortable seat to watch the scenery go by, the city quickly left behind as we streak through undulating countryside, dotted with small towns and villages. Fractious children now settled, playing on must-have gadgets, not a colouring book in sight.

I open my eyes to find my head propped on Enzo's shoulder. "Welcome back, hungry?"

"Mm, what time is it?"

"One-forty. Lunch?"

The buffet-car is a hive of activity, families refuelling for the journey ahead, no curling, dry cheese sandwiches here. We choose from the tempting fayre on offer and return to our seats while quietly people watching. I hand Enzo the catalogue for the auction tomorrow, it seems my entries have been broken down into several lots, with a few items left as individuals. They must know what they're doing; unlike me, clueless.

"Here we are, Paris," Enzo says, handing me my luggage.

"I've never really been, I only left the station briefly to get a taxi across to my connecting train on the other side of the city."

"We're here to change that; business and pleasure," he says, kissing me in the back of a taxi. "Not far to the hotel, we'll get rid of the bags then explore; where would you like to go?"

"The tower, Notre-Dame, Versailles, Montmartre…"

"Hey, stop; we only have two days; the auction will take up tomorrow morning, but I'll do my best."

The hotel is central and small, our room adequate; somewhere clean to sleep, though I'm not sure we'll get much sleep. First stop is Notre-Dame. "Oh, no, look at the queue!" I say exasperated.

"It moves quickly, I've been before, we need to head straight for the cathedrals' tower before it gets dark, the view is amazing."

"Wow! Thank you, it's stunning," I say later, looking around me at the Paris skyline shrouded by the fast-approaching dusk, so romantic. I reward him with a heated kiss. We wander through the cathedral like a pair of love-struck tourists taking in the architecture and history, the crowds receding into the background. This is our time. Outside, we enjoy coffee and sweet crepes as darkness falls.

"Need to get a move on," Enzo says, taking me by the hand and waving down a taxi.

"Where are we going?"

I don't get an answer; it's a surprise. Ten minutes later and I am at the Eiffel Tower, Enzo squeezes my hand and pays the driver before helping me out. I lean back to take it all in; the lights are mesmerising. Another long queue but I say nothing, just make my way towards it. "Booked in advance, no need to queue," he says, producing tickets from his wallet.

"I feel so small and insignificant up here," I whisper, trying to catch my breath after the long climb. Enzo squeezes my hand and pulls me in for a hug, a cold wind causes my eyes to run, which makes the river Seine sparkle even more vibrantly. Standing amid the throng and noise of tourists and lovers, words not needed, watching the light show, and the city below. Trying to commit the moment to my memory bank.

Back on terra-firma, I'm still in a daze, tired, hungry, and on sensory overload. I really have become a bit of a recluse since arriving in France. "Dinner," Enzo says, guiding me down the small side streets, gradually leaving the crowds behind.

"I'll have French onion soup followed by steak frites," I say fingering the gingham tablecloths. Enzo has the same but manages chocolate mousse for dessert, and together we sink a bottle of the house red. I catch the waiter's eye and pay the bill while Enzo visits the restrooms.

"That was sneaky of you!" He chastises as we leave.

"Look, you've paid for the tower and Notre-Dame…"

"You paid for your own train ticket, and the hotel…"

"Yes, that's the business part, let's get back to pleasure," I say, silencing him with a sensual kiss.

It's still dark, but the smell of coffee invades my nostrils. Opening my eyes, I smile, remembering our night of passion. Enzo, clad only in boxers is stood looking out of the small window onto the city below; its seven-thirty but busy already. "Let's find a café by the river for breakfast," he says, handing me coffee.

An hour later and we're sat upstairs in a window looking down over the river, watching various boats, in a variety of colours passing by, brightening up the grey morning. Enzo has crepes with bacon, but I opt for eggs benedict and cinnamon toast, quite a feast washed down with a large mug of hot chocolate, very decadent, more calories than

I'm used to of late but no doubt I'll work it off later.

Finding a vacant taxi takes a while in the busy streets, buzzing with tourists and commuters but at last, we are dropped outside a mansion on the outskirts of the city, it's imposing and makes my Chateau look like a dolls house. Stepping into the vast hall, a sea of colours adorning the well-heeled smacks me in the face. We must stand out like a sore finger, wearing comfortable, casual clothes and sensible footwear.

"Laura, how lovely to see you again, glad you could make it," says a familiar voice. "This is my wife, Cecilia," he continues, holding the elbow of a petite blond lady with a pale complexion. Leo, I'd almost forgotten about him; he came to view the Chateau with his sister Valentina when I was considering selling it. He's in the wine trade, they gave me the details for the auction house, and now it's happening; one of the many dreams turning into a reality.

"Hello, Leo, lovely to meet you, Cecilia," I say, regaining my composure. "Is your sister here?"

"Unfortunately, she couldn't make it; work commitments."

Remembering my manners, I introduce them to Enzo, and we make our way into the venue, just in time for the bidding to start. It's all very confusing, and I find it quite challenging to follow, but Leo explains things as the morning progresses. My lots are next; glancing over at Enzo, he takes my hand and tucks me into his side while the auctioneer starts his spiel, and the room goes quiet.

The first lot is a dozen bottles of red, pre-war; displayed beautifully and on a big screen too, the dust and cobwebs from their former home gone. The bidding starts at thirty thousand and rapidly rises in increments of five hundred. I'm stunned into silence; my breath becomes shallower, and my heart feels like it's trying to escape from its bony cage.

Becoming light-headed, my eyes scan the room for exit signs, then I hear the words "Sold to a client on the internet."

Leo looks at me, smiling. "Well done, that's a good start."

Gulping for air, I ask how much it went for.

"Fifty-five thousand… are you okay?"

"Could I have some water, please?"

Leo strides over to a table and returns with a bottle of water, "Here, drink this, the next lot is up now."

Enzo whispers, "Do you want to go?" I don't know how to answer, I didn't think I'd feel emotional, but I have a sense of guilt, shouldn't the wine have stayed at the Chateau? For whom though? It's too late now anyway; the bidding continues fast and furious, and I'm unable to keep up, while lot after lot goes under the hammer.

After the auction, Leo guides me through the palatial house, out on to the terrace with

Cecilia and Enzo, into a waiting car. Still in a trance, but seemingly a few hundred thousand Euros better off, we arrive outside a swanky hotel. "Wow," Enzo whispers as we climb the few steps to the door, which is opened swiftly by a young man in a smart uniform. Leo ushers us to a lift where we're elevated to the penthouse. The door opens into a different world. Opulence envelops us.

"I think you need a drink," Leo says, handing me a glass of what smells like brandy. Enzo accepts a beer as we sink into the leather sofa and I begin to relax a little, sipping the warming drink while waiting for my brain to start functioning correctly. "Better?" Leo asks, a few moments later.

"Yes, thank you, I don't know what came over me."

"It's a lot to take in, don't worry; I believe it's the Bugatti next month, will you be coming?"

"Err, I hadn't realised it was so soon, I'm not sure…"

"We'll give it some thought," Enzo interrupts, saving me.

After a civil length of time, we make our farewells, promising to keep in touch and exit the posh hotel onto the busy streets of Paris, feeling a little shaken. "How about a boat trip?" Enzo asks.

"Yes, that would be a nice gentle activity, and a cup of tea."

I try to concentrate on the French commentary about the iconic landmarks that float serenely by, giving my mind something to do rather than thinking about the auction, and all the wine that no longer resides in the cellar at the Chateau. Will it even stay in France? Where was the person purchasing via the internet? It might end up on the other side of the world! Have I done the right thing? Too late now. It's gone. Forever. I'm vaguely aware of a voice in the distance coming through the fog. "Hey, come back… where are you?" I hear Enzo say, beside me.

"Sorry; I was miles away."

"I can tell; what's bothering you?"

I look up, sighing, to see little rivulets of condensation running down inside the glass canopy. "Have I made the right decision? Shouldn't the wine have stayed at the Chateau? It's part of its heritage, what right have…"

He silences me with a kiss then holds me close. "Just think logically; if you hadn't sold the wine, and other items, you wouldn't have been able to start renovating the Chateau, and it would have gradually crumbled away. Or, you would have had to sell up; the likeliest scenario is that it would have been converted into a hotel, removing its character, leaving Alice, Gus, and Xavier without a home, or an income. I think you have taken the kindest path. Damage limitation. You have kept some of the important items, and it will look fabulous when it's finished. Just think of the long-term plan. It will still be a beautiful building; and home, at the heart of the local community. What's more important, bottles of wine or a sturdy roof to see it through another hundred years?"

Sagging, I lean into him and try to put the Chateau out of my mind; he's right, and we have only one night left to enjoy Paris.

In no time at all, we're back on the train, streaking south through the countryside, away from the hustle and bustle. I've had a lovely time, but I'm exhausted and eager to get back to peace and quiet, with Shadow; I hadn't realised just how fond I've grown of him.

10

Enzo drops me off and carries my bag inside, kissing me gently. "Thank you for a super weekend; sorry about the guilt trip," I say.

"No apology required. I've really enjoyed it too. I've got Thursday off, are you free?"

"I'll make sure I am," I reply, watching him drive away.

I call at the farmhouse to collect Shadow, but he's not there. I assume they're out hunting, but a glance at Alice has me concerned. She looks ashen and avoids eye contact. "What's the matter, Alice; where's Xavier and Shadow?"

She shakes her head, unable to answer; panicking, I ask again, louder. Gus arrives from the lounge, and he, too, looks upset. "Gus, what's wrong?"

With downcast eyes lacking their usual sparkle, he says, "Papa let Shadow out last night, and he didn't come back; we've looked everywhere. Papa's out now looking for him."

"Where have you looked?" My voice raising as the panic sets in.

"All over the estate and Chateau, and searched the woods; all the usual places," he says, holding his hands up in dismay, reminding me so much of his father.

"Where is your dad, now?"

"Papa has gone to see someone."

"Who?" I say, trying to calm my voice a little. After all, it's not Gus's fault.

"I don't know; he wouldn't tell me, but he was furious."

Alice tries to break the tension and makes me a cup of tea, which I can't drink. I pace the kitchen, trying to think of what to do. Grabbing my coat impulsively, I head for the door. "Where are you going?" Alice asks in a shrill voice.

"To look for him!"

Finally, with downcast eyes, she replies, "You won't find him; he's not here."

I ring Enzo and tell him the terrible news, and he assures me he'll circulate a photo of Shadow to all the other vets in the area, as well as the SPA, and other shelters, while reminding me that he has a microchip. After ringing everyone I can think of to ask them to look out for him, I pull on my outdoor gear and grab a large lamp, then spend the next couple of hours scouring the grounds and outbuildings; to no avail. They're empty. He's not here. Next, the Chateau, searching every nook and cranny, but I know it's futile. Feeling totally hopeless, I slide slowly down my bedroom wall and sit at the side of his empty bed, sobbing. I awake to blackness while enveloped in Enzo's arms.

"Hi," he whispers as I try to sit up, pins and needles crippling my feet.

"Have you heard anything?"

Enzo doesn't answer, just helps me to my feet as my circulation slowly returns. "Let me help you to bed."

"What time is it? You have to be at work at eight."

"Two-twenty; come on, let's go to bed, I'll go to work from here."

A ringing phone wakes me at seven, my stomach drops as I realise it's only Enzo's alarm.

"Keep me posted, and eat," he says, hugging me as he leaves. Breakfast is the last thing on my mind. I stride over to the farmhouse without my Shadow by my side, trying to put on a brave face for Alice. I'm shocked to see Xavier in the kitchen. He tries to turn away from me, but I decide to confront him.

"What happened… have you found him?"

He looks at the floor, before slowly raising his eyes to meet mine. "No, but I zink, I might know who 'as 'im."

"Who?" I demand. Alice brings coffee and motions for us to sit at the table, the bitter liquid burns my empty stomach, and I start to retch. Alice scurries off and returns with a warm croissant, placing it down firmly in front of me; no words needed. I pick at it while Xavier tells me his account.

"Do you remember at ze truffle market… two men were discussing ze best way to find ze truffles?" I just nod, and he carries on. "Well, one of zem said 'e 'ad a friend who 'ad lost 'iz truffle dog… I zink 'e 'as been and taken ze dog."

"But how would he know where to find him?"

"You put up ze posters when you were trying to find 'iz owner, yes? I saw two men loitering 'ere at ze weekend but didn't zink too much about zem at ze time," he replies, slowly leaning back in his chair.

I sit in stunned silence. Shadow has been kidnapped! Then the penny drops; he was never really my dog anyway, he belonged to this other person before me. "What do they want? I'll give them money if they give him back… they can have all the truffles…"

He states, resting his forehead in his hands, "Zey are mean. Shadow escaped from zem… we need to get 'im back."

"How?"

Clasping his hands on the table, and slowly raising his head to look at me, he says, "I 'ave ze plan."

"What plan? Do you know his location? Do you want some money?"

"I am meeting someone later… 'e can 'elp… you stay wiz Mama… pick Gus up from ze bus and don't contact me," he says, getting louder in rapid succession; then stands and leaves, taking his big dog, Beau with him. The kitchen feels empty without his presence.

Alice remains quiet for a while then suggests we keep busy to distract ourselves; only then does it dawn on me that Xavier is putting himself in danger. "Perhaps we should inform Monsieur le Maire?" I say.

"I've already told him," she replies, flushing a little. Of course, I remember; they used to be lovers.

The day drags by with no word from Xavier, I'm desperate to ring him but heed his words, not wanting to make things worse. Poor Shadow, I hope they aren't mistreating him.

"Have you found him?" Gus asks as I collect him from the bus stop.

"No, not yet, but your dad is still out looking."

Gus walks beside me silently, kicking a stone along the path. We do our best to carry on, but as dusk falls, Alice looks increasingly worried. Perhaps I shouldn't have let Xavier go, what if he's injured somewhere, or worse. Should I ring him? Just as I dig in my pocket for my phone, it rings; its Enzo.

"Any news?" He asks.

"No… I'm concerned, should I ring him?"

"Best to sit tight and wait…"

I'm interrupted by banging and a rattling chain. Whipping around, I see Xavier stood in the doorway with his cousin Bert, both looking dishevelled. Xavier has a swollen bruised eye and Bert has a burst lip. Following in behind is Shadow, covered in mud with a heavy chain chaffing his neck, and Beau with a nasty cut on his shoulder. I drop my phone and rush over to them, not knowing who to comfort first. Alice chooses her son, so I tend to the dogs. Beau needs stitches. Enzo… is he still on the line?

"Hello?" I say retrieving my phone.

"I'm on my way, are they bad?" Enzo replies.

"Beau needs stitches, I can't see any blood on Shadow. Be careful."

Xavier refuses his mother's ministrations and strides out to the garage for a pair of bolt cutters. Enzo arrives just as Xavier gets the heavy chain from around Shadow's slender neck, revealing a red welt. Enzo sets to work immediately, assessing both dogs and finds a couple of puncture wounds near Beau's cut, saying, "These are dog bites," while gently tending to the injured dog. Apart from the red mark, Shadow seems unharmed, unlike his saviours, who refuse Enzo's generous offer to tend to their injuries.

"Brandy is ze only medicine we need," Xavier says.

"Who are these men?" Enzo asks.

"I cannot say, but she is not staying alone in ze Chateau tonight," Xavier says, pouring Bert a large brandy and pointing in my direction with his free hand.

"I'll be okay…"

"Not happening; I'll stay with you until this is sorted out," Enzo says, raising his eyes momentarily from his task.

"What about your work?"

"What about it? I can commute from here – and be on-call from here – not a problem. Now, will you tell us what happened?" he asks Xavier.

"In ze morning; but make sure you lock all ze doors and windows tonight," Xavier replies, looking into his glass.

We drive back to the Chateau in the Land Rover, then give Shadow a warm bath using the parasite shampoo, just in case. He eats with gusto, then curls up in his bed; the same one that I sat next to sobbing last night. Poor Shadow. He must have had a horrible time. I sit in the corner next to him and gently scratch his head while he falls asleep, unable to stop yawning myself.

"Come on sleepy head, you need an early night. Sorry, but I just might get called out, would you prefer me to sleep in another room?"

"No way! I'm so tired. I probably won't hear you."

Enzo is asleep in no time. I, on the other hand, lie awake, imagining all the possible scenarios in my head. There must have been other dogs involved because Beau had bite wounds. I hope they are okay; Beau is fiercely loyal and can be very protective of his 'pack'. I peer over to check on Shadow, but he's fast asleep where he belongs.

Enzo is up at seven, and I join him for breakfast. He accompanies Shadow in the garden for a quick stroll before leaving. "Ring up a security company and organise cameras and an alarm. I'll call home for some gear then be back later," he says, glancing back while opening the Land Rover door, then hesitating before reluctantly climbing inside.

Just as I'm getting out of the shower, I hear banging on my front door, and Shadow barking. I quickly make my myself decent then grab a large brass candlestick before going down the stairs. The banging has stopped, but Shadow is sat behind the door. Finding my phone, I ring Xavier.

"'Tiz okay. 'Tiz only me, will you let me in?" Slowly opening the door, I peer out to see him stood there, sporting a shiner. I wince in sympathy. He starts to gesture with his hands in his familiar French way, "I need ze key to ze back door, zen I can get in and see you are okay, yes?" He has a point; I'll get a couple of them cut and give one to Enzo as well.

Eventually, I take my eyes from his bruised face and stroll across the hall to the kitchen, saying, "Okay, sit down and tell me what happened."

Sighing, he looks at me then starts to recount his experience. "I 'ad a good idea who was behind it, Big Cyrille; 'e 'az a mouth to match 'iz size. I 'ad a tip-off zat 'e 'ad ze dog back…" He looks up at me, grimacing, then continues, "I know where 'e goes looking for ze truffles on a private estate, so knew 'e would be back out wiz ze dog straight away. It's nearly ze end of ze season." He stops and looks up at me again, then shakes his head.

"You don't need ze details of what 'appened; ze dog is back safe."

"How's Beau?" I ask.

"'E iz good as new. Strong and resilient; like ze dog should be!"

"Go home to your family, take a day off… and thank you."

"I will quickly do ze animals zen go…" he replies, pulling on his padded camouflage jacket, looking like a soldier returning from conflict.

11

Alone again, I busy myself with jobs, the first being the security company who tell me they will come out to discuss my options. After lunch, I put Shadow on his lead and let him out for a few minutes in the back yard; he can have a proper walk this evening when Enzo returns. Later, just as the light begins to fade, Enzo bangs the front door shut; his face is flushed, and jaw clenched.

Hey, what's wrong?" I ask, approaching him slowly.

Slamming his keys on the kitchen table, he growls, "Bloody press!"

Rubbing his shoulder, attempting to calm him down, I ask, "What do you mean?"

"There's two of them near the front gate post. Of course, I got out to see who they were. That was a mistake." Shaking his head, he continues, "They asked if I was your boyfriend, offering me money in return for your 'rags to riches story'. Haven't they got anything better to do? They mentioned the Bugatti!"

I watch as he gets two mugs out of the cupboard, then puts the kettle on, slowly getting calmer; more like the Enzo that I know and love. "Have they gone; how did they find out about me?"

Sitting at the table, he sighs then reaches across, gently taking both of my hands in his. "Something to do with Gus's mothers' family; sounded complicated. They mentioned a court case; a name, LeBeau – yes, Phillipe LeBeau."

I can feel the blood draining from my head as my heart picks up its pace, trying hard to return it back where it belongs. With a look of concern, Enzo stands and strides around the kitchen table, putting his arms around me. "What is it? You've gone sheet white. Do you know this person?"

I quickly take a gulp of the hot coffee, burning my tongue as my mind drags me back to the letter I received from the same man some time ago; wanting to purchase the Chateau – and its contents for a piddly sum. I know I still have it; somewhere. Slowly, I stand, feeling a little dizzy, and make my way to the desk in the hall. "I think I put it in here."

Rummaging frantically, I am unsuccessful. Stepping in front of me, Enzo says, "May I?" Retreating, I watch as he methodically opens each letter, reads the signature at the end before returning them to their envelopes. "Here it is!" He exclaims, handing it to me several letters later.

Taking it with shaking hands, as if on autopilot, I return to the table, flop down on my chair to reacquaint myself with its contents.

To the new owner of 'The Chateau'

First, permit me to introduce myself. I am Monsieur Phillippe LeBeau, Gus Besnard's estranged biological grandfather. I have heard that your distant relative, Miss Mary Whitehead has sadly deceased and that you have inherited the old property; which I believe to be in a state of disrepair.

I understand what a daunting prospect this must be, and expect you are eager to secure a buyer; so, you can complete the sale quickly, and return to your busy life.

With that in mind, I would like to make you a sincere offer of 500,000 Euros cash, for the whole estate and contents as it stands. I think you will find, considering its current condition, that this is a fair and reasonable amount and would save you the considerable trouble of having to dispose of the contents yourself.

I look forward to hearing your response.

Kind regards,

Monsieur Phillipe LeBeau.

Enzo looks on expectantly as I take a moment to calm my thoughts. I hand him the offending letter, which he takes and reads. "What a cheek! I wonder why he's so interested in the place? We need to get to the bottom of this; let's take Shadow for a walk over to the farmhouse."

"Is it safe? Do you think they have anything to do with Shadow going missing?" I ask.

Retrieving our coats from the hall, he tries to reassure me that he thinks the two incidents aren't connected, but still puts Shadow on his long lead before stepping out into the dusk and locking the door. Taking no chances.

I'm shocked to find both Monsieur le Maire and Monsieur Bertrand in the warm kitchen with Xavier and Alice. "Oh sorry – I didn't know you had company; we'll call back later," I say, turning to leave.

"Laura, how delightful to see you again my dear," Monsieur le Maire says, turning on the charm. "Please stay; we're about to leave – aren't we, Monsieur Bertrand?" Monsieur Bertrand confirms with a nod and a thin smile, shaking hands with Alice and Xavier; the four of them then process towards the front door.

"A word of warning if I may; the press is snooping about," Enzo informs them, then continues with caution, "that's why we're here actually, they mentioned a court case with Phillipe LeBeau." Alice halts and puts her hands over her face, trying to suppress a sob, Monsieur le Maire is at her side instantly, offering her comfort. Something is definitely amiss, and I intend to find out what.

"Okay, what's going on?" I ask, not mincing my words, as soon as the two men leave, and Alice and Xavier have returned to the kitchen. Alice pretends to be busy washing four mugs in the sink bottom, and Xavier turns to his nearly empty bottle of brandy.

"Zey were just passing…"

"That's bull-shit Xavier, and you know it! What the hell is going on?" I ask louder, with my hands on my hips. "Has it got anything to do with this?" I ask, fishing the letter from Phillipe LeBeau out of my pocket.

Alice dries her hands on her apron then takes it from me, sits at the table and puts her glasses on, "It's in English; will you translate it for me, please?"

Sitting beside her, I do my best to read it out in French. "Oh boy; he's sly," Alice says, looking at me as I finish.

Xavier voices his feelings in a string of French swear words, which has his mother tutting, she then slips a hand into the deep pocket on the front of her apron and hands me an official-looking letter. The thing that strikes me first is the date, fourteenth of December; they have been sitting on this problem – whatever it may be, for some time.

Again, I do my best to understand its content, written in French legalese, while Enzo stands uncomfortably by the door with his hands tucked inside his jacket pockets. "Would you like me to take Shadow for a walk?"

"Stay," Xavier says, gesturing to a chair and holding up an empty glass. Enzo shakes his head but sits as instructed.

Sometime later I put the letter down on the table; horrified. Bile burns the back of my throat as I look at Alice, a single tear has escaped from the corner of her eye and runs down her cheek, splashing onto the letter on the table. No one speaks, I stand and pour the dregs of the bottle into the empty glass and down it in one. The sensation competes with the bile, but wins, as it warms its way down to my empty stomach, but the comfort is fleeting. Sighing, I sit, stand, then sit down again, agitation taking over. "What's it got to do with the Chateau and me?"

Xavier looks at the floor, but Alice decides to speak, hesitantly at first but gains momentum as she continues, "LeBeau's father was a distant relative of the general; he is bitter, dangerous and wealthy; his family contested the will when the Chateau was left to your great aunt… they lost, of course, but now he wants his pound of flesh."

Enzo, sensing something is wrong, stands and asks, "Do you feel like sharing it with me?"

I look over to Xavier, his shoulders have sagged, defeated; steepling his hands under his chin, he gives an almost imperceptible nod.

Enzo sits back down, elbows on table and waits. Taking a big breath, I somehow manage to speak. "It appears that Phillipe LeBeau is fighting for custody of Gus…"

Enzo jumps up from his chair, knocking the big table and tipping the brandy bottle over, then runs his hands through his hair and paces up and down several times. "That's ridiculous!" he says, then, standing still, he puts his hands in the air, "but he's got no chance… right?"

Xavier swirls the ice in his drink. Round and round. Round and round. Eventually, he says, "In two weeks, Gus might 'ave to go and live in Paris – wiv iz grandfazer." The pain on his face evident as he stands and strides outside, beckoning his big dog to follow.

I, too stand and try to follow him.

"Let him go," Alice says, unable to keep the wobble from her voice.

"How can I help? Monsieur Bertrand – surely, he can help." I say, sitting back down.

Alice quietly tells us that Monsieur Bertrand isn't qualified in family law so can't represent them, although he has offered advice and given them the name of a colleague in Valance who specialises in custody cases. "He is expensive – we can't afford…"

"No, but I can!" I state, jumping up and taking the letter from the table. "Give me his details, I'll contact him in the morning; two weeks isn't very long – we have to stop him." The obvious suddenly smacks me in the face. "Where's Gus? Does he know?" Alice tells me that he's gone to sleep the night at his friend's house and that he knows nothing. "Okay, let's keep it that way for as long as possible – I'll see what I can do."

We wait quietly with Alice until we hear Xavier coming back, then leave them alone for the evening. Now I know what's been troubling them; why didn't they tell me? We could have sorted it out sooner. It makes Shadow's kidnapping episode seem like a storm in a teacup.

I email all the information and relevant correspondence to Monsieur Pierre Robert, our new solicitor in Valance; and at two-thirty the following day I'm sat in his waiting room with an anxious Xavier; who's barely spoken a word all the way here. It's surprising how quickly you can get an appointment when you own a Chateau and a Bugatti! Glancing around me, I can tell it's going to be expensive, lots of polished glass and stainless steel; not to mention the luxurious chairs, but what's money? It's people that matter. Family. And these people are my family now.

"Monsieur Besnard, Miss Mackley, please come in," says Monsieur Robert, introducing himself, and showing us into his swanky office. A tray containing sculptured confectionery and a cafetière sits neatly on the desk in front of us. "Help yourselves," he says, his long, suited arm gliding in our direction. "Now, down to business," he continues, as he talks directly to Xavier, looking over to me occasionally, to make sure I understand what's being said.

"I've sent an email to Phillipe LeBeau's solicitor in Paris, but don't expect to hear from him for some time," he gestures vaguely, "it's standard practice to procrastinate. I have, however, requested an extension from the court, which I expect to be granted; so, we will have more time to prepare." He then advises Xavier of the other information required, saying, "I will need a detailed history of Gus's life and the circumstances that led to his mother leaving. Witness statements from professional people who can vouch that you are telling the truth, and a character reference from Monsieur Bertrand. Also, a letter from your family doctor, stating that Alice, Gus's grandmother, is now well enough to care for him."

Monsieur Robert turns to me, saying, "Miss Mackley, you need to write a letter, providing proof of employment and income for Xavier, as they are likely to suggest he can't afford to keep Gus." Okay, that's easy enough. I nod in agreement. Xavier at last speaks, but only to give his permission for Monsieur Robert to correspond with me by email. And, at last, we leave.

"Well, zat was a long way for ze half-hour conversation zat could 'ave been said on ze phone," he says, staring out of the window into the drizzle.

"Yes, but worth it, I have a good feeling – we have to stay positive," I say, more optimistically than I feel. "You need to sit with Alice and write a true account of what happened. Who will you ask to be a witness?"

He doesn't answer, just continues staring into the grey afternoon, as passing vehicles cover us with spray. Looking over to me he shrugs then says, "Don't know. I'll give it ze sought."

12

I try to stay away from the farmhouse as much as possible, allowing them some space to complete the task. I can be of little help, knowing only what I've heard from Rose; perhaps she would be a reliable witness, I'm sure she'd be willing to help. I'll mention it next time I visit.

The security company visits and explains my various options; I choose the cheapest: cameras facing in all four directions, mounted on the Chateau, cameras on all gate posts, with small beams set into them which will set off a bell in the Chateau every time anyone enters, and an alarm on all the doors of the Chateau. Quite expensive, but necessary. I do hope the Bugatti sells for a reasonable price or the renovations will have to be delayed.

The days pass slowly, as we try to return to some semblance of normality; whatever that is. A week later, I receive my first e-mail from Pierre Robert.

Good morning Miss Mackley,

I'm writing to inform you that Phillipe LeBeau's solicitor has responded, asking for the following, some of the items we had already anticipated:

Proof of employment and income.

A doctor's report regarding Alice Besnard.

The latest school report for Gus Besnard.

I would appreciate if you could forward me the above items, along with a detailed account of Gus's life, with witness statements where possible to back up the information, as discussed.

Regards

Pierre Robert.

A trip to the farmhouse is required. I have my statement prepared, but I don't know where Xavier and Alice have got to with theirs; they assured me they were on to it the last time we spoke. Luckily, Sylvie is Gus's teacher, so a letter from her won't be a problem. There are times when this small, tight-knit community seems more of a blessing than others.

"Morning, I have an e-mail for you," I say, handing a printed copy to Alice, who is peeling potatoes at the sink. "Where's Xavier?"

Wiping her hands on her apron and taking the sheet of paper, she asks, "Is it good or bad?"

"Nothing to worry about; if you've done the tasks."

Her forehead wrinkles as she hurries over to the dresser, taking a large folder out of a drawer. "I hope it's good enough," she says, handing it to me, then heads to put the kettle on. Alice makes coffee while I look through the contents.

"Do you mind if I read these?"

"Sure," Xavier's voice says, sounding happier than of late, making me jump at the unexpected sound. "Sorry, I was upstairs, I didn't mean to startle you."

"Oh, we need Gus's latest school report – do you have it?" I ask, waving a hand dismissing Xavier's apology. Alice gets to her feet and searches in a cupboard. Returning, beaming with pride, she hands it to me.

"He is very bright - I don't know where he gets it from; his mother's side probably."

"Don't put yourself down; you've both done an amazing job. Gus is thriving under your care." I say, opening the report. It is of course, exemplary, I continue looking at the other items. A detailed account of Gus's life, a doctor's letter regarding Alice and witness accounts from both Monsieur le Maire and Monsieur Bertrand – smart move; both men of influence. "Excellent," I say as I prepare to leave, "I'll take these home to read – if I may?

I'll also ask Sylvie for an accompanying letter, then get them sent off."

Later, the sound of the alarm that tells me someone or something has entered the drive activates with a loud 'beep-beep'. Peering out of the dining room window, I see the familiar Land Rover. I silence the alarm as he climbs out of his vehicle and up the stairs. "Just passing; I thought I'd grab a coffee break with you," Enzo says, planting a kiss on the top of my head when he walks through the door.

"Good idea. I was just wading through the letters for the solicitor; everything appears to be in order." I head to the cupboard and grab a mug, pour some coffee from the pot into it and pass it to him.

Dunking a ginger biscuit from the packet on the table in his steaming mug, Enzo asks, "How's Xavier?"

"Better; I just hope we've got enough, the enormity of the situation is just starting to sink in. Failure isn't an option." I feel myself getting angry. Enzo shuffles his chair closer and rubs my back, the contact instantly lifting my spirits.

"I'm sure it will work out in the end."

"I wish I could do more."

"Hey, you've done everything you possibly can; they wouldn't have managed without you," he says, gently. "I know they appreciate your help."

"Xavier insists he'll find a way to pay me back," I say, watching as Enzo dunks another biscuit and it disintegrates and drops into his coffee. "We'll see, perhaps I could take twenty Euros a month from his wage – it would take a long time, but it might make him feel better."

Enzo's phone buzzes in his pocket before he could respond.

"Got to go," he says after answering his phone, "Are you sure you don't need me to sleep over tonight? I don't mind."

"No, it's very kind of you, but the security is in place now and seems to work well; I'll be fine." Sensing his disappointment, I add, "How about your next night off – I could come and stay at yours." Enzo nods and heads out the door.

The beep alerts me to the fact that Enzo has left, and I get down to work; lots of e-mails to respond to. John Burrows has requested a pitch on the caravan site for a week at Easter; he stayed with his family for a while last year by accident after his car had a puncture. I remember vividly the day he discovered the Bugatti hidden behind a false wall in the carriage house, which I managed to accidentally knock a hole in with the tractor. It seems like a lifetime ago; so much has happened since then, I don't even feel like the same person. The site won't be ready for Easter, but they can use my facilities, like last time.

Another e-mail informs me that the contractors are eager to start work and will be sending someone to survey the ground; to assess whether it's dried out enough after the bad weather. That's exciting; progress at last.

An e-mail from Sylvie with an accompanying letter about Gus arrives; that was quick. I have all I need now to return to Pierre Robert, my next job.

After a late lunch, another beep gets my attention. A quick look at the camera shows a small lorry turning in through the gate posts – what can it be? A couple of minutes later, I'm stood at the front door watching, as a short, stocky man in a woolly cap climbs out of his cab with a clipboard. Holding a piece of paper out for me to sign, he says, "Trees."

Of course! I'd forgotten about them; it must be a couple of weeks since I ordered the fruit trees, so much has happened since. Wrapping my cardigan around myself, I approach the lorry. "I'm not signing until they're unloaded," I say, gesturing as I continue, "I want them behind the Chateau, please. I'll get someone to help you."

It takes Xavier and the man an hour or so to unload one hundred mixed fruit saplings. I'm sure it will take us a lot longer to plant them. With the light fading and the lorry no longer here, Xavier surveys the scene, looking at me as though I'm a child, "Zey will need protection; ze boar and deer will feast on zem."

"I see you're back on form – I'll order some tree protectors, though I've never seen a boar, or a deer on the estate yet."

When his eyebrows rise, I can tell he's about to rant, but he remembers his manners in time. "Yes, zat will 'elp wiz ze rabbits, but ze boar will just dig zem up, I 'ave ze electric fence zat I used wiz ze sheep, I will bring it in ze morning."

"Well, that will keep us busy for a few days; Gus can help too," I say, trying to lighten the mood. "Come on, it's too late now, we can't plant them in the dark," I add, turning to leave.

13

It's my first night alone since Shadow disappeared. I have mixed feelings. I enjoy Enzo's company; he's funny, caring and quite romantic, but I also like being on my own with Shadow. Xavier took him out before he left, so, he'll be okay until bedtime. The heavy curtains are all closed and the fires roaring, so we'll be nice and cosy; I settle down in the small sitting room to check e-mails. The contractors confirm they are sending a man out tomorrow to survey the site, and I have an enquiry for a thirtieth birthday party; a friend of a friend of Jacques. It will probably turn out to be quite a drunken affair, but it's business.

In need of an early night, I accompany Shadow for a quick stroll in the back yard before settling into bed with a mug of hot chocolate. A beeping noise permeates through my dreams and disrupts my slumber. Shadow jumps up and barks. What was that? Beep. Beep. It does it again. The beam has been broken on the gate posts. I'm not expecting visitors! I jump out of bed and scramble through the papers on my dressing table, locating my tablet to look at the grainy image. What on earth is it? It beeps again as another creature appears on the screen, digging in the soil. Of course! It's a boar, well two of them. Much larger than I thought, at least a meter high. Sagging with relief, I reassure Shadow and climb back into bed. Less than an hour later, it happens again, a quick glance at the screen reassures me that it's the boars once more. This carries on for some time; rather annoyingly, until I stop looking and try to ignore the beeps. Who thought that this was a good idea?

The following morning, I answer the door bleary-eyed to a middle-aged man in baggy jeans and lumberjack shirt, introducing himself as the surveyor. Having been kept up most of the night by pigs, I missed the arrival of his van. He follows me over to the designated site at the side of the carriage house and starts pacing over the field, kicking at the odd tuft of grass, and stamping in any hollows. "Don't you have any equipment with you to test the ground?" I ask, rather optimistically.

He looks up at me and shrugs, walks a few meters to an old discarded branch, snaps a length off, comes back towards me and pokes it into the soft earth. Looking at me with a grin, showing several missing teeth, he says, "Yes, it's okay." Walking away, he lights up a cigarette which provokes a coughing fit. Recovering slowly, he wanders back to his van. He nods at an inner thought and climbs in then winds the window down and says, "The equipment will arrive shortly." Well, that was very technical, I hope they know what they're doing. Monsieur le Maire recommended them; he probably owed them a favour. It is, after all, only groundworks; what could possibly go wrong?

Walking briskly back towards the Chateau, I encounter Xavier milking the goats. "Morning," I shout across the paddock to him.

"Come 'ere. Look," Xavier gestures towards one of the goat's waiting in line.

"What's wrong?" I ask, "Shall I call Enzo?"

"No, I sink she iz pregnant, look – she 'az stopped producing ze milk and iz getting big."

"How did that happen?"

"Ze usual way," he says dryly, not looking up from his task.

"Obviously, but the males are in a separate paddock."

Once he's finished his task, he looks at me and says, "Yes, and I told you zat ze big male escapes. 'E iz ze nuisance."

"Well, if we're going to make more cheese to sell, we'll need more goats."

"Only if zey are girls; and it takes a long time, she will need her milk for ze babies; so, we will 'ave less milk for ze chevre."

Mm, I hadn't thought of that; I'll get Enzo to check them over when he calls. Oh, there were boar in the garden last night, they kept setting the alarm off when they came through the gate." I add as an afterthought.

His eyes light up. "Excellent, what time?"

"I can't remember exactly; I'll have to look at the images again to find the times." I turn and head for the house. He stands, picks up the buckets and stool and follows me back home. "I'll fetch my tablet while you load the buckets in your truck to take to Alice," I say once we get inside.

Xavier looks through the images, getting quite excited; noting the times, which seems a strange thing to do, but I decide not to question him. Soon after, he starts to swear loudly. "What's wrong?" I ask alarmed.

He looks at me, concerned, then tries to change the subject, "Nozing; shall we make a start wiz ze trees?"

"Okay." He is weird. While he's in the garage collecting the tools, I take another look at the images on the tablet. Nothing unusual; several pictures of wild boar. Just as I'm about to turn it off, I see two shapes on the last image. Enlarging it, I can just about make out two men in dark clothes. Four-twenty in the morning. I wonder who they are. This must be what Xavier saw; why didn't he tell me? I don my coat and wellies and follow him into the meadow where the trees are to be planted. "Okay, who are they?" I demand.

"Who?" He asks, pretending to examine a small tree.

"You know very well; the two men in the pictures." Slowly, he digs a small hole and plants a sapling, avoiding eye contact. "Well?" I ask again when he doesn't answer immediately.

"You are like ze dog wiv ze bone!"

"If you don't tell me, I'll ring the police."

That has the desired effect; his head whips up, and he looks into my eyes. "Police are ze last zing you need; keep out of zis, I will deal wiz it."

"Okay, only if you tell me who they are."

Picking up another sapling he sighs, and replies, "Big Cyrille, ze man who took Shadow."

"What are you going to do? He's dangerous – you can't confront him again!"

"I 'ave a plan – I need you to send me ze image, and I can sort it," he replies, planting another tree.

"Look, this is not your problem…"

Snapping his head up and staring at me, he interrupts, "No, and Gus is not your problem; zis iz 'ow we work, yes?"

Softening my stance, I look at him, "Xavier – you, Gus, and Alice are like family to me."

"Touché!" He replies, signalling the end of the conversation. Okay, I'm going to get nowhere with this, he's so stubborn. I'll let it drop, for now, he might have won this battle, but the war's not over; I can't let him confront these people again, it might not end so well next time.

Over the next few days, we manage to plant the trees; Gus places small tree protectors around the saplings and Xavier rigs up an electric fence to keep the larger animals out. Tired but satisfied, I make my way up to the top of the mound to survey my new orchard. It looks stunning with the bright afternoon sun low in the sky, scattering light through the bare branches. I close my eyes and try to picture it in spring, covered with frothy blossom; not long to wait now. Then, in summer, the meadow will be a riot of colour from the wildflowers. I can't wait to see it. When I arrived last summer, it had already withered to a mass of brown seed heads, with only the odd brave flower left scorching in the fierce heat. This is the exact spot that I had my encounter with the viper; I wonder where it is now? Asleep underground no doubt. What a long way we've come since then; but there's still so much more to do.

I take my time and enjoy the walk back home with Shadow – still on his lead – calling in to check on the walled garden. Xavier has been busy in here too, the greenhouses are full of seed trays and pots which are starting to sprout, and the prepared beds are covered in horticultural fleece to warm the soil up ready to plant this year's vegetable and salad crops. I know he's finished pruning the vines and olive trees; so, he's got a bit more time now. I've ordered a dozen more beehives that should arrive next week, the bees though won't be ready until March. I've never been stung by a bee, but I'm sure that will be rectified shortly.

14

My phone ringing in my pocket breaks the quiet spell.

"Hi, I've finished now for two days, would you like to do something?" Enzo asks.

"Oh sorry, I'm helping Xavier tomorrow; we're giving the drawing room a makeover, as they're coming to hang the chandeliers next week."

"Oh, okay. I'll come and help," Enzo replies, trying to hide his disappointment.

"That's really kind of you – but I would understand if you've got something better to do."

"No, nothing planned; I'll be there about seven."

I'd better get back and invent something for dinner; I was just going to get a pizza out of the freezer.

The following morning, the backdoor beeps at eight-thirty; its Xavier, dressed in dirty overalls and carrying a set of ladders. "Would you like breakfast?" I ask, pointing to the table set for two.

"I breakfasted two hours ago," he replies dryly.

"Morning," Enzo says cheerily as he arrives downstairs.

Xavier offers a curt nod and walks past with his ladder in the direction of the drawing room. We eat hastily and join him, setting to work lifting the rugs and moving what little furniture I have into the centre of the room, before covering them and the piano with dust sheets. Starting with a thorough clean, I remove the accumulations of dust and cobwebs before beginning to paint, a combination of pale pink and light grey. If Aunt Mary is watching, I hope she approves. By early afternoon, the first coat is on, but it looks a little patchy.

"We will 'ave to do it again tomorrow. Now we 'ave time to do ze hall; it won't take long, it's not 'az big." Xavier announces, carrying the ladder through.

"That man is more like a machine," Enzo says, rolling his neck and shoulders. "I'm knackered."

I look at him sympathetically, and massage his shoulders, "Have a break, take Shadow for a walk."

Later, exhausted, we fall into bed just after ten. "Sorry, not much of a day off, was it?" I say, cuddling into him.

"Mm, you smell of paint and toothpaste," he replies before kissing me.

Our sleep is disturbed by a loud crack. Sitting up quickly, I survey the room; Shadow is stood by the door, wanting to get out. The familiar noise starts again. Gunshots. Enzo jumps out of bed and looks out of the window.

"It's too dark to see anything," he says.

I grab my tablet to look at the camera. There are two men with guns, but I can't identify them. I don't think its Big Cyrille, neither of them looks rotund enough. "What should we do?" I ask while pacing the room.

Climbing back into bed, Enzo says, "Nothing; but I've got an idea that will take your mind off the situation…"

I grin and head back to bed.

Xavier arrives again at eight-thirty the next morning, and thankfully, we finish our decorating and have tidied up by mid-afternoon.

"Ze second coat doesn't take az long," Xavier announces, washing the now pink rollers and trays, before departing quickly.

"He seemed in a hurry," I say.

"Fine by me; a hot bath I think, come on," Enzo says, taking my hand.

Later, we stroll through the grounds with Shadow before darkness falls, he seems quite excited and drags us up the drive. "It's not like him, he usually prefers the woods," Enzo says puzzled. I try to distract him and take him towards the pond, but he's having none of it. "Let's follow him," Enzo suggests. A short while later Enzo bends down and picks up an object.

"What is it?" I ask.

He passes it to me, "A spent cartridge from a rifle; that's what we heard last night." Shadow gets faster as we near an area of flattened grass, "Look – blood." Enzo says, bending down to examine a dark patch. Pointing, he continues, "Wheel tracks too. I'd say someone has been poaching here. Show those images to Xavier, he might recognise them."

We head back towards the Chateau. Kissing Enzo before he leaves for his night shift, I say, "Sorry to ambush your days off, but thank you for your help."

"I've actually enjoyed it, though I do still ache a little."

"I owe you," I reply, blowing him a kiss.

The following morning I'm at the farmhouse at eight, I want to catch Xavier before he heads out onto the estate. Shadow stops at one of the outbuildings behind the farmhouse, sniffing the bottom of the door eagerly. "Come on, boy," I say tugging him a little, but he refuses to budge. "Come on

Shadow," I repeat, pulling harder at his lead, but he's going nowhere. "Mm, what's got you so excited?" I say, tentatively trying the door. It opens, and I step inside warily, the scent of death heavy in the air.

Gradually, my eyes adjust to the gloom of the dank building. Shadow jumps up and down at my side, working himself into a frenzy. Two massive objects appear to be hung from the ceiling, finding my phone I use it as a torch. "Whoa!" I jump back, startled, as I realise that I'm stood next to two large, dead Boar hung from the rafters on fierce looking hooks; their throats slit. Still covered in hair. Of course, the gunshots. It was Xavier, but he wasn't alone. I wonder who helped him? I forcefully drag Shadow out of the building and run the few yards to the farmhouse, bursting through the door.

Xavier jumps up from the table and rushes towards me. "What iz ze matter?" He asks alarmed.

"You!" I shout, pointing to him then back to the door. "The boar – hung up out there!" I continue gesturing wildly.

Visibly sagging with relief, he returns to his breakfast, "Zey are good – yes?"

"Who helped you?" I ask, finally calming down.

"Friend."

"You could have warned me…"

"Why? You would not 'ave been pleased – now we 'ave good meat and zey will not eat ze crops," he says between mouthfuls of sausage. "I will butcher zem tomorrow and bring you some for ze freezer."

Alice, I notice, keeps quiet, busying herself with the dishes, obviously party to the event. Changing the subject, I say, "Enzo says the goats are okay, and he's left some traps out to try and catch the feral cats, so we can get them neutered; will you check them for me a few times a day? I don't want to leave them in the traps longer than necessary."

Stuffing his mouth with the remains of his breakfast, he says, "Can't today – going out."

"Where?"

"Friend."

Another conversation that he's not willing to have, where is he going? Not getting any further, I bid everyone goodbye and head back to the Chateau. Just as I get past the pond on my journey home, I think I can hear a heavy grumbling noise. Shadow lifts his head and looks around; nothing to see. Once over the small bridge, I can feel vibrations in the ground – I don't think earthquakes are an issue here. The noise gets louder, and a metallic clanking joins the rumpus, followed by shouting. Moments later, I arrive on the drive to see a low-loader trundling towards me with large earth moving machinery on board. The procession comes to a halt, and an older man climbs out of his cab and approaches me.

"Is he in?"

I stand still, look at him and reply, "Who exactly are you looking for?"

"The boss," he says louder, as though I'm stupid.

"I am the boss, this is my estate," I say, equally as exaggerated.

His mouth drops open, and he stares at me before continuing, "Are you sure? It says 'Xavier Besnard' on my worksheet."

"He is my estate manager, but it's his day off – so you're stuck with me, I'm afraid."

The poor man's mouth drops even further, then his demeanour becomes more business-like and respectful. "Where do you want them – Mademoiselle?"

"At the side of the carriage house, please; follow me." Once on site, a young man emerges and helps him to unload the heavy machinery. While they do that, I head to the kitchen to make coffee. When it's ready, I hand them the coffee and ask, "When will the work-force arrive?"

"Nothing to do with me, Mademoiselle, I don't know – I only hire out the machinery."

Oh well, at least it's a start. An e-mail to the contractors is required.

15

I get my reply a few hours later, they will be starting on Monday; not long to wait. I also have an e-mail from Valentina, Leo's sister. She is going to the classic car auction in Paris and asks if I'd like to accompany her. I respond.

Thank you for asking, but it's too far away. Enzo will be working, and the contractors will be here, so I can't take much time off.

It's a shame, she's a great person, and I think we'd get along well, but I'm too busy at the moment. She answers.

I won't take no for an answer; I'll pick you up at seven on Saturday morning.

Perhaps she's been drinking the wine instead of selling it, the auction starts at ten! I send a reply.

Have you got a Tardis?

Mm, I wonder how much it will sell for, I want to place the order to have a new kitchen fitted, but I need about thirty thousand Euros, and the roof needs replacing, that's another fifty thousand and the bathrooms… My email beeps with her message.

Just be ready.

"What is that noise?" I say to Shadow early Saturday morning as we stroll through the back yard. It gets louder, a thudding, whirring noise. Shadow doesn't like it and rushes back inside, whimpering. It sounds to be at the front of the Chateau. I peer out of the dining room window as dawn breaks to see flashing lights dropping out of the sky onto the front lawn. A helicopter! It comes to a halt, and the rotor blades slow down and stop. Valentina! She didn't tell me she was coming in a helicopter! I rush outside to see her being helped out of the machine, waving as she approaches.

"Wow! You didn't mention a helicopter!" I shout.

"Laura, how lovely to see you again – are you ready?"

"Yes; I'll just get my bag," I say, running into the hall.

Valentina introduces me to the pilot, who helps me to strap myself in securely and hands me a set of headphones with a microphone. My eyes don't know where to look first as we leave the ground, I take lots of photos of the Chateau and estate as it gets smaller, beginning to look like a toy village. "This is amazing, thank you," I gush, "I can use these photos for my website, but you shouldn't have come all this way just to get me."

"No trouble at all, I was down on the coast on business, so it's not out of my way. I'll get a friend of mine to come out and take some professional photos for you when you're ready. Oh look, we're nearly there."

"In Paris?" I ask.

"No, we're catching a jet in Valence, it's much quicker."

"Oh, I haven't got a ticket…"

"You don't need one." Valentina interrupts.

The pilot starts talking to someone, and I look about me, puzzled. "It's only air traffic control, we're cleared to land," Valentina explains. My stomach suddenly feels as though it's in my mouth as we start to descend. Fifteen minutes later and I'm strapped into the seat of yet another aircraft as we are catapulted along the runway at speed. Lifting steeply up into the air. How the other half lives; Enzo will be so jealous! What would Gran think if she could see me now – in a private jet?

We are met on arrival by Monsieur Levant, the man who came to value the Bugatti. "How delightful to see you both again, do let me show you around," he says. Swiftly avoiding the crowds, he takes us via a short cut into a vast exhibition hall made of glass, housing the cars for sale. It's mesmerising. A profusion of colour. Vehicles of all different shapes and sizes lined up. Monsieur Levant hands Valentina a catalogue and politely asks, "What exactly are you looking for today?"

"Well, I'm looking for a car to enter into historic rallying events, but first we'd like coffee." She says.

"Of course, how very remiss of me," he replies, guiding us over to the VIP hospitality area, accompanying us to a table beautifully set on a mezzanine level looking down over the collection.

A smartly dressed middle-aged man sat alone on the next table stands and offers his hand to me. "Miss Mackley, how nice to meet you at last." I take his hand a little confused and offer a smile in return. How does he know my name? "I am Phillipe LeBeau – you may recall I made you an offer for your property last summer, but alas, you didn't respond."

A little shaken, I square my shoulders and choose my words carefully, "Yes, thank you for your interest; I do recall the letter, but the Chateau is not for sale."

"I see the Bugatti is, though."

Sensing my discomfort, Monsieur Levant stands, "Yes, it's there; shall we go and take a look?"

I nod, and we all head towards the cars, leaving Phillipe LeBeau at his table.

"Wow, I wouldn't have recognised it," I reply, composing myself, as we arrive at its side. "I can't believe it's the same car!"

"Our team have done an excellent job of preparing it while retaining the originality." Monsieur Levant replies. "The auction will be starting shortly; would you like to look at the other cars first?"

"Yes, please," Valentina interrupts, "I'm after the little blue Alpine A110; would you bid for me? One hundred thousand is my ceiling."

"Excellent choice." Monsieur Levant replies, leading us over to the exhibit. It seems a lot of money for a little car, but I manage to keep my thoughts to myself. Next, he looks at me and continues, "The Bugatti is last; the grand finale, there has been a lot of interest."

Valentina looks over to a small group of men with cameras that are being hustled to the side. "Damn, Paparazzi! They get everywhere; I'm afraid you're likely to be in the newspapers tomorrow," she says, looking at me in concern.

"Why would they be in the slightest bit interested in me?"

"Well, firstly, they have nothing better to do. Secondly, the Bugatti is big news, and – I'm afraid – you're with me; they adore reporting what I do next, waiting like vultures to capture any unladylike moments." Of course, I'd forgotten that her brother Leo, is a count. I've seen pictures of their ancestral pile; it makes my Chateau look like an outbuilding. I'm not used to the company of A-listers.

The noise from the well-heeled hushes as the auctioneer takes his place and the cars, one by one, go under the hammer; some at eyewatering prices. Valentina seems quite pleased as she gets the little blue car slightly under her ceiling price.

The auctioneer says, "Ladies and gentlemen, now to the star of the show…" He introduces the Bugatti, adding a list of details about its provenance. "Who will start me at one and a half million?"

What? Do I hear correctly? I look at Monsieur Levant, who smiles back at me warmly, not in the least bit put out. I, on the other hand, feel as though I'm about to faint. "Could we go back to our table," I whisper to Valentina. "Has that man gone?"

"Certainly – yes, he's down here; in fact, he was the first to bid."

Monsieur Levant orders coffee as we watch the proceedings, it feels like an out of body experience as the price escalates and passes three million.

"This is insane," I whisper to him.

"It's a rarity with a unique history, we expected at least three million, everything from now on is a bonus; competition is fierce," he says. My brain begins to shut down, as it usually does when I'm way out of my depth.

"Sold in the room for three million, three hundred and fifty thousand Euros!" Shouts the auctioneer, tapping his hammer on the lectern.

I look up from my coffee cup just as a bright flash explodes in front of me. "What was that?"

"Paparazzi, I'm afraid; it was inevitable," Valentina says. "It seems they are more interested in you than me for a change. Just think of it as free publicity for your business; it might be worth making a small statement."

"Me? Make a statement? I wouldn't have a clue."

"Yes, it really could be advantageous, perhaps you should do an exclusive for one of the upmarket glossy mags. Then you'd get paid to promote your venture. Win-win."

I look back at her a little bewildered. "I wouldn't know where to start."

She picks up her cup and drains it, looks at her watch and says, "Time to go; give it some thought. Sophie, my cousin, deals with our PR, she would help – it's not that difficult."

We head back to the airport.

"Thank you for the lift," I say later, as I'm assisted out of the helicopter in front of the Chateau into the impending dusk. "You're very welcome to stay the night," I add as an afterthought, then immediately wish I hadn't. She won't be used to my lack of facilities.

"No worries, I'm glad you enjoyed it; I'm meeting Leo and Cecilia at the villa, they're staying there for the weekend with the twins – you must join us sometime. Oh, and give some thought to the publicity opportunity, but you'll need to act fast, they get bored and move on quickly."

I retreat to the front door and watch as they lift off into the pink sky and slowly disappear. Wow, what a life she must lead! Inside, Shadow greets me enthusiastically, I can see he has been fed by the gnawed bones left near his bowl; Xavier must have been and fed him. I quickly change out of my finery and back into comfortable clothes and stick a pizza in the oven. The contrast is stark. Would I want her lifestyle? Shadow comes across and licks the back of my hand; no, I wouldn't swap what I have here.

16

I'm back safely, what a day! How're things with you? x

I know Enzo is on-call, so he might be too busy to reply. Should I tell him how much the

Bugatti made? No, I won't … unless he asks. Now for Xavier – what should I tell him? I don't think I've processed it myself yet. Now I can afford to start renovating the Chateau, but I mustn't get blasé; I still have a big tax bill to settle first. Shadow is curled up on the rug in front of the crackling fire, while I research which kitchen appliances I want; it's too easy to get carried away, but I'm going to stick to my original budget. I'm not expecting to make a profit in my first year.

Great news. All OK here, missing you! Xx

I'm tired and sleep in late the following morning, and woken by a bleep – the back door; someone has come inside. I grab my robe and arm myself with my trusted candlestick, popping my head over the galleried landing to hear Xavier chuntering to himself.

"Coming!" I shout, taking the steps two at a time.

"Good afternoon," he says dryly.

"It is Sunday, and only nine-twenty."

"Mama is making ze lunch, and you are invited."

"That's kind, one o'clock?"

"Well?" He asks quizzically.

"Well, what?"

"What does it feel like to be ze millionaire?"

"Oh, the Bugatti; I've not had time to think about it… how do you know, anyway?"

He doesn't answer but slaps a newspaper down on the table. The headline reads, LOCAL HEIRESS – RAGS TO RICHES! With a photo of me, sitting next to Valentina. I look up at him, shocked, then pick the paper up and begin to scan the article.

English incomer, Laura Mackley, the new owner of the Chateau has made nearly three and a half million Euros by selling the vintage Bugatti she found on her estate to an unnamed recipient in Paris. It is believed she has also sold numerous other items from the Chateau to further increase her wealth. The Chateau once belonged to the 'Deford family' which included a long line of brave military personnel.

She is pictured here socialising with Valentina Carboni, multi-millionairess and daughter of a count from Italy...

I put the paper down and sag, "Well, that's not very complimentary."

"What did you expect?" Xavier replies, raising his eyebrows.

"I hadn't given it any thought; I don't understand why they're interested."

"You 'ad better get used to it, zey are camped at ze bottom of ze drive."

"What?" I shout, standing and walking towards the front door.

Xavier steps in front of me, blocking my progress, "Don't be stupid, do you want ze picture tomorrow to be you in zis?" He says, picking up the collar of my fleece dressing gown. He's right of course, but what should I do now? "Do not go out or open ze front door, I'll come back for you at lunchtime." Xavier turns and walks out, closing the door behind him. Now what? A prisoner in my own home! Surely, they'll get bored and go soon, and its Sunday; don't they have families to go home to?

"Are they still here?" I ask Xavier when he arrives back later. He just nods and whistles for Shadow, who appears instantly by his side. "I'll just get his lead," I say.

"No need, 'Big Cyrille' won't be bozering you again."

I stand tall and square my shoulders, "Why Xavier? What have you done now?" I say, examining his face for signs of bruising.

"Sorted it."

"How?"

"Can't you just accept it's over?"

"No! What have you done?"

His face softens a little for just a moment before he tells me, "I took ze photo of 'im trespassing on your land wiv ze gun to Monsieur le Maire, who 'appens to be ze brozer of ze man who owns a productive estate where 'Big Cyrille' is granted permission to hunt for ze truffles. 'E told 'im if 'e causes any more trouble 'e will not allow 'im back on 'iz land – simple – yes?"

I do hope it's that simple with no repercussions… but I now know how this community works – and all favours are called in at some time. Shadow enjoys his freedom on the short walk to the farmhouse. Thankfully, the press has stayed at the gate and not ventured onto the estate. The contractors will be back in the morning; perhaps they'll get rid of them for me.

"This is lovely Alice, thank you," I say, tucking into a bowl of tasty stew.

Xavier looks up from his food and gives his mother a knowing look while Gus has a fit of giggles. Alice nudges his elbow, and he stops abruptly, looking at his empty dish. Whatever the joke is, I'm clearly not going to be included. We spend a couple of hours discussing the progress the contractors have made with the ground works; the pitches have been dug out, and the gravel is due on-site tomorrow for the hard standing. Water pipes and the septic tank are still to be installed, as is the small toilet and shower block, which is to be made inside a 'log-cabin'. They assure me it will be ready for Easter. I haven't taken any bookings for the campsite until the end of April, apart from my friends, the Burrows' family. Hopefully, we'll be up and running by late spring.

I have my first official function in a few weeks; a small wedding reception for Philip and Joelle, who live and work in Paris, but have a second home here in the Ardeche, where Philip's mother lives. Phillip's mother,

Edith, is paying for the event and wants the same menu that she enjoyed at the 'old folks' Christmas party that I hosted for the village in December. That should be easy, I've hired a clever 'hog-roast' machine that is basically an oven in a trailer, powered by bottled gas that stays outside. If I like it, I'll see if I can find a second-hand one for sale.

Beeping the following morning alerts me to the fact that the contractors are here, I wonder how they got on with the press? I saw Xavier stroll across earlier, so he can deal with them. I join them later, just in time to witness the gravel being laid; my first few pitches are now ready, but there's still a lot to do.

"Good afternoon, it's progressing well," I say to the foreman, the same chap that came out to do a not so high-tech survey of the ground a couple of weeks ago.

"Starting to dig out for the septic tank tomorrow," he says, between puffs of his cigarette.

I smile and nod, leaving them to their work. Apparently, most of the press has gone, only a couple of tenacious guys left. I expect they have realised that I live a mundane life, and not much excitement is going to happen here. My next stop is the paddock to visit the goats, Enzo wasn't sure when my pregnant nanny is due to give birth, so I'm keeping a close eye on her. Thankfully, she seems okay, and the cats have recovered well and are back on rodent duty. There's only one billy goat in the other paddock, the biggest one is missing; he must have escaped again! Shadow joins me in the hunt for Big Billy, I know he likes the walled garden, so that's my first stop. Xavier has repaired the gate, and it's closed. Opening it, I poke my head in, but he's not here. Where next? If I were a greedy goat, where would I go? The orchard: no sign of him here either, now I'm puzzled. I send a text to Xavier.

Big Billy is missing again.

Xavier might have better luck than me.

It's okay, I know where 'e iz.

One problem less, I'll let him deal with it. Enzo is coming for supper, I'm making a stew with the meat Alice gave me yesterday, it was so tasty; she's given me the recipe: lamb, bacon, onions, garlic, carrots, potatoes, mushrooms, chopped tomatoes, and fresh herbs.

"Mm, something smells good," Enzo says, taking his big coat off. "How's your day been?"

Over dinner, he asks about my trip to Paris. He thinks an article in a magazine would be good publicity if it was done right, and suggests I ask Valentina for her help. Tomorrow's job.

"I'm going to need a few more nanny goats for milk, do you know anyone who is selling any?" I ask later once the dishes are washed and we're sitting in the living room.

"I'll make some calls in the morning. If not, we could go to a farmer's market, we're bound to find some ... but right now I have other plans," he says, lifting me off the couch and carrying me upstairs.

17

I load a tray with goodies and treat Enzo to breakfast in bed, which goes down well; he does a lot for me, keeping an eye on my animals and refusing payment. One thing leads to another and an hour passes by.

"Going for a shower; I must get on," I say, leaving him in bed.

Jobs to do – first I email Valentina, asking her to set up a meeting with Sophie, her cousin and PR person. Next, I ring several kitchen companies, asking them to come out and give me quotes. The land-line rings with its shrill piercing tone.

"You 'ave to get 'ere, now!"

"Hello, Xavier. Where is here, exactly?"

"On-site, ze emergency!"

That's all I get before he hangs up.

"Grab your bag; emergency on-site," I shout to Enzo as he finally appears downstairs.

I run across as fast as my wellies permit. Enzo gets there before me, expecting some sort of traumatic injury to one of the men. I arrive panting to find Xavier and several men staring into a big hole. "What's wrong?" I manage once I've got my breath back. I peer into the bottom of the hole to see a substantial metal chest with its lid curled open like a sardine can, revealing its contents – guns; lots of them, and hand-grenades.

"Oh, my God!" I say, "What are they doing here?"

I start to make my way towards it, but Xavier stops me, "Zay are old and could explode any moment – we will 'ave to ring ze police."

"Are they from the war?" I ask, then suddenly remember. "There was an old map of the estate with some of the war memorabilia; it had a few crosses marked on it, I put it back in the bureau – didn't give it another thought."

"Go and find it, and ring ze police, I will evacuate ze site." Xavier orders, as he takes charge.

I hear the sirens in the distance getting louder and louder, as I locate the old map in the bureau after phoning the police. The contractors are now huddled at the top of the drive with the press. Oh dear! I'd forgotten about them; I'll be in the news again tomorrow!

"It's a good job that your contractors only took the top off the chest; if they had dug it out of the ground, it would have exploded –

very unstable. We need bomb disposal experts." One of the officer's in charge says. I give the police officer the map, and he confirms that the cross does match the same spot that the ammunition was discovered. "We have to assume that the other crosses are potential sites for explosives – I'm sorry Mademoiselle, you will have to evacuate the estate, you have half an hour to collect your belongings then we will have to cordon the whole estate off."

"Come on, let me help you; you can stay with me," Enzo says.

"I need to be here – and what about Xavier, Alice, and Gus? Where will they go?"

"My place is too small; don't they have some family?" My mind flashes to Cruella Deville! Will she have them? I don't think so! I shake my head in despair.

True to his word, the police officer allows me only thirty minutes then I am evicted from the area. Xavier, on the other hand, refuses to go;

insisting he has the animals to tend to, telling the officer that the goat is due to give birth any day now. I quickly help Alice to pack a few things for her and Gus. Apparently, Monsieur Le Maire has kindly offered to take them in for a few nights, then we are escorted off the estate. Once safely away, I text Xavier.

Keep me posted, I want to know everything that happens.

Luckily, the suspected sites are in the wooded area, nowhere near the farmyard.

Zey won't tell me, ze bomb squad are 'ere – and more press.

What about the animals? Will they be blown up? Enzo tries to put my mind at rest. "The ammunition has been there for an exceptionally long time, it's unlikely that it will explode, they're just being cautious. I'm going to ring a few contacts to see if we can find you some more nanny goats."

Two hours later, we are on our way to one of Enzo's clients who has a large goat herd further up in the hills. I try to relax and look at the scenery as we drive out of the valley. "Looks familiar," I say, as we round the bend where I had my accident in Dolly in the deep snow; it seems quite different now, in the sunshine. The Land Rover stops at the top of a steep drive near some dilapidated outbuildings. An old man with skin like leather appears out of a shed holding an old-fashioned crook. A proper shepherd. "This is Henri, he's your man for goats."

Henri nods and gives me an almost toothless grin, his nicotine-stained fingers clutching his polished crook. He shows us into one of his sheds where a nanny goat has recently given birth to two, still wet twins. She carries on bleating and licking her babies, unconcerned by our presence. "Oh, they are adorable!" I squeal.

"You might have some of your own by the time you get home," Enzo says.

"I don't know how to look after them!" I say, starting to panic.

"No, but their mother does. You won't have to do anything except give extra feed and keep them in for a while; it's still cold at night."

With the cooing over, Henri takes us to a small field where lots of goats are happily eating grass. He explains that they have recently had their weaned kids taken from them and produce excellent milk. Enzo checks them over and suggests several that he thinks would be good. Most of them are white, but one has small black spots, she looks so cute, and I know I must have her.

After much dithering, I eventually choose five others and tell Henri that I'll be back to collect them when the ammunition has been removed, and the estate declared safe again. "Yes, there was lots of activity in your village, I was a boy during the war; too young to fight but old enough to be of help to the local resistance," he says as a frown creases his face.

I tell him about some of the things that I've found at the Chateau, his face lights up, and the creases drop away, "When I come for the goats, I'll take you back with me to have a look – in return for your stories."

"Deal," he says, shaking my hand, as we drop him back at his cosy cottage.

Climbing back into our car Enzo turns and takes my hand, "Where now?"

"Valentina recommended a small bistro that they frequent, it's a bit of a drive – would you like to go? My treat."

"Sure, do you know where?"

I put the address into the sat-nav and enjoy the journey up into the hills. A couple of hours later, Enzo parks in a small cobbled square by a river; it's quiet here – the tourists are still further up in the ski resorts. A bell tings above the door as we enter, and a small, stocky man appears, introducing himself as Gino. When I tell him I'm a friend of Valentina's, he makes a fuss and shows us to a small table set into an alcove and brings us a complimentary drink. "Anyone who is a friend of the Carboni family is a friend of mine," he says, kissing me on both cheeks.

"Not quite what I was expecting," I say, as I look about the small, cosy room. "Apparently, Gino's famous locally for his ice-cream, you should get on well."

"A bit of a long way to travel for an ice-cream, we'll have to come for a weekend in the summer." I prevent myself from reminding him that he'll have gone back home by summer; an uncomfortable feeling starts in my stomach. I'd allowed myself to quietly neglect that thought, and now it's decided to jump out and bite me. As we sit and eat our dinner, Enzo asks, "You've gone quiet; are you okay?"

"Sorry – yes; I was just thinking about the ammunition and guns; I hope I can get back tomorrow; I've got so much to do."

Thankfully, by lunchtime the following day, I get a call from the police saying the guns and ammunition have been safely removed and that the other two sites on the map have been excavated – one was already empty, and the other was a chest containing tinned food, which they have left in-situ for me. "Excellent news, I can go home," I say to Enzo, wanting to put a little distance between us; I don't want to become dependent on him, I need to remind myself that our relationship is temporary. I send a text to Xavier, who is waiting for me when I get back.

"Quick, ze goat is going to 'ave ze baby soon." We head quickly to the stable and arrive just in time to see that two tiny kids have been born; still pink and wet.

"Aww, I want to cuddle them!" I squeal.

"Well you can't – they seem okay, keep an eye on them and keep them inside for a while," Enzo says after he's checked them over. "Don't usually have problems with goats, they're good mothers."

Xavier then leads us into the wooded area, where we stand and stare in amazement at a large hole containing yet another old metal chest – full of old tins. "Probably bully beef," Enzo says, wiping at the unreadable labels. "What are you going to do with it?"

"I'm not sure, but we need to get it inside, or it will deteriorate now it's exposed. We'll ask the contractors; they've got lifting equipment." After a negotiating session, they agree to move the chest for a crate of wine, and it's soon safe in the kitchen. Next, I get a call from the police, who say I can have the guns and grenades back once they are disarmed.

"Why do you want zem?" Xavier asks, puzzled.

"I'm thinking of turning the attic into a small museum; that should attract clients who are interested in military memorabilia. If we can get a few stories from Henri to go along with them, it could be good for business."

"Meanwhile, we 'ave ze big holes to fill in," Xavier says, leaving with a sigh.

"Yes, and I need you to fence off another paddock for six new goats, please," I call after him. "Poor Xavier," I say once he's left, "I suppose it's good for him to keep busy; take his mind off the looming court case – only a few days to go!"

After dinner, we go back to check on the new kids; they are already standing and exploring their new home, and mummy goat seems well. Just another day at the Chateau!

The following morning, I am once again the headline of the local newspaper; this time it's about the discovery of the ammunition from the war. More good publicity I suppose, and it ties in nicely with Sophie's visit tomorrow.

She has already contacted a magazine, and they are interested in running an article about me. Who would have thought my life would have turned out to be exciting enough for people to read about?

Enzo is up and off early to work while I busy myself doing housework before Sophie arrives, she lives down on the French Riviera; so, I suppose she'll drop in by helicopter too. I feel her arrival before I hear and see her; I'm glad the press have gone! She's a friendly woman – difficult to age; possibly late thirties.

"Hello, Laura, how lovely to meet you at last; Valentina has told me so much about your exciting journey!" She enthuses in fluent English, with only a hint of an accent. I'm glad to see she's wearing warm clothes and sensible footwear when she asks to look around the estate.

I start with the farmyard area and the baby goats, followed by the carriage house, the holes where the metal chests were found, the vines and walled garden, all the while telling her about my adventures. Back at the Chateau, she especially wants to see the attic and old wine cellar, making notes and taking photos as she goes along. I send her some pictures of the Bugatti, from when it was still in the carriage house and the treasures that were in the attic, which she thinks the magazine will want to feature. The day flies past, and she leaves to write her notes for the article, saying, "Someone will probably want to come out and take some 'official' photos, I'll be in touch."

18

The next few days pass by in a blur of activity; from dealing with issues arising from the contractors, and visiting Sylvie, to making sure we are prepared for tomorrow's court case; thankfully it's being held at a small court in the local town, as it's all about Gus and not his grandfather. Monsieur Robert will be there representing us, I know Alice is upset but managing to put on a brave face. Poor Gus has now been told, and he has prepared a written statement which he did at school with Sylvie and a child social worker, stating that he wishes to remain where he is; it's quite short but to the point. Sylvie will read it out as an impartial witness. I arrive at the farmhouse in good time to pick Xavier and Alice up to take them to court.

"You can't wear that!" I shout as Xavier comes downstairs.

"It's clean."

"I don't care; haven't you got a suit?"

Alice just looks at me and shakes her head. I swiftly turn tail and head back to the Chateau; Enzo has left some of his clothes at mine. Rummaging through I find a pair of smart trousers, a shirt, and a jacket. A quick call to Monsieur le Maire and a tie is organised. Not a perfect fit but better than ripped jeans and a tatty fleece.

We enter the old stone building and are shown into a compact waiting room, Monsieur Robert, and the other witnesses arrive soon after. Apparently, Phillipe LeBeau and his entourage have been given a separate room to wait in. Alice sits and stares at the floor wringing her hands, while Xavier paces up and down the small space, tugging at his shirt collar. Thankfully, it's not long before we're called in and shown into the courtroom. It's far less intimidating than I imagined; nothing like you see on TV. No public gallery, just the immediate family concerned, witnesses and solicitors.

Phillipe LeBeau, dressed to kill, with his solicitor in tow, is shown to a row of seats at the other side of us. He nods curtly as he passes but doesn't speak; his solicitor follows confidently behind him. Why do I want to poke his eyes out? The judge arrives and introduces herself, taking her seat at the front, then proceedings begin swiftly; Xavier is invited to speak first, and he reads out his prepared statement like a robot, recounting Gus's life since birth. Stating how Gus's mother abandoned the child as a baby and has made no effort to contact him since.

LeBeau is next; questioning Xavier's ability to parent, showing a recent photograph of him with a black eye; suggesting he tends to become violent. We didn't see that one coming! How did he get that picture? Slowly the penny drops – it must have been LeBeau who informed the press about the Bugatti and me. What a snake!

"Monsieur Besnard, please explain the circumstances leading to your injury?" asks the judge. Xavier just looks at me and shrugs, looking like a lost little boy. But Monsieur Robert saves the day.

"Mademoiselle Mackley, perhaps you could explain to the court about the kidnapping of your dog, Shadow, and how Xavier Besnard was beaten by the violent thugs when trying to retrieve the poor animal?" Glad to help, I recount the event. The judge just nods and listens intently, as a secretary minutes my every word.

She then questions LeBeau, giving him a hard time about his previous, non-existent, contact with Gus and the whereabouts of his daughter, Gus's mother. It turns out that she married a wealthy Arab and now lives in Saudi Arabia and has no contact with her family. "Should you be granted custody of Gus, what are your plans to educate him?" The judge asks next.

I watch Xavier clench his hands into fists until his knuckles whiten as LeBeau boasts to the judge and answers smugly, "I have secured a place at a prestigious boarding school near Paris for the boy." I gently reach across to

Xavier's lap and take hold of his hand while listening to the sickening man.

The judge also asks the witnesses to read their statements and is particularly interested to hear from Sylvie, Gus's teacher. "Gus is doing very well at school, achieving his expected targets. He participates well in class and has many friends. He enjoys school and is a delightful member of our community."

"What about you, Mademoiselle Mackley?" asks the judge. "I'd like to hear about the stability of Monsieur Besnard's employment and residence. Will he be able to care for his son financially?"

I stand and say, "I have only been a member of this caring community for six months, and my business is in its infancy, but I have enough assets to keep the business afloat for a year, after which we should be making a reasonable profit to take us forward. I have no intention of making Monsieur Besnard or his family homeless."

At last, it's over, and we are asked to leave the courtroom and are shown back to the little waiting room, which now feels claustrophobic. Xavier continues pacing, and Alice can take no more, bursting into floods of tears. I stare at the ticking clock on the wall, trying to calm my breathing as time stands still. Our heads snap up in anticipation as the door opens; a small older man appears and invites Xavier and Monsieur Robert back to hear the verdict. The rest of us are left sat staring at each other in silence, for what feels like an eternity.

Eventually, the two men return, beaming; and I know we've won. Alice bursts into more tears and I can't help but join in. Sylvie is the first to speak, choking back her own feelings, "Sorry, I have to get back to school. Do you want me to tell Gus? I know he'll ask me."

I look over to Xavier, who just offers a quick nod. He's in no fit state to speak. "Yes, I think it would be cruel to make him wait longer than necessary. Thank you," I add. A camera flash goes off in our faces as we leave the building a short while later. They are so insensitive; why can't they leave us alone at a time like this?

Once back at the farmhouse, Xavier strides straight through the kitchen and upstairs, returning a few minutes later wearing his usual tatty clothes. Enzo's borrowed items are draped over his outstretched arm, he nods and drops them onto a chair; gets three glasses from the dresser and fills them with brandy. Still standing, he drains his drink in one gulp then pours another.

"Steady on," I say.

Pulling a chair out, he slowly sits and raises his glass. "Zis one, I will savour." He slowly sips the brown liquid then adds, "Zank you!"

Alice steps forward and hugs me tightly. "Thank you so very much for your help – we will forever be in your debt."

Xavier arrives the following morning with a bunch of flowers and the local paper.

ENGLISH MILLIONAIRESS STEPS IN TO HELP LOCAL BOY STAY WITH FATHER AFTER BITTER CUSTODY BATTLE

Underneath the headline is an unflattering photo of LeBeau trying to hide his face from the camera. "What a cold, callous, individual; I do hope this is all over with now and we never have to see him again," I say looking up at Xavier. "How could his daughter go and leave her baby like that?"

Xavier sighs and with a pained expression says, "She didn't want ze baby, I 'ad to beg 'er to keep it."

"Why was she here in the first place?"

"'er fazer, 'e sent 'er down for ze summer to try and worm 'er way into to ze affections of your aunt; it didn't work. Zey took an instant dislike of each ozer; she wasn't a nice person."

"Why?"

"Ze Chateau, of course! 'e wanted it; I zink 'e knew about ze 'idden treasures."

"I'm sorry Xavier, did you love her?"

He runs his hands through his unruly hair then hesitates before saying, "I zought I did at ze time; but I was young and naive – as was she. I don't blame 'er, it was a long time ago. I 'ope she's 'appy now."

19

The days are beginning to get longer, the nights aren't quite as cold, and spring flowers are tentatively peeping through the barren earth; a sign of things to come. We need to start thinking about the few events that we have booked so far; the small wedding is in two weeks, and I need to order flowers. Joelle, the bride, seems very laid back and isn't bothered about choosing them, so I've spoken to the groom's mother, Edith. She is footing the bill and wants lilies; I'll do my best, but the flowers are out of season, it will be so much simpler in summer.

That gives me another idea – I'll suggest we grow our own flowers for future events, like lavender, roses and freesia, my Gran's favourite. More research needed; that's a suitable job for Alice, she'll know what grows best in this area. All fifteen pitches are now finished, the septic tank is in, and the water pipes laid. All that's left is mains electricity and the small shower block with solar panels on the roof. The contractors reckon they'll be finished in a few weeks.

My website is now up and running, generating enquiries, and I'm starting to take bookings for the campsite. I've ordered my kitchen cabinets and appliances. Unfortunately, they won't be here until after the wedding, but I've hired a hog-roast oven, so we'll manage. I'm only catering for thirty; I need to ask Xavier to get me the tables that are stored in the carriage house, they'll need a good clean before the wedding.

Enzo is bringing my new goats today, and Henri is coming with him, I've defrosted the last of the meat that Alice gave me and put it in the oven; I'm sure he'll be happy to share a casserole with us. It's not long until the beep from the gatepost signals their arrival and I rush out to meet them at the farmyard. Enzo and Henri herd the six frisky animals into the new paddock, they make a dash for the feed trough and get down to the business of producing milk. We take Henri to see the new kids, he checks them for me and tells me I have a boy and a girl, but he's keen to move on to the war memorabilia.

First, I show him the chest of tinned food that was dug up in the woods. He's fascinated, telling me that it would have been dropped by a British aircraft during the night for the resistance, who would have buried them for leaner times. "I remember one of my neighbours who used to be involved in shining lights into the night sky to assist them, it was a dangerous activity; if they had been caught, they would have been tortured then killed," he says. He's keen to see the diary written by Sergeant Harry King, about the night his plane was shot down too. "You need to have this on display; the brave things these people did should never be forgotten," he says. "And the uniforms in the chest, get them out and do something with them." He then goes on to tell me stories of the things he did as a boy in the war to help the local resistance. "I was issued with two jumpers, one red and one blue. I was given an instruction by a local priest as to which jumper I should wear and which path to walk while wearing it. Sometimes it would be raining or even snowing, but I still had to go out and walk up onto certain hills in just a jumper. I've since learned that red was a signal to the resistance to stay put, and blue was an instruction to proceed."

His stories are fascinating, so many people risked their lives and that of their families to aid the war effort. Lots of young men were killed or tortured, and their families still won't talk about it. "My older brother, Paul, was one of the unlucky ones; my mother was never the same again," he says, looking down at his crook. Henri then kindly agrees to have his photo taken with the chest of tinned food for my website.

"Once I get sorted, I'm going to open up a small museum in the attic; I'd appreciate your advice," I say, and Henri beams in pleasure.

We tuck into dinner, and Henri complements me on my casserole, "Tasty this; nice bit of goat."

I look up from my plate and smile, "It's lamb Henri, I've had it in the oven for a couple of hours. Otherwise, it's a bit tough."

"Definitely goat – I should know. It has a distinct texture; if you mix a bit of rosemary in with their feed, it improves the flavour."

Suddenly the piece of meat in my mouth gets bigger and bigger as I try to chew it and put on a brave face. Enzo looks over to me and winces. Realisation dawns; I'm eating my own goat! When Xavier told me that he knew where Big Billy was, I'd wrongly assumed that he'd moved him to a safer location to prevent him mating with the nannies. It's no good; I just can't swallow and have to spit it out into my serviette. "Yes, it is a bit tough," I say, starting to feel queasy. "Shadow can have the rest."

"Don't waste it, I'll take it home for my supper," Henri says grinning.

I tip the remains of the casserole into an old ice-cream tub for Henri and clear the table while Enzo takes him back home. I can't believe I've been obliviously eating my own animal; how could he do this to me? Indigestion sets in and I struggle to sleep thinking about 'Big Billy'.

Preparation for the wedding keeps me busy for the next couple of weeks as well as all the other jobs. We have plenty of milk, which keeps Alice on her toes, making cheese and ice-cream. Valentina is purchasing a bulk order for one of her hotels 'The Lemon Tree', down on the Riviera, a courier is coming to collect it tomorrow; she's going to place a regular order if it goes down well.

The bees will be arriving next week, they should be just in time to pollinate the orchard, although fruit will be thin on the ground for a few years until it's established. The trees in the walled garden that are protected by the elements are showing signs of life, and the few sheep we have will be lambing soon. It's exciting to be at the start of a new season. I'm beginning to feel as though I belong here now, but it's been a steep learning curve.

I'm surprised to find I have an e-mail from Joelle, the bride.

Sorry, its short notice but I was wondering if I could stay at the Chateau on the night before the wedding, with my two sisters who are bridesmaids?

That's the day after tomorrow; so little time to prepare! The bedrooms haven't been refurbished yet. What should I say? Well, I suppose it's business and good practice to have guests paying. How much should I charge?

Hello Joelle. You are very welcome to stay if you understand that the rooms are quite basic and haven't been refurbished yet. You would have to share the house bathroom.

That will probably put them off.

That's okay, we'll see you on Friday afternoon. Thank you.

Oh, my goodness! Along with all my other jobs, I've now got three rooms to prepare and the extra meals.

20

With all hands to the pump, we manage to be ready on time. Alice and Rose have done a fantastic job with Xavier's help, decorating the Chateau with flowers, candles, and ribbons. It all looks fabulous. The three guest rooms are ready with flowers, champagne, and chocolate; personal touches that I hope will be appreciated. Thirty is undoubtedly pushing it a little for the dining room. I will need to hire a marquee for more significant events. I quickly change into smarter clothes and greet Joelle and her sisters, Louise, and Chloe, who seem relaxed and laid back, and show them to their rooms, which thankfully, meet with their approval. Their partners are staying at the holiday home they own further down the valley. Apparently, Edith didn't think it suitable for the bride to stay with the groom on the evening before their wedding.

"Would you like afternoon tea in the drawing room in half an hour?" I ask.

"Yes, please, if it's not too much trouble?"

"Not at all, make yourselves at home and just shout if you need anything."

I prepare a pretty, vintage, tiered cake stand piled high with Alice's homemade shortbread and scones and make a pot of tea and coffee for the girls, leaving them to settle in, before heading back to the kitchen to finish preparing the vegetables for tomorrow's feast. Xavier has got the hog and goose ready to roast; I no longer ask where the meat comes from, and he doesn't volunteer the information. All my goats were still here this morning. That's a bonus! Dinner is set for seven-thirty, and the girls request an informal affair; I make coq-au-vin and serve it with crusty bread and our own red wine, which goes down a treat.

"The car will be here at eleven fifty-five tomorrow morning, so can we have breakfast at eight-thirty?" Joelle asks.

"No problem, any special requests?"

"Whatever you have; something light."

I leave my guests chatting in the drawing room with a bottle of wine and a roaring fire, then retire with Shadow. The girls were happy to have his company, but I'm going to leave him at the farmhouse with Beau tomorrow; I can't risk him getting in the way or upsetting anyone. Not everyone likes dogs.

"Something smells delicious," Joelle says as she enters the kitchen with her sisters for breakfast. The girls enthuse over my truffle flavoured scrambled eggs, asking for the recipe. One to add to my breakfast menu when I get started. So much to think about. Xavier arrives at the back door dressed in his usual scruff, I suggest he goes off to check on the animals until the girls have finished and started their preparations for the big day.

He returns a while later looking disgruntled. "Xavier, you need to get changed, why aren't you wearing the black trousers and white shirt I got for you? We have paying guests. Go and get changed."

He leaves, muttering under his breath, then returns shortly, looking uncomfortable, but he's just going to have to get used to it. I've ordered uniforms for all of us with our logo embroidered on the shirt. Alice and Rose arrive soon after and get to work in the kitchen. Dinner for thirty to cook! A black taxi pulls up outside, and a grey-haired man gets out, this must be Joelle's father. I introduce myself and offer him a drink, which he declines. "I'll go and tell the girls you're here." I head towards the stairs after ensuring Joelle's father is comfortable. I can hear giggling coming from their room so gently knock on the door.

"Come in," Joelle calls.

I pop my head into the room, to see the girls helping Joelle into her dress. "You all look amazing!" I say.

Joelle looks at me in the mirror. "Thank you, would you take a photo of the three of us, please?"

"Of course – where would you like it?" We spend the next fifteen minutes taking pictures in various locations, as well as some with their father Georges, whom they requested come up to the room before they all get into the taxi and head for the church.

"Right, I reckon we have about an hour before the guests arrive, what's left to do?" I head back to the kitchen to look at my to-do list and finish preparing. Fifty minutes later and the taxi returns followed by at least twenty other cars – parking! I hadn't thought of that and quickly dispatch Xavier to decide upon a suitable location for the vehicles; at least the grass is dry.

Philip helps his bride out of the car, and the photographer abandons his Jeep and rushes out to take photos, which seems to take an age. Rose and Alice stand in the hall greeting guests with champagne and showing them into the drawing room, where they stand in small groups chatting and making a fuss of Edith, their matriarch, who is very much enjoying the attention.

A little girl of about six or seven skips up to me and asks where the toilets are. I escort her to the cloakroom where she stands and stares at me in amazement. "But... where are the toilets?" I take her into a cubicle and lift the lid of the antique toilet seat to reveal the porcelain bowl. She bursts into a fit of giggles and proceeds to lift her pink taffeta dress; I turn and leave as her mother comes looking for her, apologising profusely. A little while later, a queue has formed to visit the 'strange' toilets as the word spreads.

With photographs and comfort breaks finished, we start seating the party for dinner, with Edith in charge; everyone is assigned a seat as per her plan, and we begin with soup. After dessert, the few children are excused so they can play, while I serve coffee to the adults in the dining room. My ears alert me to the familiar sound of piano music. I pass my task on to Rose while I go and investigate, creeping slowly towards the drawing room. Once again peering through the crack in the door, I witness the little girl in the pink dress sitting on the piano stool, smiling up at someone that I can't see, while the piano appears to be playing by itself. Catlike, I tread as lightly as possible and stealthily enter the room. The music stops dead.

"Where have you gone?" Shouts the little girl, quite confused. She stands and walks towards me, "Where has she gone?"

"If you mean Aunt Mary, she's very old and tires quickly. Probably gone for a rest. Did she speak to you?"

"No, and she didn't say goodbye. Will she come back?"

"I'm sure she'll be back another day. Did she seem happy?"

"Oh, yes, can I come back and see her again?"

I nod, and smile, then try and distract her, "Would you like to see my baby goats?"

The little girl squeals excitedly and rushes off to ask her mum. As I walk towards the paddocks with the children, I notice Shadow and Beau race across the lawn, chasing a smaller dog with Gus running after them. When we catch up with them, Shadow has mounted the dog and is mating with it. "That's Pipi, Auntie Sara's dog, it's her princess. Look, she's trying to give your dog a piggyback ride!" The little girl says. Lost for words, I help Gus as we try to part the two animals: with little success.

"No, silly, it's humping it!" The older boy from the party shouts excitedly, rushing off; no doubt to tell Auntie Sara all about it!

Auntie Sara is beside herself when the news gets out, but half an hour and a double brandy later, she seems quite pleased when Xavier offers her fifty Euros for every puppy that results from the union. Slightly annoyed, I gesture towards the kitchen, and once we reach the privacy of the room, I ask him, "What are we going to do with a pack of mongrels?"

"Make a 'andsome profit – once I and Shadow 'ave trained zem to be ze truffle dogs!"

This does nothing to ease my annoyance, but there's nothing I can do, so I shrug it off and re-join the festivities. Joelle and Philip leave in a shower of petals soon after; heading down to the Riviera for a few days.

"Thank you so much; we've had a fantastic day!" Joelle says as she turns and throws her small bouquet into the crowd of well-wishers.

It misses by a mile and comes straight in my direction, time stands still; should I catch it or let it land on the floor? Decision made; it's way too pretty to destroy. I take a small step forward and reach out my hands as it falls gently in my grasp. The crowd clap and cheer just as Enzo appears from around the corner. I didn't see him arrive.

My cheeks match the colour of the pink roses in my hands as he steps forward and places a soft kiss on my lips, which incites more clapping and cheering. Joelle looks at me and winks before climbing into the red Alfa Spider that Philip brought earlier. "I wasn't expecting you so soon," I say, as Enzo stands at my side grinning like a child.

"Thought you might like some help with the clearing up. Many hands make light work."

The rest of the guests leave in dribs and drabs, and we get down to clearing away the aftermath. Later, I recount the story of the unfortunate dog incident, which Enzo thinks is priceless. "Xavier is quite excited about the prospect of training some puppies to become truffle dogs, but I'm not sure what Princess Pipi thinks about the situation," I say, trying to stifle a yawn.

"Talking of princesses; I have some worshipping of my own to take care of," he says, taking my hand and leading me upstairs. I look back over the top of the landing, and my eyes pick out Joelle's pink bouquet on the hall table. My first wedding, it's been a superb day!

21

"A day off; where would you like to go?" Enzo asks as we munch breakfast in bed.

"I need to buy new beds for paying guests; the ones we have are lumpy and uncomfortable."

"I can vouch for that, but you can get them online; probably cheaper too. I mean a proper day off! A colleague was telling me about some amazing caves – Grottes de Saint Marcel; a couple of hours away. It's on my to-do list. Would you like to go? Think of it as research if it makes you feel better, and you deserve a day off after yesterday."

It sounds lovely, so I agree. The drive takes us through some fantastic scenery, and some quite scary roads; with twisting hairpin bends and terrifying drops; plummeting into the valley bottoms. I'm glad I'm not driving, but Enzo doesn't seem phased.

"There's quite a queue," I say, with a sense of déjà vu as we arrive.

"I'm assured it's well worth the wait, and we get to taste some wine while we're down there!" Enzo replies, full of enthusiasm.

Once inside it takes a little while for our eyes to adjust to the light, it's a noticeable descent, and the floor is wet; chilly too. We follow on behind the guided tour to find ourselves in an enchanted world with ginormous chambers, decorated with stunning rock formations and glassy pools, some illuminated in multiple colours; causing the hairs on the back of my neck to stand up as tingles travel down my spine. I look over to Enzo, and I can tell he feels the same. "Wow! This is otherworldly," he says, his eyes darting everywhere.

"Awesome! I'm so glad you persuaded me to come." I say, straining to listen to the guide as she imparts her knowledge. We continue with the tour, passing through lofty galleries; some with evocative names and one containing a stunning fountain. I stop to take pictures along the way, tourist information for my future guests.

"On to the wine tasting," our guide says. We are led into another gallery; now used as a wine cellar. Here we're given more information about the unique qualities of the cave that enhance the maturation of the wine, before being offered a glass. Then the lights go out. Pitch black. I've never experienced darkness like this before.

I'm so glad I'm holding Enzo's hand, this is just the sort of situation that would typically induce a panic attack, but I feel calm and serene. Taking a lungful of the humid air, I slowly exhale, then raise the glass to my nose. It smells incredible, plums and cherries, with a hint of liquorice. The aroma permeates through my nose into my lungs, and I can't wait any longer to taste the red liquid. It doesn't disappoint. Dark and intense.

Chocolate and coffee. Amazing! The lights come back on, Enzo has his eyes closed and a broad smile across his face. "This one's a winner!" He says.

"Definitely, better than our own wine." I waste no time emptying my glass before the process starts again with the next bottle.

The ascent is much harder; especially after two glasses of wine. I don't know how Enzo had the resolve to only taste both drinks and not indulge like me. He obviously has masses of self-control. Though pricey, we treat ourselves to a couple of bottles in the obligatory shop on the way out, and Enzo asks for a bundle of leaflets to display at the Chateau.

"You know – you need to keep all of the receipts for visits like this; you can claim them as expenses when you start making a profit," he says as we climb wearily back into the Land Rover. I lean back and let my head flop onto the headrest.

"I can't even begin to think about work; I'm exhausted."

Enzo smiles and starts the engine while I snooze most of the way home.

22

Enzo needs to be up at seven for work; it's a good job really, as a journalist and photographer are due at ten to interview me for the magazine article. Thankfully, Sophie is coming too. I have a couple of hours to make myself look presentable. The Chateau appears as good as it can; the flowers from the wedding still surviving, if a little past their best.

Sophie arrives first, this time by car. "You look lovely, but perhaps we could put your hair in a chignon, and I've brought you an outfit that I think will suit you," she says, floating effortlessly into the hall, carrying a large coffee machine and setting it to work instantly. Next, she puts the oven on and fills it with part baked bread and pastries. I look at her quizzically. "Tricks of the trade, think of it as aromatherapy."

Fifteen minutes later, and I'm stood looking at my reflection. I'm wearing skinny navy jeans; they're designer label, of course. A cream silk blouse and a long, cashmere coffee-coloured cardigan that has one chunky, wooden button fastening asymmetrically below my neck. Knee-length leather, practical looking boots complete the illusion. "How did you know what to get?" I ask, looking at the stranger staring back at me in the mirror.

"It's my job to know," she replies casually, fussing with my hair. A loud beep alerts us to the impending arrival of our visitors. "You're amazing, just be yourself. They've got the story already, they're just looking for a few quotes and personal touches," she says, sensing my nervousness. As we get to the bottom of the stairs, the smell coming from the kitchen is divine. Now I know what she meant. I need to invest in a fancy coffee machine! "Now, you go and relax in the drawing room, and I'll show them in." She gently nudges me in the direction she wants me to go.

The first thing I notice when I enter the room is the artfully placed, expensive looking throws and rugs, and new impressive floral arrangements – when did she do that? "Glad you managed to find us – do come in," Sophie's voice floats into the room from the hall.

"Sophie, super to see you again," comes the reply in fluent English, followed by the low tone of a man's voice that I can't make out. The next sound I hear is the voice of a small child babbling in French.

"Papa, Papa, bicik."

"I'm sure we can find a biscuit and some juice, do come on through," Sophie says, as the group enters the drawing room. I stand and walk towards them holding out my hand as Sophie introduces me to Mirelle, the tall, willowy journalist, and Gabriel, the photographer, who is holding a small boy of about two and a half.

"I'm so sorry, this is my son, Ben. His nursery has closed – it was last minute. An outbreak of some sort." Gabriel says, holding out his hand.

"It was either bring him along or cancel; so sorry," Mirelle says, looking most uncomfortable.

"Oh, Laura doesn't mind children; she used to be a nurse," Sophies says, looking optimistically at me for a reply.

"Not a problem, everyone is welcome here," I reply quickly. "Do come and take a seat; Sophie is about to bring refreshments; would a goats milk ice-lolly be acceptable for Ben?"

With refreshments sorted, we sit down on my new chairs, chatting, while Ben sits on one of Sophie's fluffy throws and tackles his lolly. Gabriel wastes no time taking pictures and patiently encourages me into various poses in strategic locations – the drawing room, dining room, and staircase. He's good at his job and makes me feel comfortable and at ease.

With the photo shoot over, Mirelle starts her questions. "What does it feel like to be wealthy, after starting life as an ordinary working girl? A bit like winning the lottery I should imagine; or are you out of your depth?"

Sophie's eyes nearly pop out of her head as I look over to her for guidance. "Well – err – I don't think of myself as wealthy," I say tentatively at first but then begin to feel a little annoyed. "I'm still very much a working girl; I have taken on the challenge as custodian of this amazing piece of history."

"Yes, but you have the money from the sale of the Bugatti…"

"That money is about to be ploughed straight back into the Chateau. Work starts next week to replace the entire roof, which currently leaks like a sieve, causing severe damp issues. The bedrooms are going to be refurbished for guests, and the kitchen is to be replaced and divided into a small breakfast room – amongst many other projects that are currently taking place."

"What about the artefacts and antiques? Haven't you sold them all off?" Again, Sophie is lost for words as she stares at me in open-mouthed shock at the rudeness.

"Yes, some of the antiques had to be sold to pay the big tax bill that I inherited along with the estate; but I've kept as much as I possibly could. All of the war memorabilia is still here, and I intend to open a small museum to display the items."

"So, that's another commercial venture?"

"Not at all, it will be free to locals and guests…"

Then it happens – the piano begins playing, but this time it's not the soft tinkling music we're used to; it's loud and rowdy, like the music from a horror movie. Everyone stops and looks over to the piano, including me. I know she's here, I can feel her, but I can't see her. Ben, however, seems to be able to and stands and toddles towards the noise, which gradually quietens down and returns to a melodious tune before stopping. He points and giggles, as though Aunt Mary has made some type of gesture. I hope it was a rude one directed at Mirelle.

"What was that?" Mirelle asks nervously.

"Whatever you want it to be; I rather fancy it was my great Aunt Mary, but who knows?"

"Does it happen a lot?"

"No, just occasionally, when she's happy or angry; but I think it was the latter today though."

"Aren't you afraid – living here alone?"

"Not at all, I feel very comfortable striving to save this place from decline; ensuring it has a place in the future, as well as the past."

Sophie has, at last, found her voice, "Yes, Laura is doing an amazing job. She could have taken the easy way out and sold the whole estate to the highest bidder; it would have then been turned into another hotel or apartment block with the loss of livelihoods and homes for some of the locals. She has achieved some amazing things in her short time here and has been most benevolent towards the locals and her staff."

"Yes, I heard about the custody battle; would you like to tell me more?"

I stand as tall and straight as possible. "Thank you for coming, I hope you've got what you want," I say, signalling the end of the interview. Gabriel jumps up and grabs his camera gear in one arm and Ben in the other and mouths his hasty goodbye from the doorway. Mirelle, on the other hand, lingers and holds out her hand, which I don't take.

"I like you – I like you a lot," she says, then shouts to Gabriel, "one more shot of Laura leaning over the piano! Oh, and tell me about the Scottish vet; are you planning your own fairy-tale wedding?"

"Enzo and I are both far too busy with our work to consider a future together," I reply, then immediately wished I hadn't. Too late, the damage is done.

Sophie leans on the door and heaves a sigh of relief once they have gone, "Oh my goodness – what just happened there?"

"You tell me, it was supposed to be just a few quotes and personal touches; that woman was evil!"

"I didn't mean Mirelle, though I do agree with you; journalists can be like that. No, I meant the piano thing. What was that about?"

"Oh, like I said, just great Aunt Mary making an appearance…"

"But I couldn't see anyone – could you?"

"No, I could sense her presence, but I couldn't actually see her; it seems that only children can. She's appeared several times now but only when children are present. Come on, let's get some coffee, and I'll tell you about her visits." I say, leading Sophie to the kitchen.

Sophie is fascinated by my story, but I'm not entirely sure that she believes in ghosts. Come to think of it, neither am I, but what other explanation is there? Poor Aunt Mary, she must have been distraught to reveal herself in front of Mirelle like that. I wonder – perhaps she's here all the time quietly watching me. Did she know where the key for the bureau was hidden? Was she observing me search for it? Is she only in the drawing room, or does she travel about? So many questions. Sophie leaves soon after, and I'm left with my thoughts whirling. I suddenly feel restless now that Sophie's gone and start to wander from room to room looking about me, but what am I looking for? Shadow takes an interest and joins me; can he see her? We search everywhere, even the attic but can't see anything unusual. Oh well, no doubt she'll come back when she's ready.

As I head back down from the attic, I remember the comment about Enzo. Why did I say that? I'd like nothing more than him to stay here in France with me, but I can't ask that of him. He's at the beginning of a great career with an excellent opportunity to work at a practice in his hometown. I can't let him walk away from that. I don't know how he feels about me. I know he enjoys my company, but he's never mentioned the 'love' word. Come to think of it, neither have I. Well, not to him anyway. When I see him again, I'll tell him what I said and explain that it was just a way to cut Mirelle off and get her to leave. Nothing personal. After all, it's none of her business. I'm distracted by the beep that tells me the back door has just opened. Rushing down the stairs, I find Xavier tinkering with the fancy coffee machine that Sophie brought.

"'Ow much was zis?" He asks sarcastically.

"Oh, it's not mine. Sophie brought it for the interview, she must have forgotten to take it with her," I say, then realise I'm still wearing her clothes. Perhaps she can pick them up when she next passes through.

"Zey are coming to put ze scaffolding up tomorrow, but today I'm planting crops; are you coming to 'elp?"

"Yes, the bees will be here soon, we'll need lots of flowers for them," I say, as my phone alerts me to a text from Sophie.

I forgot to mention – Valentina has two hot tubs that she's replacing and wants to know if you'd like them.

"Is zere a problem?" Xavier asks, looking at my shocked expression.

"Erm, no – do we want two hot tubs?" I ask.

"Well, I don't want one," he replies.

"Have you ever been in one? It would be another facility to add to our list for the guests," I say.

"No, and I don't want to. 'Ow would we get zem? And I don't know 'ow to maintain zem; zey need chemicals – yes?"

Sounds terrific, thank you, but how would I get them here?

Sophie replies instantly.

Leave that to me.

23

I'm up early the following morning and ready when Gustave arrives to instruct the scaffolders of his requirements. There's lots of frenetic activity, and it takes six men all day to erect the scaffolding, which rather spoils the appearance of the old building, but the result will be worth it. They manage to finish as the dusk descends. Xavier turns to face me as he's about to return to the farmhouse, as though it's an afterthought, and says with a weary sigh, "I trust you will not try to climb up ze scaffolding when I 'ave left?" I pretend to be busy and don't respond. "Well?" He prods a little louder.

This man gets under my skin, why can't he drop it? "No Xavier, I won't – and there are no storms forecast either," I reply sarcastically. "Though I intend to go up during the day to paint the upstairs shutters," I add quietly as he disappears.

I'm woken early the next morning by shouting and loud clanging sounds, there is nothing to see out of the front, so, I make my way across the landing to look out of the back. Several large skips are being unloaded in the backyard, with Xavier and Gustave shouting out instructions. As I reach the kitchen, another van pulls up, and several unkempt looking men pile out. I feel outnumbered and overrun by their presence. Xavier pops his head inside, "Ze labourers' 'ave arrived, zey are going to remove ze roof."

"So I gathered, I hope I'm not expected to supply endless cups of coffee. Anyway, I need to go to town. The kitchen company wants to go over last-minute details with me; they begin after the Easter break. I'm going to be living in a building site for a while. Then it's the refurbishment of the bedrooms. Can you look after the roofers?" I ask.

Xavier nods his head in agreement. I step outside, and the warm rays of the early spring sunshine lift my spirits. The front of the Chateau looks strange shrouded in scaffolding, but I won't let it get me down. I've survived the workmen being here for ages, building the campsite, which is now finished ahead of schedule, just in time for Easter. John Burrows and his family will be arriving next week, it's a shame it coincides with the mess at the Chateau, but we can spend time outside now that it's beginning to warm up a little. Lily will adore the baby goats. And who knows, perhaps she can tempt Aunt Mary to play for her again. The children will have some playmates too, I have four other families booked on site for Easter: two Dutch, one German and one French.

Looking up at the clear blue sky makes me think of Dolly, should I get her back out now the risk of snow has gone? One glance over to the Yeti makes my mind up for me. No, I've got used to the comfort and safety of a modern car; I'll save Dolly for short journeys down to the village. My phone pings – a text from Enzo.

Sorry, I'm not going to make it this evening, we're testing a large herd of cattle for TB and won't finish until late. x

Oh, no! We haven't managed to see much of each other over the last few days, we're always so busy. And, I was planning to mention my throw-away remark to Mirelle about our relationship. Oh well, next time.

I'm sorry to hear that, I hope it goes well, we'll have to re-arrange. X

I return home to find that a copy of the magazine has arrived through the post. That was quick! I hastily put my shopping away and sit at the kitchen table with a cup of tea, rapidly leafing my way through the pages until I reach the article about the Chateau. It's unnerving to see myself staring out of the pages; there's a small photo of me stood looking over the galleried landing towards the large window, but, it's the full-page photo of me laid across the piano that I find disturbing. Behind me is a shape – a grainy, pale-grey image that could possibly resemble a person. I look closer, but frustratingly I can't make out any details. Surely this is photo-shopped! I read the headlines.

LAURA'S HAUNTED CHATEAU

The article is quite short and briefly mentions how I inherited the Chateau, stating that I've made a fortune from selling its contents. I put the magazine down, feeling deflated and disappointed; it was meant to be more about the history of the Chateau and the role it played during the war, rather than about me. There's plenty of speculation about the ghost of Aunt Mary, but no mention of the diary that Sergeant Harry King wrote, but it's the closing sentence that upsets me the most.

Laura is currently having a fling with a local vet, but she says she hasn't the time or the inclination for a serious relationship.

"Oh, no! I'll have to speak to Enzo before he sees this." I immediately dial his number, but it goes to voicemail. Should I leave a message? He did say he was busy with a herd of cattle. No, I'd better not. I'll try again later. After all, it's not like he's going to go out and buy a magazine aimed at middle-class women, is it?

I'm brought back to the present by a loud crash, followed by several more. Of course! The roofers. I walk across the kitchen and look out of the window to see a weird, plastic chute, that seems slightly homemade. It consists of dozens of plastic buckets and traffic cones with the bottoms removed, tied together to form a long tube-like structure, which the roofers are using to tip the old roof tiles down into a gigantic skip, billowing with clouds of dust. Very Heath Robinson, but it seems to work. I open the back door and stick my head out, only to be shouted at by a man sawing through a hefty piece of timber, "Tres dangereux!" I close the door quickly, as more dust swirls about; I suppose I should have known better. I must remember to only use the front door for now. I do a sweep of the Chateau to check that all the windows are closed, it takes an age to dust this old building without the added mess from the roofers. I need to get out of here, I'll take a walk with Shadow in the grounds.

Later, I try ringing Enzo again before I retire for the night, but he's still not answering. I hope he's okay.

24

Several days pass by in a blur of noise and dust, with still no word from Enzo. I've sent texts and left messages, but he's not responding. The only option left now is to call in and see him. But why should I? He's the one behaving like a child. What should I do? I need a distraction. I'll go and see Alice. I find her in the garden hanging washing on the line. She asks as I walk up to her, "Laura, I was just thinking about you; I've finished a batch of chèvre for Valentina at The Lemon Tree, are they collecting today?"

"Yes, mid-morning, I believe," I reply, then enter the kitchen to make coffee. We sit at the table in silence while I pick at a croissant. Eventually, Alice removes her glasses and leans back in her chair.

"When are you going to tell me what's bothering you?"

"Nothing is bothering me, I'm fine," I say, more sharply than I intended.

"That's rubbish, and you know it! You've had a long face now for a few days; are the roofers getting on your nerves? Or, has Xavier done something to upset you again?"

Sighing, I put the croissant back on the plate and look at her, "Perhaps a little; the dust is getting everywhere, but the messy part is over, at last. They're putting the new tiles on now. And no, Xavier's not to blame this time." After another lengthy pause, I continue, "It's Enzo; he won't return my calls."

"Oh, dear; have you two had a row?"

"No, but he's avoiding me."

Looking concerned, Alice asks, "Why would he do that? It's not like him. Perhaps he's not very well."

"Oh, Alice, if only that were the case. It's because of the silly comment in the magazine article about being too busy for a relationship. He's obviously seen it and is feeling hurt. It was just a throw-away remark to stop Mirelle from digging into my personal life, but she took it out of context," I say, looking into her motherly face. She stands and walks towards me, enveloping me in a hug, which has the effect of opening the flood gates. I start to cry, quietly at first; but it's not long before my cries turn into sobs – big ugly ones.

"There, my dear, a good cry will do you good. It must be tough for you, having taken on so much responsibility all on your own. You let it all out now." Alice continues holding me until my sobbing subsides, making no sounds, only slowly rocking me side-to-side, as though comforting a small child. When I finally stop, she lets go and passes me a box of tissues. "Now, why don't you finish your breakfast, tidy yourself up. Then, drive over to the practice to talk to him? I'm sure it's just a simple misunderstanding." I nod, sniffling the last of my tears. Slowly, under Alice's watchful gaze, I manage to finish my croissant. "There now, off you go… and let me know how you get on. If he upsets you, just come back, and I'll give him a piece of my mind," she says sternly. I've grown so fond of her; she's rapidly becoming a substitute mother figure in my life. One I need right now.

I wait for an hour for the courier collecting the chèvre, and for the blotches to disappear from my face, before climbing into my Yeti and driving down the valley to the vet's practice. I park in the grounds outside Enzo's cabin and hesitate for a while before ringing the doorbell, but there's no answer, and his car's not here. Walking down the side of his lodgings, I peer in through the lounge window. There's no sign of life. Wearily climbing back into my car, I drive further down the lane to the practice; perhaps he's working. Someone will know where he is. I park in the small carpark with three other vehicles, but Enzo's Land Rover isn't one of them. Making my way over to the old stone building, I have a sinking feeling. I know he's not here.

As I walk in, the busty brunette behind the reception desk says, "Bonjour, I'm sorry, we're just closing for lunch."

"Oh... err... I'm looking for Enzo. Is he out on a call?"

"Enzo? No, he's on annual leave at the moment," she frowns and flicks through a big diary on the desk. "He's not due back until next week. Would you like to make an appointment with one of the other vets?" She asks with a perfect smile.

"Um, no, thank you, it's not important," I say quickly, turning and rushing for the door. Once in the safety of my car, I lean back and close my eyes. I can see his image – smiling and carefree, not a worry in the world. Why didn't he tell me? Not even a text. Nothing. Then I remember Alice's comment about him not being well and wonder if there's a problem back home with his family. Surely, he would have let me know, wouldn't he? I decide to give him the benefit of my doubt and ring him again, but it goes to voicemail.

"Hello Enzo, I've just called in to see you at work, they told me that you'd taken some holiday. I do hope everything's okay back home. Ring me when you can. Bye." There, right or wrong I've done it, now it's up to him.

I try to keep myself busy preparing for the arrival of my first guests tomorrow at the campsite, a French family in a motorhome with two small children. The Burrows' are due the day after, and I'm looking forward to seeing them again; so much has changed since their last visit. As I'm taking my dinner out of the oven, I hear my phone alert me to an incoming text. It's from Enzo!

Sorry I missed your call. I'm travelling through Europe for a couple of weeks with an interrail pass. I was going to ask you to accompany me, but it seems that you are too busy with work.

Really, is that all? Damn right, I'm too busy with work! I've got a campsite to run and a Chateau to restore. I can't just swan off when the fancy takes me – unlike some people! Trying to calm myself down, I inhale deeply and sit at the table. Cold pizza for one doesn't seem very appetising anymore.

25

After a restless night, I step outside into the spring sunshine and walk over to the campsite, making a final check in the shower block. Everything is finally ready, and I try to put Enzo out of my mind as I mentally prepare myself for the arrival of my first guests and the official opening of my campsite. It's an informal affair, with no ribbon cutting or prepared speeches, when, shortly after lunch, a large Hymer motor home slowly makes its way down the drive, through the tree arch – now peppered with bright green foliage – and following my new signs, makes a left turn into the campsite. I check my reflection in the large hall mirror, pleased with my new turquoise polo-shirt embellished with the words 'Le Petit Chateau Campsite'. I then walk over to greet my guests. "Welcome, I'm Laura, please make yourselves at home," I say, offering my hand through the open window. A young woman shakes my hand, then climbs out while her husband clambers into the rear of the vehicle releasing two young children. Once outside, the children squeal with delight and head straight for the small play area with their father following closely behind.

"What a super place; the children will love it here, thank you," she says. Then continues, "Sorry, I'm Danielle, and my husband is called Paul."

"I'll show you around then leave you to settle in. If you need anything, don't hesitate to come and ask," I say, as I give Danielle a quick tour, showing her where the necessary facilities are. "I also have a folder containing tourist information – leaflets of places of interest to visit in the area," I add as I'm leaving.

"Thank you, but I think the children will be happy to play for the rest of the day, we've been travelling for a few hours."

"You can walk anywhere on the estate, and we have a small farmyard that you're welcome to visit," I add as an afterthought.

Back at the Chateau, I send Xavier a text to inform him of our first arrival and remind him to wear one of our official shirts, instead of his usual scruffy attire.

I am wiv ze sheep, we 'ave lambs.

My first thought is to text Enzo and tell him, he might want to check them over, then my stomach spasms as I remember that he's gone away, and we're no longer an item. Were we ever? Did I read too much into our relationship? Perhaps it was just a fling. Two lonely people in a foreign land – a holiday romance. Picking up my phone, I reply to Xavier.

Fantastic. I'm on my way.

I pull on my wellies and paste a smile on my face, before making my way to the new paddock housing the pregnant ewes. As I approach, I can see at least three white lambs in the paddock close to their mothers, with Xavier crouched down over another ewe laid on her side. I open the gate and walk over to him just in time to witness the birth. Xavier stands back as the mother turns and licks her baby, and soon it's on its feet, bleating. "Oh, they're amazing!" I say, trying unsuccessfully to control my emotions, as a single tear rolls down my cheek.

Xavier looks at me and raises his eyes skywards, "You are too soft, you will 'ave to toughen up if you are going to succeed."

"I have every intention of succeeding!" I say sharply, turning away from him to compose myself. "Are there any more due today?"

"We 'ave no way of knowing. Zey were all put wiz ze ram at ze same time, could be today or in ze next few days. I will keep a watch over zem."

"Okay, I'll help, I can walk over every hour, but what about the night?" I ask, concerned.

"Two of ze ozers were born last night and managed wizout our 'elp. Zey will be fine." Offering one of his usual shrugs while looking at an incoming text. "It's Gustave on ze roof; 'e is saying 'e expects to finish by ze end of ze week."

"Good news," I say, smiling, "it's not taken as long as we expected. At least the roofers will be gone in time for the kitchen re-fit." I'm somewhat relieved. Distracted by the sound of the excited squeals of children, we both turn and look in the direction of the campsite. "Sounds like someone's having fun," I say, trying to remain upbeat.

"I 'ave work to do; ze rose bushes and ze plants 'ave arrived zat Mama chose. I need to get zem in ze ground," he says, closing the paddock gate behind us.

"Yes, I must get on, too," I add, walking away purposefully.

Back at the Chateau, I stroll through the rooms looking for jobs, but everything is up to date. Slumping down on the window seat, I stare out of my bedroom window, overwhelmed by a sense of loneliness. The dogs are out with Xavier. Alice is busy baking and cooking – stocking the freezer for the coming season, she tells me – and caring for Gus, as well as tending her garden. I really do need to pull myself together. The Burrows' will be arriving tomorrow, that's something to look forward to. Standing abruptly, I decide to take a trip up to the attic to inspect the roof. I've not been up there for a long while. Xavier said it would be safer if I stayed out of their way.

I'm pleasantly surprised, it's a lot lighter now all the paint has been removed from the windows. Other than that, it doesn't look much different from the inside. I can see where a few of the old timbers have been replaced, but the off-white ceilings with their flaking paint are pretty much intact. It's a bit dusty, but nothing that a good spring clean won't sort out. I open the doors into the small rooms, which appear unchanged except the one with the roof light and squirrel hole. The hole has been filled in and the window replaced with a bigger version. It looks amazing! It's double glazed, with a blind trapped between the glass panels. A sturdy flight of new steps leads up to it, with large grab handles at either side. I can hear the men working outside. Opening the blind, I crane my neck and can see one of the roofers just outside the window. I take hold of the catch and attempt to open the window, but it's locked. The roofer's head snaps up, and he gestures for me to go back down the steps. Feeling foolish, I turn and climb back down into the attic. It seems I'm not even allowed on my own roof now! The attic feels empty with the treasures gone. My eyes land on the old chest containing the military uniforms.

Henri, the goat shepherd, comes to mind; I promised him that I'd display these items and make a small museum. The photographs of the military memorabilia and a short history of the role of the Chateau through the war years are now on the website, so I really should do something about it. I'm distracted by a text from Xavier.

How are ze sheep?

Of course, I'm supposed to be keeping an eye on them. With thoughts of the museum behind me, I grab a fleece and my wellies and rush back to the farmyard. Another of the ewes is laid on her side, labouring. Panicking, I look up. Xavier's truck is here, but I can't see him. "Xavier!" I shout but get no reply. Locating my phone, I ring him. "You need to get here quickly, one of the sheep is in labour."

"I am over on ze ozer side of ze estate, is she in distress?"

"I don't know. I'm used to patients that can talk to me."

"You will be okay, just stay wiz 'er. Phone back if you 'ave ze problem," he says before ending the call.

I stand close by the panting animal, praying that she won't need my intervention. Time seems to stand still as the poor thing continues to pant and strain. It feels like hours have gone by before she makes any progress, but gradually, a small bulge appears out of her back end. She immediately stands as the lamb appears feet first; still encased in its amniotic sac. Slowly, it emerges and drops to the ground, unmoving. It lies motionless in its watery cocoon while its mother walks away, seemingly clueless and makes no attempts to help it. I've been present at several births in my short career, but I've never been in charge, I've always had a midwife with me. Looking around for assistance, I realise I'm alone this time. Should I ring Xavier? By the time he gets here, it will be too late – no, it's a matter of life and death, and it's down to me.

Bending down, I swiftly burst the sac and clear the membrane away from its face. It's not breathing! I can't give it mouth to mouth resuscitation, so I lay it across my lap, head down, and start rubbing its chest vigorously. Still, nothing happens. I pluck a blade of long grass and tickle its nostrils. Eureka! The lifeless animal starts to sneeze, then takes its first lungful of air. I free it from the rest of its membranes and rub it dry with some soft hay. It slowly struggles to its feet and starts bleating, looking for its mother. Picking it up, I quietly approach mummy sheep and place it by her side then stand back, but she ignores it, seemingly more interested in the spring grass.

What should I do? Thinking on my feet, I decide to walk away and watch from the farmyard, giving the new mum some space and time. After ten minutes of the poor lamb bleating for the comfort of its mother, I'm beside myself. I want to go back in and embrace the poor thing. Should I just gather it up and take it back to the kitchen? It could sleep in a box by the range, and I could bottle feed it. No, the best place for it is with its mother. I'll give it a little longer. A few minutes later, with the lamb persisting, its mother looks at it a little shocked before deciding that she needs to do something. She turns in its direction and starts to sniff at it. She then licks it several times before bleating loudly, which has the little lamb scrabbling underneath her, finding a teat and beginning to suckle. I breathe a massive sigh of relief as another tear streaks down my face. Only then do I realise that Xavier is standing about two feet away from me, with a goofy grin splitting his face. Feeling silly, I dry my eyes and ask, "How long have you been here?"

"Long enough," he replies, smiling at me. "You know, I do believe now zat you will succeed. You did everysing zat you should 'ave. Well done."

Feeling a little embarrassed by his praise, I ask, "What should we do now?"

"We leave zem alone," he replies, looking at his watch. "It will be dark soon; Mama 'az cooked lots, join us for supper."

I call at the Chateau to shower and change before strolling over to the farmhouse with Shadow. It's like walking into a farmer's market. Every available surface is covered in foods of every description. Pies and quiches, pâtés and cheeses, cakes, and pastries. "Alice, you've been busy," I say in surprise as I take in the scene.

"Yes, just getting a head start, so we have food for any short notice events," she replies, looking over at the spread proudly. "I'll freeze it all when it's gone cold."

"It smells divine, and I'm starving!" I reply.

"Yes, farming is hard work, and you did a great job today," Xavier says, then proceeds to tell Alice and Gus about my lambing experience. "Zere is five more sheep still to lamb, it should be over in a day or two."

"I'll help," cries Gus with a mouthful of pie.

"You 'ave school tomorrow, but ze next day is Saturday, you can be in charge zen. I will check a couple of times tonight, and Laura can be in charge tomorrow." Xavier says.

"But the Burrows' are coming tomorrow afternoon," I say.

"Good, zey can 'elp too," he replies, tucking into his mother's mouth-watering dishes.

"Papa, school finished today, it's Good Friday tomorrow; I will help Laura," Gus says between mouthfuls of cake.

After supper, I walk over to check on the sheep with Xavier. All appears quiet, with no sign of any imminent births, the new mothers are settled down with their babies tucked into their sides. "I'll set the alarm and come out in a few hours; let's go and get some rest now," Xavier says as he leaves me at the Chateau.

I'm exhausted. So much has happened today. I have my first paying guests on the campsite, and I've delivered my first lamb. Feeling pleased with myself, I fall into a deep sleep with little thought of Enzo and his sulking behaviour.

26

I wake refreshed on Friday morning and rush over to the sheep before breakfast. Two more lambs have arrived, and one of them is black! I wonder if Xavier was here to help them or if they managed alone? I don't have long to ponder as his truck pulls into the farmyard. "Is all okay?" He asks through his open window.

"Yes, it appears to be. Were you here when they were born?" I ask, pointing to the two new lambs.

"Only ze white one, ze black one wasn't 'ere when I checked at five zis morning."

"Well, it seems to be doing fine on its own. Take the morning off; get some rest," I say.

"I need to talk to Gustave, zen, I will go back 'ome for a while."

"Yes, I'd like to have a look at the roof myself—"

"No! You must not go up zere today," he snaps, "zey are working by ze new window, its tres dangerous! I will show you tomorrow when it's finished and safe. And, you are on sheep duty today."

I refuse to get angry. "Okay, if you say so. Another day won't make much difference, and I've got the Burrows' arriving after lunch. Plenty to get on with." I say. He puts the truck in gear and drives in the direction of the

Chateau. I stay a while longer, gazing at the sheep and marvelling at the new lives just beginning.

The swallows have returned and are busy building their mud nests in the stables and any other suitable overhangs, it's such a beautiful morning, and I can't think of anywhere I'd rather be. Then, I suddenly remember Enzo and immediately feel guilty for not missing him. Only a few days ago, I was miserable, and now I'm feeling better already. Perhaps I'm as fickle as he is. No, that's not fair, he didn't promise any type of commitment; he was honest from the start and told me he would be leaving in the Summer. I'm glad he's gone away for a while, the distance will be good for us, but he could have informed me… My thoughts are interrupted by the sound of delighted squeals, looking over my shoulder, I can see Danielle and Paul arriving with their two small children.

"Good morning!" Paul shouts.

"Good morning, I hope you had a peaceful night," I reply.

"Yes, thank you, as peaceful as you can with three-year-old twins," Danielle adds.

"I'm just going to collect the eggs; would you like to help?" My question is met with more squeals of delight as the two small girls rush over to join in the hunt. An hour later, I return to the Chateau with a basket of eggs for Alice, minus the four that I gave to my guests for their breakfast; Alice seems to have got through so many eggs this week. As I put them on the kitchen table, I notice a note that Xavier has left for me.

Can you organise an Easter egg hunt for ze children?

It's Good Friday today, so I have until Sunday. That's tomorrow morning taken care of, then. I'll have to drive to town for chocolate eggs and decorations. The visit to the roof will have to wait until the afternoon now. I'll ask Alice if she'll make an Easter cake for me to hand out to the guests, she seems to enjoy baking. Looking out of the window I can see that Xavier's truck has gone, I do hope he's gone to get some rest. After enjoying my scrambled eggs for breakfast, I ring Alice. "Morning, do you have time to make an Easter cake for the families staying at the campsite?"

"Err, yes, I suppose I can. Gus can help me to decorate it."

"Talking of Gus, is he coming to watch over the sheep? Only three left. If there's a problem, ring me."

"Yes, I'll send him over."

Poor Alice, she does sound flustered. Do I ask too much of her? She is going a bit overboard with the cooking just now; we won't have any space left in the freezers if she carries on.

A beep alerts me to a vehicle entering the drive. Peering out of the window, I can see a caravan; it must be the Burrows'! I rush out to meet them with Shadow eagerly following me. I arrive at the campsite in time to see Dylan and Lily rushing over to the small play area. Dylan turns and waves before climbing on to the trampoline. Lily turns and rushes back towards me, shouting, "Has the old lady been back?"

Lost for words, I gather Lily in my arms and hug her. "Hello, Lily, you've grown…"

"Yes, but not as much as Mummy; her tummy is ginormous! And I've lost my two front teeth. Look," she replies, poking her small pink tongue through the gap, then rushing over to join in the fun with her brother.

John is out of the car next. He smiles at me, then walks around the car to the passenger side and helps Jackie out. "Oh, I see what Lily means," I say as I approach them both for a hug.

"Wow, you have been busy," John says, looking around in interest.

"Not as busy as you!" I reply, laughing. "Congratulations, when is the baby due?"

"Only another three weeks to go… and I can't wait; I'm getting fed up of looking and feeling like a hippopotamus!" Jackie replies.

"Yes, we had to come via the tunnel; the ferries wouldn't take Jackie in her condition. But she'll be fine. Dylan and Lily were both nearly two weeks late and had to be induced, and we'll be back home in a couple of weeks." John says, then adds, "This is amazing, better than I anticipated, and I can see you have a new roof at last."

"Yes, but I haven't been up to see it yet; apparently, I'm not allowed to inspect it until tomorrow. Would you come with me to give your professional opinion?"

"I most certainly will. Now, where do you want us to site the caravan?"

"Take any pitch you want; I've got two more families arriving later today."

John inspects the pitches and chooses one near the play area, "We can sit and keep an eye on the children from here with a glass of wine. We're having a barbeque this evening, you must join us. Six o'clock." John says, rubbing his hands together like an excited child.

"Thank you, that will be lovely. Wrap up warm, though; it still gets quite chilly once the sun goes down."

Just as I arrive back at the Chateau, another caravan enters the drive, and I'm trotting back over to the campsite to welcome more guests — a German family with a young boy of about eight years of age. While showing them the facilities, I hear Gus shouting, "Laura! Laura! Where are you? Come quickly!" I hastily excuse myself and dash over to the farmyard to see Gus in a panic, crouched at the side of a recumbent ewe that has already produced a lamb; which is thankfully breathing, but still wet and getting cold. Grabbing a handful of soft hay, I instruct Gus to dry the lamb off while I inspect its mother, who remains on her side, panting and looking uncomfortable.

"I think she's having another one; twins!" I say. "I wonder where your dad is?"

"Cool, I didn't think of that. He was going into town to collect some things for tomorrow," Gus replies.

"Tomorrow? Why, what's happening tomorrow?"

"Err, um, oh, I don't know; they didn't say," he replies, blushing.

A loud bleating noise grabs my attention as the stricken ewe strains and gives birth to a second, smaller lamb. I quickly clear away the membranes and proceed to dry the little lamb with more hay. At last, it starts to breathe by itself and makes a feeble noise. Its twin is up on its feet and nuzzling its mother, who begins to take an interest and smells at her new offspring. Once the ewe has got to its feet, I repeat yesterday's actions and step out of the paddock with Gus as we observe the expanded family. Within a few minutes, the bigger lamb has found its mother's teats and is suckling greedily, but the smaller one is standing off to the side, looking a little hunched. "What should we do now?" Gus asks, "I wish Dad were here."

"Don't worry, let's give it some time," I reply, feeling less optimistic than I sound; secretly wishing that Xavier was here too. Again, time seems to pass slowly. After fifteen minutes, there's no progress; the tiny lamb is making no attempt to find its mother's teats. "I'm just going to give it a nudge," I say as I make my way back over to it, gently steering the creature in the direction of its mother. Shockingly, she turns and butts it away to the side of the paddock and proceeds to ignore it. "Oh, my goodness!" I say, collecting the small creature up in my arms, "It's so cold and thin."

"Nana usually puts them in the side oven," Gus says.

"In the oven? We're not going to eat it!"

"No, silly, not to cook; only to warm it up a little, then she bottle feeds them. Most of them survive; we only eat them when they're bigger," Gus grins at me.

"Come on then, let's take this to her," I say, ignoring his last comment as we walk over to the farmhouse. We arrive at an empty kitchen with a note on the table. 'I've gone down to the village, ask Laura if you need anything.'

"Oh, dear; now what?" Gus asks, looking worried.

"Where do you keep the feeding bottles?" I ask. Gus disappears, returning shortly with a large bottle and rubber teat from an outbuilding, which I wash and sterilise with boiling water. He then produces a grubby container of white powder that he assures me is dried milk for lambs. "How old is that?" I ask, curling up my nose. "Wait a minute! We have plenty of goats milk, lets warm up some of that!"

"But, do lambs drink goats milk?" He questions.

"Only one way to find out," I say, wrapping the tiny creature in a warm towel and offering it some of the lukewarm goats' milk. At first, it ignores the teat, so I squeeze some of the liquid onto my finger and place it gently into its mouth. It doesn't react instantly, so I wiggle my finger a little. Slowly, it starts to suck, and I carefully replace my finger with the teat. It manages to drink a small amount of the milk, but some of it trickles down my leg, leaving a sticky feeling. I can't help but smile as I say to Gus, "This reminds me of the morning you tried to teach me how to milk the goats when I first arrived, do you remember?" He looks at me, giggling, and nods.

"Yes, and look 'ow far you've come since zen; we will make a farmer of you yet," says a familiar voice.

"Xavier! How long have you been watching?"

Shrugging, in his peculiar fashion, he replies, "Long enough."

"Oh, what happened to its mother?" Alice asks as she enters the kitchen carrying a large floral display. Gus jumps up and proceeds to recount the story of the younger twin, rejected by its mother. "Well, it looks like you're doing a fine job of lamb sitting," Alice says, before dispatching Xavier to go and check on the rest of the flock. I reluctantly hand my charge over to Alice, who carefully places it in the side oven.

"Yes, and I need to get back to the campsite; I'm expecting a Dutch family," I say.

27

The Dutch family consists of a young couple with a little girl about the same age as Lily. They have already pitched a large tent near the shower block, and decline my offer of assistance, so I head over to the sheep to catch up with developments. Xavier appears to have everything under control and is putting out more feed to supplement their grazing. "I've been invited to a barbeque with the Burrows' this evening, and I'm going into town in the morning to get the chocolate eggs for the Easter egg hunt. You can still ring me this evening if you need any help."

"'Ave a nice time, I'll be okay 'ere – ze ozer two sheep look like zey are starting in labour, it should all be over by bedtime," he says.

"Thank goodness for that. I think we've had enough births; first the goats, now the sheep, and it won't be long before Shadow's puppies are born."

"Well, it is zat time of year!" I nod and make my way back to the Chateau, change into warm clothes, ready to spend an evening with my friends.

"Something smells good," I say as I arrive with a couple of bottles of our house wine. Jackie takes them from me and puts them under the caravan while John continues to turn the steaks on the barbeque. "Dylan and Lily seem to be having a good time on the trampoline," I add.

"Yes, they love it – no doubt we'll have to get one when we get home," Jackie says, looking over at John, who nods in agreement. We spend the evening chatting, and they are eager to hear my news about the Chateau and the progress that's been made. I tell them about the guns and ammunition we found, and the work we've done so far.

"We've got some new lambs; the children are welcome to visit them. We have a sickly lamb that Alice is bottle feeding. When it gets a bit stronger, they can come and help to feed it," I say.

"Laura, where is your dog?" Dylan asks enthusiastically.

"Shadow; he's called Shadow, and I've left him at home," I say.

"Can I take him for a walk? I've always wanted a dog." Lily asks.

I look across to Jackie, who immediately says, "We're not going to have a dog! I won't be able to look after it when the baby arrives!" The children whine in protest.

"Yes, they take a lot of looking after, but you can come over and help me to look after Shadow," I reply. This seems to placate the children as they tuck into their food. Darkness falls, and I make my way back to the Chateau for an early night, I've got a busy day tomorrow.

I awake at seven-thirty with a text from Xavier.

All ze lambs 'ave arrived safely, I'll check on ze guests if you want to go to town.

Gosh, it's like he's had a personality transplant. I don't know if I preferred the old belligerent Xavier or the new more amicable one.

Thank you, I'll be back at lunchtime to inspect the roof.

The morning whizzes by as I trawl the shops for Easter chicks and chocolate eggs. It's a struggle, as many of the shops have almost sold out; I suppose I have left it a bit late. Easter was never really a big event back home, only an excuse to eat chocolate, but here it seems to be important; it's all about family. Seeing all of the chocolate is making me hungry; time to go home for lunch.

The Chateau door is wide open when I arrive, that's strange. Alice pops her head out and then turns quickly and goes back inside. I do hope everything's okay. I abandon my car and collect my shopping then step inside. I'm blown away. My hall is full of people! Xavier, Alice, and Gus are at the front of the queue; this is so weird! Alice steps forward and embraces me. "Congratulations, we're all so proud of you."

Xavier is next. He doesn't speak but leans in and gives me a quick peck on the cheek, looking somewhat awkward. Then Gus. "Love you lots," he whispers, then adds in a louder voice, "can we eat now?"

Alice shushes him as the rest of the crowd break into "Hip-hip-hooray!" Some in English and some in French.

"What… why…?" I stutter, then I notice Monsieur le Maire stood at the side of

Gustave with a glass of bubbly. He steps forward and raises his glass.

"To Laura and her new life here in France. I'd like to take this opportunity to wish you every success with your new venture, and officially welcome you into our community. You've had highs – and lows – but you've weathered the storms and persevered. Well done." More applause follows as I stand like a statue, looking at the bewildering array of guests.

The spell is broken by Gus, who takes my hand and leads me into the dining room – it is a visual delight. Floral displays and Easter decorations adorn every surface, and bunting is hung from the ceiling. The huge table is covered in food – now I know why Alice has been so busy! A three-tier cake dominates the centre of the table, covered in yellow icing and Easter bunnies. I can't move. I feel as though my legs are paralysed; rooted to the spot. In the drawing room, I hear the familiar tinkle of the piano as the hairs stand up on the back of my neck, and I know Aunt Mary approves. "Tuck in everyone, while it's still warm," Alice says, as the labourers who worked on the roof appear out of the kitchen.

Xavier steps forward, handing me a plate. "It's ze 'topping off ceremony' for ze roof – it's a tradition." My hunger seems to have disappeared as I stand back and watch all these people; friends, enjoying their lunch. So many familiar faces. Monsieur Bertrand; the first person I met when I arrived. Pedro, Rose, Sylvie and her partner, Jacques, the mechanic, along with the Burrows' family and many of the locals I've encountered along the way. I think I'm in shock.

"Is Enzo working?" Jacques asks as he approaches and stands beside me. I just shake my head; I don't want to think about him at the moment. This is too special to spoil. I look around the room, and my eyes fix on Xavier; he's stood looking at me, smiling, then averts his eyes. He seems different, somehow.

"I can't believe that he organised all this without me knowing," I say to Jacques.

"He's a good man…"

"Hi, guys! Sorry, I'm a little late. What have I missed?" A familiar voice says from the doorway.

"Jenny!" Jacques rushes over and lifts her off the floor. I walk over, joining in with the group hug.

"How… why…?" I, again, stutter.

"A certain French farmer contacted me and said that there was going to be a party; you know parties and me! Come on, I need a drink!"

As Jacques heads off to fetch Jenny her drink, I say, "But… I only Skyped you a few days ago, and you never mentioned anything!" Jenny winks mischievously at me. Jacques is attentively back at her side with a glass of bubbly a moment later.

I slowly make my way across the room, thanking all my guests as I go. "Did you know about this?" I ask John and Jackie as I pass by them. I don't get an answer, just a knowing smile. It seems everyone knew except me. It's Alice's turn next, "Thank you so much for doing this, it's so thoughtful."

"Don't thank me – it was Xavier's idea, I just helped to make it happen," Alice replies. My eyes scan the dining room, but I can't see him. Knowingly, she adds, "He's outside with Gustave and the rest of the roofers."

I leave the chatter behind me and step outside to see Xavier sat on the stone wall drinking a beer with Gustave. Slowly, he stands and approaches me. "Thank you for all of this," I say gesturing towards the party.

"No big deal," he replies, shrugging.

"Well, it's a big deal to me. Thank you, though I still don't know how you managed to keep it a secret from me." Prodding his shoulder, I say, "This is new, you look dapper.

Have you had your hair cut?" He just smiles. "Can I see the roof now?" Nodding, he takes my hand and leads me through the hall, thronged with my friends enjoying themselves. I stop short. "Oh, John wanted to see it too. I'll go and get him."

Bypassing the crowds, he says, "First, I want to show it to you myself, zen anyone can come." I follow on behind him up the stairs into the attic. He pauses at the bottom of the new steps that lead up to the window in the roof, which now has a red ribbon tied with a neat bow across it. Looking back, he produces a pair of scissors. "Are you ready?"

Feeling a little giddy, I take the scissors, climb the steps and cut the ribbon, saying with a giggle, "I declare this roof open! God bless her and all that stay under her." I hear laughter followed by clapping as I turn to see Alice, Gus, Sylvie, and Jenny stood in the attic, beaming. Reaching up, I examine the catch, which unlocks with a series of satisfying clicks as the window opens in front of me.

Feeling brave, I slowly pop my head out. I'm blown away. The window opens onto a small balcony with a plain glass balustrade surrounding it. Two small wrought-iron chairs and a low fancy table are artfully placed off to one side. "Wow! I didn't ask for this! How much more will it cost me?" I ask.

"Nothing, it's already paid for," Gustave's voice says in the near distance. "Go on out and take a look," he adds, entering the attic behind my friends.

I cautiously climb out onto the balcony, with Xavier following on behind. I can see for miles; the farmhouse off to my left with the village beyond, the drive and campsite with the valley disappearing into infinity to my right. "Wow, this is amazing, but who's idea was it, and who paid for it?" Xavier stands beside me silently, looking a little uncomfortable. "It was you wasn't it?" I accuse gently.

He sighs, before replying, "You 'ave done so much for my family and me, now I 'ave done something for you." Lost for words, I put my arms around him and give him a peck on his cheek. Embarrassed, he steps back and opens a small gate at the side that leads onto the roof itself. Striding through it, he holds out his hand, "Come on, but be careful; I don't want to find you stuck up 'ere again," he says with a mischievous glint in his eye.

"I think I will stay here on the balcony, where I'm safe. I can see most of the roof from here." He turns and joins me, closing the gate behind him, and we stand in silence, taking in the view.

The spell is broken by Jenny, who quietly arrives behind us. She asks, winking, "Am I interrupting an intimate moment?" She looks around, taking in the view. "Oh, my God! This is freaking awesome, my favourite new drinking hole."

Xavier steps to the side. "Not too much drinking 'ere; we don't want any more accidents on ze roof." As he leaves, he says, "I'll go and get John."

Jenny turns to look at me then says, "Wow! I can feel the tension; you could cut it with a knife! Are you two 'friends with benefits' now? And what happened to Enzo? I can't keep up with your exploits!"

"No, we are not! Enzo and I aren't together anymore… it's a long story; I'll fill you in later." I say as John's head appears through the window.

28

"…So, that's the story of how our relationship ended," I say to Jenny the next morning, after explaining about the magazine article and Enzo's reaction; going on a jaunt through Europe for a couple of weeks to avoid me.

"Did you love him? I mean… you don't look broken-hearted to me."

"Hmm, I'm not too sure now; I thought I did at the time."

"Any regrets?"

"No, I don't think so; we had a great time, but he'll be going back home in a few months anyway. And I've still got so much to do here. The kitchen company starts on Wednesday, so, I'm afraid it will be a bit of a mess. I'm going to have my meals at the farmhouse until it's finished. Alice will be thrilled to have you there as well."

Grinning, she says, "Count me out. Jacques has this week off, and he's taking me down to the coast tomorrow until Friday, then I fly home next Saturday."

"Are you two getting serious?"

She laughs. "No, like you; just friends with benefits!"

"Come on, it's Easter Sunday; we've got chocolate eggs to hide," I say, rolling my eyes and handing Jenny her jumper.

John helps us to hide the eggs while Jackie rests. Later, Dylan, Lily, and the other children have a fantastic time finding and eating them. "Can we go and feed the baby lamb now?" Lily asks after the chocolate eggs are gone.

"Yes, come on; Mummy can have another rest," John says, standing up.

"You can both have a rest; we'll take them," I say, looking across to Jenny.

Alice is thrilled to see the children and shows them how to feed the small lamb, which is looking stronger already. "He's so cute. What is he called?" Lily enquires.

"You choose a name, and she's a girl," Alice says.

"Mary, let's call her Mary after the old lady," Lily shouts excitedly.

"Okay, Mary, it is," I reply, as my phone rings.

"Laura, come quickly! I think the baby is coming!" John's panic is evident.

"I'm on my way, I'll ring for an ambulance," I reply, as I hear Jackie swearing in the background.

The children jump up and down excitedly, though I make them stay with Alice, while Jenny and I climb into Xavier's truck and rush over to the campsite. As we approach the caravan, we can hear Jackie shouting and enter to find her laid on the bed with the baby's head just visible. Jenny and I look at each other, then go into professional mode. I wash my hands while Jenny boils a kettle and instructs John to find clean towels and linens. "Where's the ambulance, I need gas and air!" Jackie wails.

"It's too late for pain relief; you're doing just fine, now with your next contraction I want you to push," I say, trying to calm her down a little. Thankfully, it works, and within minutes the baby's head slowly emerges. "Pant, Jackie, I need you to pant now while I look for the baby's cord," I say. John joins in, panting beside his wife. I gently feel for the baby's neck and try to remain calm as I discover the cord wrapped around it. I look over to Jenny, who grimaces back at me.

"What's wrong? Tell me what's wrong?" John raises his voice in alarm.

I look back at Jenny, who puts her hand on John's shoulder and quietly tells him, "The cord is wrapped around the baby's neck, which isn't always a problem. We need you to stay calm for Jackie's sake."

"Okay Jackie, you're doing really well, but we need the next stage to go slowly, so with your next contraction I need you to push gently but listen to my instructions and stop if I ask you to," I say to poor Jackie, who is looking exhausted.

"It's coming!" Jackie wails as she starts to push.

"Woah! Slow down, Jackie; take it really slowly." Jackie gives a loud groan and starts to push again. "Slowly, just go slowly now," I caution, as the baby's shoulders appear. Jenny leans over me and supports the baby's shoulders as I manage to free the cord and loop it back over its head. "Good girl, now you can push." The rest of the baby emerges with a swish of fluid. "Well done, it's a little girl," I say as I clear away the mucus from her mouth and lay the baby on Jackie's chest. We all hold our breath for what feels like an eternity until we hear her cry.

John looks on, slightly bewildered. "Is she okay?"

"She seems to be," I reply, as we hear the ambulance pulling up outside. Jenny rushes out and shows a paramedic inside.

"You're too late," John says, beaming while stroking his daughter's face.

Jenny and I step outside to give them some privacy while the paramedic checks mother and baby over and cuts the cord, declaring them both fit and well, but suggesting they go to the hospital as a precaution. Moments later Xavier arrives on a bicycle.

"Is everything okay?"

"Yes, fine," I say slowly.

Xavier takes his jacket off and places it over my shoulders. "You don't look fine; you're shaking, and you look very pale."

"I'm okay, though I could do with sitting down, my legs feel like jelly." He puts his arms around me and gently lifts me into his truck while Jenny climbs in the back. Back at the farmhouse, Alice, Dylan, and Lily come rushing out.

"Where's Mummy? I want Mummy!" Lily wails.

Jenny hugs Lily and explains what has happened. "She'll be back soon… with your new sister."

"I would have preferred a dog!" Lily says with a pout and walks over to sit next to Xavier's big dog, Beau.

"Well done," Alice says to Jenny.

"Oh, it wasn't me. Laura took charge and had everything under control, she's a natural midwife," Jenny replies.

Alice smiles and passes me a cup of tea, "I've put sugar in it, it will help with the shakes." Xavier sits by my side, gently rubbing my back.

"I'll be fine. It's just the adrenaline leaving my body," I say, while secretly enjoying the contact. My phone pings with an incoming text.

Thank you for everything! Will you please watch the children until I get back?

I show the children the message from their father. "Cool! Can we sleep in the Chateau?" Dylan asks excitedly.

"Yes, of course, you can. Let's go and collect your things from your caravan," I reply, beginning to feel better.

Later, when the children are finally tucked up asleep, and Jenny and I are sitting in the lounge, John phones, "I'm on my way back, I'll call in for the children."

"They're already in bed now. How's Jackie and the baby?"

"They're both fine and should be able to come out in the morning, thanks to you."

"It was Jackie that did the hard work, not me. You can come and stay here with the children if you wish, I can make up another bedroom."

"Thank you, that's very kind, but I'll stay in the caravan tonight. I'll come over for breakfast with the children if that's okay?"

"Of course, see you then," I say, adding, "sleep well."

"I don't know about you, but I need a stiff drink; lets wet the baby's head!" Jenny suggests.

"I'll give it a miss, I'm responsible for the children tonight; tomorrow perhaps," I say.

"I understand. You always were super-sensible, but I'll be down on the Riviera living it up tomorrow!"

"I wonder if they have any clothes for the new baby? I hope Jackie plans to breastfeed; there won't be any shops open tomorrow, it's Easter Monday."

"Mm, what about nappies?" Jenny adds, then starts to laugh. "We'll worry about that tomorrow. I'm ready for bed. What a day!"

29

The sound of bickering wakes me from my slumber. Lily and Dylan! I jump out of bed and look at my watch, seven-fifteen. Grabbing a robe on my way out, I find the children charging across the landing, "Hey! Slow down, you might fall," I say.

"We're looking for ghosts!" shouts Dylan.

"Well, the only ghost here won't come out if you're running about, she likes children to behave," I say. "Come on, let's go and make breakfast; what would you like?"

By the time John arrives, the kitchen is covered in flour as the children help me to make pancakes. "Daddy!" Lily shouts as she runs into his arms, "I'm making pancakes, come and have one; shall we save one for the baby?"

"But not that one," Dylan adds, pointing to one on the draining board, "it's for Shadow. Lily tossed it onto the floor." The children finish eating and continue with their ghost hunt while I have coffee with John.

"Do you have any clothes and nappies for the baby?" I ask.

John shakes his head and grimaces, "No, we weren't anticipating needing any; they're all at home."

"Oh, dear, the shops will be closed. Is Jackie going to feed the baby herself?" I ask.

"We bottle fed the other two," he says, scratching his stubbly chin. Distracted by the beeping alarm, he looks out of the window. "Xavier's here in his truck." I stand and walk over to the window to see him lifting an old-styled pram out of the back, along with a large suitcase and a car seat. Meanwhile, Alice and Gus climb out of the front with Beau following behind.

"It looks like you have a pram now, I'll give it a good clean," I say as the family arrives in the hall.

"I've already given it a good clean and washed the sheets and blankets. I've also put together a bundle of baby clothes; I'm sorry, most of them are blue," Alice says, before adding, "Congratulations! What are you going to call her?"

"That's so kind of you, Alice. Thank you. I don't know; It's only just beginning to sink in," he says, looking bewildered. His phone rings and he excuses himself and stands in the hall, coming back a few minutes later, smiling. "That was Jackie, they're ready to come home. Apparently, there's a pharmacy open near the hospital where we'll be able to get nappies and feeding equipment. Would you look after the children until we get back?"

Jacques arrives soon after John leaves and whisks Jenny off down to the coast while Alice and the children make even more mess, baking a cake for the arrival of the new baby. "I'm going to prepare a room for Jackie and John, they can't stay in a caravan with a new baby," I say.

Xavier is behind me in an instant. "I'll 'elp you; ze top of ze pram turns into a carry-cot. I'll bring it up, zen you can get it ready for ze baby." The rest of the morning is taken up with preparing for the arrival of the new mother and baby. Xavier brings two bottles of bubbly out of the cellar while Alice makes lunch and I take Shadow for a walk with the children.

"Mummy! Look, Mummy and Daddy are here!" Lily shouts as their car comes to a halt outside the front door. John helps Jackie out and carries the car seat into the hall. Shadow walks over and sniffs at the baby, obviously deciding that she is of little interest before walking away. Beau, on the other hand, walks over and sits at the infant's side. "Mummy, Mummy, we're all sleeping in the Chateau!"

Lily shouts excitedly, "There's even a pram for the baby to sleep in."

Jackie looks over to me and mouths "Thank you," then hugs her children, telling them how much she has missed them. The family settle down and enjoy the feast that Alice has prepared.

After a short while, Lily says, "I decorated the cake Mummy, can we give a piece to the baby?"

Jackie looks at Lily and then back over to me with a soft smile, "The baby has a name now, and no, she can only have milk."

"Ooh, what is she called?" Alice asks, looking over to the small bundle asleep in the oversized car seat, with Beau sat watching over her.

"Well, seeing as she was born in France, we've decided to call her Frances, and her middle name is Laura," Jackie says, bursting with pride.

"Laura! That's your name!" Lily shouts, pointing to me with wide eyes.

"Yes, thanks to Laura, Frances is safe and well," John says.

Before I get a chance to speak, Xavier chooses this moment to stand and pour everyone a glass of bubbly, diluting the children's drinks with lemonade. "Raise your glasses to Frances Laura Burrows, may she 'ave a long and 'appy life."

"Is she French or English?" Gus asks.

"Good question; I think she is dual nationality, and we have to go and visit Monsieur Le Maire to get the required papers to take her back home," John says.

The sound of crying wakes me in the middle of the night. Of course! Frances. A glance at my phone informs me it's nearly two-thirty. Twenty minutes later and the crying hasn't stopped. I tiptoe across the landing and knock quietly on Jackie and John's bedroom door.

John opens it and starts to apologise, "So sorry, we didn't want to disturb you. She just won't settle; we've fed and changed her."

"Don't worry, I'm going to put the kettle on. I'll take her for a while so you can get some sleep," I say, taking Frances out of his arms. Once downstairs, I place her over my shoulder and try to wind her, which has little effect. "You poor little thing… have you got a tummy ache?" I say. I'm suddenly startled, as the haunting sound of a familiar melody echoes out of the drawing room. It's an old nursery rhyme that I haven't heard for a very long time; my gran used to sing it to me when I was little. Slowly, I make my way towards the music and enter the drawing room, the hairs on the back of my neck begin to prickle as the tune continues. Frances gradually settles and stops crying as I stand by the large window. I can see no one. There is a full moon, bathing the room with soft, silver light; the piano continues to play by itself as Frances snuggles into my shoulder and sleeps.

I gently place her in the Moses basket loaned from one of the kind locals and lie down on the sofa next to her. I'm woken by John as he places a cup of tea by my side. "What time is it?"

"Six-thirty. Go back to bed, I'll take over now." I sit up and pick up the cup, taking a cautious sip.

"It's Wednesday, the kitchen company will be here in a couple of hours. Thankfully, Xavier has emptied the big kitchen, so there's not much to do; I think I will go for a nap." I say, standing up with my tea and walking towards the door to the hall.

"We're going into town for some bits for the baby, and we have an appointment to register her birth, so we'll be out of your way in a couple of hours, thank you. By the way, what did you do to finally get her to settle?" John asks as he follows me.

I begin climbing the stairs, "I had a little help from Aunt Mary." Stifling a yawn, I continue, "And friends are never in the way."

30

The kitchen company arrives, and the rest of the week passes by with frenetic activity and more dust. The warmer weather and lengthening days bring a flurry of inquiries and bookings for the campsite, as well as the text that I've not been looking forward to.

I'm back, would you like to go out for dinner so we can talk?

Enzo. How dare he? I'm going to leave him to stew for a few days. After all, he left me for two weeks without even bothering to tell me he was going. I don't think so! A walk over to the campsite to see my friends, the Burrows', will take my mind off him. On my way over, I receive another text. Dare I look? Phew, it's from Sophie.

The hot tubs will be arriving tomorrow.

Gosh, that was quick! Where are we going to put them and what preparation do we need? A quick text and I have my answer. Xavier will need to build a decking area to sit them on. With the dimensions required, I change direction and walk over to the farmhouse.

"I can't build two sets of decking in twenty-four hours!" He protests, frowning, then adds, "But, I can ask ze kitchen fitters to 'elp, and we 'ave ze electrician 'ere."

"I'm sure John will help too. Where shall we put them?" I ask.

"One by ze shower block on ze campsite, and one at ze back of ze Chateau," he replies, smiling.

"Good idea let's get on with it," I say as we both march towards the Chateau to get to work. And, the following afternoon, when the large lorry trundles down the drive carrying the hot tubs, the bases are indeed finished. By early evening, they are full of water, along with the required chemicals, wired up and ready to go. Several of the guests on the campsite are patiently waiting to try it out, and I can't wait to get into mine. The timing couldn't be better as Jenny will be here this evening.

Jacques drops Jenny off just after eight. After her lengthy good-bye kiss, she asks, "Have you eaten? I'm starving."

"No, I was waiting for you. I'll put the pizzas in the oven; the kitchen still isn't quite finished, but everything works."

"Wow! This is so different, I've been gone less than a week, and you've done so much," she says, examining the partition wall and new appliances.

"That's not all. I've got a surprise for you when we've eaten," I say, beaming excitedly.

"Now, what have you done? Let me guess… you're getting married," she says, laughing.

"As if!" I shout out, pouring her a glass of wine and listening while she tells me about her holiday down on the coast with Jacques, wearing a dreamy look on her face. "It sounds like you will be the one getting married," I say. She just smiles. After dinner, I take her by the hand and lead her out of the back door.

Looking at the hot tub, she squeals, "Oh-my-God! When did you get this?"

"It only arrived today, and we are going to be the first in; come on!" I say as we rush upstairs to get changed. The evening passes all too quickly, and the following morning, I drive Jenny to the airport, cutting it fine as always; she is back at work tomorrow.

I see very little of Xavier over the following week, partly because he's so busy tending to the vines and crops and partly because I try to spend my free time with the Burrows', as they leave on Friday, having booked a flight home.

They are going to leave their car and caravan here until the summer holidays and fly back down for a couple of weeks, then drive back when Frances is a bit older. "Tomorrow is your last day, why don't you take the children out and I'll take care of Frances for you?" I suggest over lunch.

"We can't ask you to do that, you've done so much for us already," John says.

"Nonsense, it will be my pleasure. Have a look online and decide where you want to go, I'll make a picnic for you," I say. "What would you like?"

I spend the afternoon baking and enjoying my new kitchen, the oven is big enough to feed a small army. Soon I have prepared a massive feast for the Burrows' to take tomorrow, and plenty for supper tonight; more than I can eat myself. I think I'll invite Alice, Gus, and Xavier over. Alice's mobile goes to voicemail, so I leave a message. "Hello Alice, I've made too much food, would you like to come over for supper?"

A short while later she rings back, "Sorry Laura, Gus has been invited to a birthday party this evening, and I'm going to visit a friend in the village while he's out, but I'll ask Xavier."

"Oh, okay, I hope you both have a nice time," I say, trying to hide my disappointment. Ten minutes later, I receive a text from Xavier accepting my invitation to dinner. Not quite the evening I had in mind. He arrives at seven, looking clean and smart.

"For you," he says, handing me a bunch of flowers, and placing three bottles of red wine on the table.

"Thank you, they are lovely; are they out of the garden?" I ask.

"Yes, and ze meadow," he adds, leaning over giving me a kiss on each cheek. "Dinner smells good, 'ow are you getting on wiz ze new oven? I 'aven't forgot about painting ze kitchen, I will do it next week." We get through supper while discussing jobs that need doing and the imminent refurbishment of the bedrooms. As he downs his third glass of wine, Xavier asks, "'Ave you been in ze 'ot tub yet?"

"Yes, it's wonderful, it helps me unwind before bed."

"Good. Come on, let's go and unwind." Xavier stands. I look up at him in amazement.

"You want to go in the hot tub?"

"Yes, why not?"

Somewhat shocked, I ask, "Have you brought your swimming trunks?"

"No, I don't 'ave any. My underwear is clean," Xavier replies, taking off his shirt.

"Oh, erm, okay – I'll go and change," I say, though I'm slightly bewildered. When I return, Xavier is already sat in the hot tub with a full bottle of wine and two glasses on the patio table. He leans over and fills the glasses, handing me one as I get comfortable in the warm water. "This feels surreal; who are you, and what have you done with Xavier?" I ask cautiously.

"Zis is still me," he says, pointing to himself, "But, like you, I 'ave changed." I continue to look at him as I finish my wine, unsure of what to say next. He then pours me another.

"I think we've had enough, don't you?" I say, starting to feel a little tipsy. He shrugs then drains the glass in one gulp.

"You need to relax. We 'ave done so much 'ard work 'ere. Surely, we can 'ave a night off," he says. Reaching over, he places the glass on the table then scoots across the hot tub and sits beside me. My skin begins to tingle as his knee gently rests next to mine. I tense and draw away. "Come 'ere, I don't bite. Just relax a little," he says, moving closer. I release the breath that I hadn't realised I was holding. He's right, we're just friends enjoying a little downtime. I lean in and rest my head on his shoulder as my body sags with the effects of the alcohol and the soothing warm bubbles. Looking up, I gaze at the inky black sky punctuated with stars, sparkling like diamonds, and give an involuntary shiver.

"It's getting cold, time to go in," he says, taking my hand and helping me out. Once the chilly evening air hits my warm body, my legs sag, and I lean on Xavier, noticing for the first time his broad, muscular torso. He gently sweeps me up in his arms and carries me into the kitchen, where he drapes a towel over my shoulders.

"When did you become so handsome?" I ask, slurring my words a little.

"I don't look any different; I zink you are wearing wine tinted spectacles. Come on, let me 'elp you upstairs." He picks me up again and carries me upstairs, depositing me outside my bedroom door. "Can you manage from 'ere?"

"Yes, thank you," I say as he steps back, giving me a good view of the rest of his body; his white cotton boxers hung low on his hips have become translucent and stuck to him like a second skin. I look at him and lick my lips, then slowly step towards him, placing my hands on his solid chest. He sucks his breath in then takes a step back. Feeling brave, I repeat his advice from earlier and try to imitate his accent. "You need to relax. We 'ave done so much 'ard work 'ere."

Xavier laughs, takes my hands off his chest and places a soft kiss on each of them, then softly says, "Now I know it's ze wine, off you go to bed; I'll lock ze door..."

I don't let him finish his sentence. I wrap my arms around his neck and stand on my toes, placing a gentle kiss on his lips. He doesn't open his mouth but stands very still, balling his fists at his side. I continue with my efforts until he eventually begins to relax and kisses me back, gently at first, then with an increasing passion. Desperate for oxygen, I break the kiss and step back, admiring his growing manhood, "That's impressive," I say, pointing to his boxers.

He takes the towel and wraps it around his waist, giving me a warning look, before saying, "Laura, I'm going now before somezing 'appens zat you might regret."

"And what if I don't regret it?" I whisper.

"You 'ave 'ad too much to drink, I will not take advantage of you," he says. Just as he's about to turn away, I throw myself into his arms and kiss him again. "You… drive… me…insane!" He says between kisses, picking me up and depositing me on my bed. I pull my wet bikini off and claw at the top of his boxers. He stills, then steps back. "Are you sure zis is what you want?" I nod and smile eagerly. "Tell me; tell me what you want, Laura."

"Xavier, I want you to make love to me. Now." This has the desired effect, and he obliges, with increasing passion.

31

A ringing phone wakes me from my slumber, it's not mine but sounds familiar. Opening my eyes, I can see a sleeping form next to me. Xavier. The events of last night flash through my memory. Oh, my God! I slept with Xavier! What was I thinking? The phone stops, obviously gone to voicemail. I sit up and look at the time, seven-twenty; Alice and Gus will be worried. Climbing out of bed, I cover myself with the still damp towel and head for the bathroom for a shower. What the hell am I going to say to him? "Oh Xavier, thank you for last night; you were wonderful." I don't think so! This is crazy. Feeling ridiculous, I return to the bedroom to find Xavier pulling his jeans and shirt back on. He looks at me cautiously and smiles, "Erm… Zat was

Mozer, she is worried. I told 'er zat I spent ze night 'unting boar, but I don't even 'ave a rabbit to take back for 'er." He grimaces then carries on, "it was ze first thing zat came to mind."

"Erm… well, I suppose it's feasible. You could tell her that you called in for breakfast and left them in the freezer here." I say, then add, "I'll make coffee while you finish in here."

Glad of the hasty retreat, I enter the kitchen to see the empty wine bottles and glasses; no wonder I have a headache. This is so awkward. In all fairness, Xavier did try to leave. This is all my fault. I drink a large glass of water staring out of the window, while I wait for the fancy coffee machine to do its thing. I can feel him enter the kitchen before I hear or see him. He makes a nervous coughing sound then pulls out a chair and sits at the table, I am unable to turn around; what am I going to say? I hesitate then slowly force myself to turn; decision made. I'll act as though nothing happened. "So, what have you got planned today?" I ask, filling two mugs with strong black coffee and placing one of them on the table in front of him.

"Really?" Cocking his head to one side, he gives me a quizzical look.

I look away. "I'm looking after baby Frances today. John and Jackie are taking the children out; it's their last day. I'm going to miss them." I say, placing butter and honey on the table.

Xavier sighs, and looks away then replies, "Okay, if zis is 'ow you want to proceed… I am working in ze vineyard today," his voice softens when he looks at me again. "Laura, I am sorry…"

I stand and walk back to the grill, feigning interest in the toast, now starting to brown. "Don't be, it was all my fault; you have nothing to be sorry for."

We pick at our breakfast in silence, then Xavier collects his jacket off the back of the chair where he left it last night. "I will call in at lunchtime to see 'ow you are getting on with Frances," he says with a smile as he walks out of the door, not giving me a chance to reply. I listen to his footsteps rhythmically crunching on the freshly laid gravel, and as they fade away, I drop my head into my hands.

What was I thinking? And what am I going to do about it? I hear my Gran's voice echoing in my head, "You can't change what's already done; learn from it and move on." Yes, she always knew how to make me feel better. I need to be on my guard when I'm with Xavier; that can't happen again. I'm distracted by the beep from the gate post informing me that the kitchen company are here to finish off. It will be a relief to get back to normal; whatever that is!

An hour later, John arrives with Frances in her pram, "Everything you need is in the basket underneath. Thank you. Ring if you have any problems; she's just been fed," he says, handing over his sleeping daughter.

"I'm sure we'll be fine, have a nice day; and don't hurry back," I say, taking the pram and equipment from him. I stand outside and watch him walk away before bending over the sleeping baby. "Well Frances, what are we going to do today? I don't know about you, but I could do with escaping," I say. "Let's go for a walk."

I pop inside for a cardigan, and my phone then set off towards the walled garden. I haven't been for a while. And I need to stay clear of the vines; I don't want an encounter with Xavier. Shadow runs on ahead, and I hear Gus shouting a greeting to him. I expect Gus is tending to the goats, he milks them at weekends and holidays. As we approach, Gus asks, "Hello Laura, did you see Dad this morning? He didn't come home last night."

"Erm... Yes. Yes, I did. He called in for breakfast; he said he'd been out hunting. How are the lambs doing?" I ask, trying to change the subject.

His face lights up as he points to the runty lamb abandoned by its mother at birth. "She's doing really well and is back with the others now. Is that Frances, where is Dylan?"

"Yes, I'm looking after her for the day; they have gone sight-seeing, it's their last day. They'll be back at teatime I should think. I'll see you later," I say as I wave and continue walking, not wanting to answer any more questions. Gus returns the gesture and turns back to milking the goats.

I reach the tranquillity of the walled garden and gently push the door open. With a bit of a struggle, I manage to get the oversized pram through the entrance and stand and stare. It's a visual delight. The fruit trees scrambling up the walls are laden with blossom; their aromatic perfume filling the garden. My eyes don't know where to look first. The small beds are brimming with early salad crops, and the greenhouse is bursting with foliage. What a change since my last visit; Xavier has obviously been very busy here. I place Frances in the shade and sit on an old stone bench while I drink in the scene. My mind takes me back to my first visit here at the end of the summer when the walls were festooned with ripe fruit. I look down at the sleeping baby and whisper, "I was sat here when I heard your daddy on the other side of the wall, looking for help after he had a puncture. That seems so long ago now; so much has happened since then. Everything was going so well; how could I have been so stupid?" I lay my head back against the old stone wall, warmed by the spring sunshine and screw my eyes tight shut; trying to quell my inner turmoil. I will not cry! Oblivious to my quandary Frances stirs, makes a little squeaking noise then settles back to sleep.

"She's in the walled garden…" A voice filters through my dream. I slowly raise my head and turn my aching neck; I must have fallen asleep! A wave of panic surges through me, making my heart race, as I look over to see Frances still sleeping soundly in her pram. "Laura! Laura!" Gus shouts as he enters the garden, "there you are, the kitchen fitter has been looking for you. He said he tried to ring, but you didn't answer."

My heart returns to normal, as I say, "Oh, sorry. No, I put my phone on silent so it wouldn't disturb Frances. Is everything okay?" Looking at my phone, I'm surprised to see it's eleven-thirty.

"Yes, he said he needed to go and get something from town, and he'll be back later," Gus says a little too loudly, which stirs Frances, and she starts to make cat-like noises.

"She must be getting hungry, I'd better get back; thank you," I say.

"Are you okay, your face is very red?" Gus asks, perceptive for his young age.

"Silly me, I should have worn a hat; you know how easily I burn," I say, brushing off his concern. "I have to go, see you later," I add, as Frances starts to cry.

I'm relieved to find the Chateau empty and turn the key in the lock behind me, craving solitude. I quickly set to work feeding and changing Frances, pleased to have a diversion; cradling the infant to sleep before placing her in the Moses basket in the drawing room. My stomach lurches, but I don't feel hungry, though I know I should try to eat. I manage a small sandwich with a glass of water, before cleaning dust off the new surfaces. Another beep alerts me to a vehicle entering the drive, it's probably the kitchen fitter. I look up a moment later to see a familiar Land Rover approaching. "Oh, shit! Enzo. Just what I need." I dash into the hall and stand to the side of the heavy front door; he won't be able to see me here. I hear the loud clunk as he climbs out and shuts the vehicle door, followed by the sound of crunching gravel. A moment later, a nervous cough precedes the inevitable dull knock on the old door. I stand stock still, almost holding my breath.

He knocks again, this time louder. When I fail to answer, I hear his familiar voice, "Laura, Laura, are you in?" I crane my head to the right as I hear another set of footsteps approaching on the new gravel. "Oh, Xavier, hello, have you seen Laura?" Enzo asks. Oh, my God! Now, what am I supposed to do? Xavier has a key to the back door. I bend down and crawl on my hands and knees into the drawing room. Frances is awake and looks up at me from her basket. Yes, I can pretend to be feeding the baby, it's not a duty I would interrupt to answer the door. I pick her up and cradle her in my arms, enjoying the contact with her warm body, while concentrating; trying to hear what the two men are saying.

"Enzo! Long time, no see," I hear Xavier say sarcastically.

"Erm, yes, I went away for a couple of weeks," Enzo replies nervously.

"So I 'erd," Xavier replies curtly. "Laura is not in; she 'as gone out wiz 'er friends, zey are going 'ome tomorrow." He adds, "Did she not tell you?"

"Erm, no, we haven't spoken in a while. I've brought Laura some flowers, I'll leave them on the step," Enzo replies. I then hear more footsteps as he retreats to his vehicle and starts the engine. I heave a sigh of relief as I watch his Land Rover disappear up the drive.

After a lengthy pause, Xavier shouts, "Ze coast is clear now, and I'll give you some space." Then I hear his footsteps fade away.

"Phew! That was close," I whisper to Frances as I hold her tight.

32

The Burrows' family return later in the afternoon, and over tea and cake tell me all about their day out. They borrow a couple of suitcases to pack their belongings, and I reassure them that I don't mind driving them to the airport in the morning. John reminds me that he will have to take his car as well, as we won't all fit into my Yeti. "Xavier said that he would come along too so he can drive my car back; he's a great bloke," John says. Oh damn! I'd forgotten that minor detail! That means I've got to endure his company once again!

The rest of the evening seems to drag, and my eyes keep landing on the jug of wildflowers in the middle of the kitchen table, a few of the petals already drooping; nothing like the fancy, elegant, arrangement from Enzo, that

I've put out of the way in the dining room. Both so very different; just like the two men causing me confusion. Do I want to be with either of them? I'm only putting off the inevitable with Enzo. I should meet up with him and clear the air; tell him it's over between us, and suggest we remain as friends until he returns home in a few months. Yes, I'll ring him tomorrow. Xavier, on the other hand, is a different matter. I'm his boss – and landlord. Is that legal, let alone ethical? No, I couldn't possibly have a relationship with him, even if I wanted to. There. Decision made. I'll apologise to Xavier, and we should be able to move on, as though it never happened.

Wearily, I climb into bed and wrap the comforting duvet over me. But I'm instantly transported back to last night by his musky aroma, which has remained on the bedclothes. I play the night over and over in my head, his tender kisses, and gentle caresses, followed by his surprisingly considerate lovemaking.

Most of the night is spent tossing and turning, with sleep nowhere in sight; and I arrive at the campsite the following morning feeling exhausted. Jackie is sat on a bench at the play area, watching the children while John moves the caravan over to store in the carriage house. "Good morning, you look worse than I feel," Jackie says, laughing.

"Yes, I had a bad night; a headache, but I'm okay now," I add, putting my sunglasses on.

"Oh, dear, self-inflicted?" I only nod and smile, letting her think I'm hungover. I wish.

John's car approaches, with Xavier, already sat in the passenger seat. He doesn't get out, but waves and I only smile back while helping Jackie load the children into my car. The journey passes quickly with the children chattering excitedly about the prospect of their first ever flight. Before long, we arrive at the airport, where John is stood waiting. He gets to work helping Jackie to unload the children and luggage. "Xavier seemed to be in a hurry," John comments.

"Yes, we have a delivery this morning; we start refurbishing the bedrooms next week. Always something to do," I say, excusing his behaviour.

"I don't want to go home, Daddy," Lily says.

"I know, but we'll be back in a few months, and I'm sure you can't wait to tell your school friends about your new sister," John replies optimistically.

"Huh, my friends would be more interested if I'd got a new dog," she moans as she takes hold of his hand.

I bob down at her side and whisper, "Shadow's puppies will be here when you come back, would you like to help with their training?" This seems to have the desired effect, brightening her mood, and she trots off behind her parents, waving until they're out of sight.

The Chateau seems lifeless without my friends; I ring Sylvie but her mother, Rose, tells me that she's gone away with her partner, Vince, for the weekend. He seems like a nice man, and I'm genuinely pleased for her. With only my thoughts and memories to keep me company, I set to work emptying the sizeable front bedroom on the opposite side of the landing to mine. I can't dismantle the big bed, and I'm not asking Xavier, the workmen will do it on Monday. Finally, I pluck up the courage to contact Enzo.

Thank you for the flowers, we need to talk; when are you free for coffee?

There, that wasn't too difficult. A short while later, I receive a reply.

I'm on call this evening, how about tomorrow morning?

Sunday, yes, I need to get this over with.

That suits me, the new ice-cream parlour in town at eleven?

Neutral territory and I can call at the supermarket on the way home; the kitchen cupboards need stocking up. And, we can talk about ice-cream, a subject he knows well; it will stop the conversation from becoming too personal.

I arrive ten minutes late, a trick I learned from Jenny; it prevents me from sitting on my own for a few minutes, clock-watching and feeling awkward. "Always keep them waiting," that was her mantra. Enzo is alone at a small table outside, next to a couple with two small children, perfect. Not too intimate. He glances nervously at his watch, no doubt wondering where I am, then he lifts his head, and our eyes meet. "Hi, sorry I'm a bit late, I had trouble parking," I say as I paste a smile on my face and pick up the menu to avoid any notion of physical contact. So far, so good.

"No worries, glad you could make it; I've meant to give this place a try." He fiddles with his keys.

"Well, what do you recommend?" I ask briskly. He raises his eyebrows and looks at me in confusion. "Oh, off the menu, I mean," I add feeling stupid.

He smiles like a little boy, all confusion forgotten. "Mm, so much choice; either the Maple creation or the white chocolate chip temptation. I know! We could get one of each and share."

Oh no, I don't think so, way too intimate. "I think I just fancy a scoop of vanilla and a plain waffle," I say, sitting back on my small, hard chair, folding my hands in my lap. Enzo stands, smiles, and enters the parlour to place our order, waiting patiently in the long queue; giving me time to mentally prepare myself for my little speech. As he returns to our table, my phone vibrates, notifying me of an e-mail. I smile apologetically and open the message, which I need to read twice. I'm absolutely astounded.

"Is everything okay?" Enzo asks, trying to read the expression on my face.

"I can't believe it. It's from a man in England called Harry Miles-King, the grandson of Sergeant Harry King who was secreted away in the attic during the war. After years of searching the internet for information, he came across my website and is eager to arrange a visit to find out all he can for his mother, who has recently been diagnosed with Alzheimer's disease."

"That's fantastic. I'll tell Henri, the goat man; he's sure to want to get involved with that," he says, as our ice-creams arrive. Enzo leans forwards and digs into his creation with enthusiasm, while I look at mine with a little apathy. "You could have chosen something a little more adventurous," he says with a mouthful, pointing his spoon in my direction.

I put my spoon down and lean back in my chair, looking into his eyes; it's now or never. I say as sympathetically as I can, "Enzo…"

He puts his spoon down too, and says cautiously, "Ah, this is the awkward bit. I guess it was only a matter of time, but I was hoping to wait until we'd eaten."

"Enzo, please hear me out. What we had was wonderful, but it's in the past…"

"Laura, I'm really sorry for running off like a fool, I don't know what came over me, it won't happen again; I promise…"

"No, Enzo, it won't because we're no longer an item; I've grown up and moved on. Let's not spoil what time you have left in France; can we at least be friends?"

He picks up his spoon and continues spooning his dessert into his mouth without looking at me. When he's finished, he slowly puts his spoon down and raises his eyes. "Is that really all that what you want – to be friends?"

"Yes, Enzo, it is," I reply softly.

He looks down at the table then back up at me before picking up his keys and standing. He pauses and runs his fingers through his hair as though looking for inspiration, then touches me lightly on the shoulder and says, "Goodbye, Laura." He hesitates, then strides away. I refrain from turning to watch him go. I can't believe he did that. A few minutes earlier he'd promised he'd never run away again, and now he just has. It appears I've made the right decision this time.

33

I call in at the supermarket on the way home but struggle to concentrate on my shopping list, my mind is elsewhere; so much to ponder. Then I arrive back to an empty Chateau, eager to tell someone of my e-mail from Harry

King's grandson. Shadow cocks his head to one side and listens as I babble on excitedly to him, but he soon loses interest and stands by the back door to be let out, so I sit down at my computer and compose my reply.

Dear Mr, Miles-King,

Thank you for your e-mail. I was thrilled to hear from you, and I'm so pleased that you found my website. I have the diary here at the Chateau along with other items of military memorabilia; some of which possibly belonged to your grandfather. You would be very welcome to come and visit. However, I am in the process of refurbishing the Chateau now and won't be able to accommodate you immediately; but I should have at least one room finished in approximately two weeks. I do have a campsite which you're welcome to use, or I could suggest alternative accommodation in the area.

I don't have all the answers to your questions, but I do know of a local man, Henri, who was involved with the resistance and may be able to tell you more. I can certainly show you the monument in the village dedicated to your grandfather's colleague, the brave pilot of the stricken plane. The local priest may also be of help but getting information about the war years is very difficult, it's still a subject that causes distress.

I look forward to hearing from you,

Regards

Laura Mackley.

"There, the job is done," I say to Shadow as I press send. Who else can I tell? Jenny won't be very interested. I could pop over and tell Alice, but I don't want to risk bumping into Xavier. No, I'll wait until I get a reply to my e-mail, I should really get on with displaying some of the items, but where? I can't have people trudging up to the attic while I've got the builders in, though I expect Mr Miles-King will want to see where his grandfather was hiding. The rest of the day is spent looking at the old artefacts; uniforms, guns, and ammunition – now made safe, of course. There's also the old chest full of tinned food, currently stashed in the back porch – and the diary. Where should I put them? I wonder from room to room, pondering. The library is hardly ever used, I could make a display in there. It's a bit dark though, with little natural light; would it be too dingy? Who can I ask? I wake up in the early hours with an idea. Sophie. She might have some suggestions. After all, they must have so many family heirlooms in their huge ancestral pile. Yes, I'll ring her tomorrow. I settle down and fall back asleep.

My alarm wakes me at seven-thirty, I need to be ready for the workforce who are starting on the bedrooms today. An hour later and they arrive, followed by a large lorry, and waste no time getting started. By early afternoon, the area for the ensuite shower room is already formed in the first bedroom with the floorboards up for the plumbing. I'm very impressed. I wonder how Alice is getting on with the new curtains that she's making for me? Perhaps I should go and see for myself; I can't avoid them forever. Yes, the sooner I get it over with, the sooner I can move on and put my silly mistake behind me. Stepping outside into the afternoon sun lifts my mood, it's far warmer outside than it is in the Chateau.

"Hello, stranger," Alice says with a hint of sarcasm.

I smile at the woman who now means so much to me, "Sorry, I've been busy with Jackie, John, and the children, as well as all the workmen I've had to endure. They've started on the bedrooms now; I came to see how the curtains are progressing."

Alice beams and lifts a large pair of heavy curtains out of a box on the floor, "I've finished the biggest pair, along with the pelmets and tails." Handing one to me.

"Oh Alice, these are beautiful, thank you. You are so clever; the only thing I can do with a needle is sticking it into people," I say laughing.

"You don't know what is possible until you try," says a familiar voice in the doorway. "I'm glad you 'ave come, Shadows puppies 'ave been born and I'm going over to inspect zem; would you like to come?" Xavier says, looking directly into my eyes.

I half turn away from him, making a fuss over folding and replacing the curtain back in its box while gathering my composure, then look back at him hoping my blush has started to fade. "No thank you, I need to get back to the Chateau, the builders will be expecting me. Another time perhaps." I'm sure he realises it's a pathetic excuse; I would have loved to see the new-born puppies, but not enough to suffer the embarrassment of spending time alone with him in the confines of his truck.

Xavier smiles sadly, then turns to leave, while Alice puts the kettle onto the stove. She looks at me and winks then says, "I've made a cake, and we need to catch up." I spend the next hour telling her about Mr Miles-King. "Oh, that's wonderful, I'll make sure Xavier gets over to the Chateau to paint the bedroom and hang the new curtains as soon as they've finished fitting the bathroom. I can't wait to see it." She somehow manages to drop Xavier's name into almost every other sentence. I'm beginning to wonder if she suspects something has happened between us, or if it's something she's always done, and I've just never noticed before. Either way, it begins to make me feel uncomfortable, and I make my excuses and leave.

Back at the Chateau, I have a voicemail message from Sophie explaining that the library would be the perfect place to create a small museum as the lack of light would help to prevent the artefacts from deteriorating, and suggests I ask the builders if they could make me some display cabinets. That sounds like a plan. I also have a reply to my e-mail from Mr Miles-King, informing me that three weeks from now fits in perfectly with his workload, and he asks if he could bring his mother with him. Gosh! Will the builders be able to finish two bedrooms by then? I load a tray with tea and cake and make my way upstairs to ask them. "But, of course! We are speedy workers," says Georges, the oldest man, who seems to be in charge. I then tell them of my idea about creating a museum in the library.

"I would be honoured to do that project for you," says Adam, a middle-aged man. He then averts his eyes and bows his head before looking back at me and saying, "You see, my grandmother was violated by a German soldier when she was only seventeen. She got pregnant and would have had to suffer the indignity of bearing a half-German baby, as well as being an unmarried mother, but a kind, local young man who was a friend of the family, married her. He would have become my grandfather, but I never got the chance to meet him. Sadly, he was killed while working for the resistance; driving the vehicle that was attempting to take the two airmen to safety."

At this, all the friendly banter ceases as his colleagues fall silent and stare at him.

"I didn't know that; I'm sorry," Georges says solemnly.

"No one did, it was a closely guarded family secret. But I feel like it's time that these stories were told – before they are forgotten and lost forever."

Adam hesitates then looks around the room, perhaps wondering if he's made the right decision. Knowing exactly how that feels, I walk over to him and rest my hand on his shoulder and say, "Well, Adam, I'll take you down to see the library; you'll probably have a better idea where to put the display cabinets than me." I'm desperate to know more of his story but sense that now is not the time to ask.

Once the workmen have left, I ring Alice and inform her of the progress I've made and that I need the curtains for the smaller bedroom too. "That's not a problem. I'll send Xavier over to measure the window. Got to go, bye," she says abruptly before ending the call, giving me no chance to object to her suggestion. Fantastic! Just what I need!

I immediately head upstairs to inspect the window, it's considerably smaller than the other one, and I'm sure I can measure it myself without the awkwardness of Xavier's presence. I drag a pair of step ladders out of the bedroom that's currently being refurbished and rummage about to find a tape measure. Then carefully climb the ladder, reaching the top step just as I hear a voice behind me.

"What are you doing? I am 'ere to do zat."

"Woah!" I'm startled by Xavier's demand, causing the ladder to wobble alarmingly.

"What is it wiz you and windows?"

He grabs me off the ladder as it topples over, preventing me from landing in a heap on the floor, before placing me gently on my feet. I look into his smiling eyes as I try to form a coherent sentence.

"I would have done just fine by myself if you hadn't startled me."

"You don't 'ave to do ze jobs by yourself – you 'ave me to 'elp you now. I will catch you when you fall," he says, gently letting go of me. He then produces a notebook and pencil and proceeds to measure the window. "Okay, now you can show me what ozer jobs need doing."

"How are the puppies doing? Did Enzo attend their birth?" I ask, thinking of something to say instead of addressing the elephant in the room.

He screws his face up and replies, "Sara is making ze big problem; no, 'e sent one of his colleagues."

"Oh, dear, what type of problem?" I ask. Xavier wastes no time and quickly gets his phone out to show me several photos of

Princess Pipi and her new offspring all cuddled together on a cerise, pink, fluffy blanket placed inside a rather grand dog bed in the shape of a mock Chateau.

"She is treating zem like royalty! We need to get zem 'ere as soon as possible so zey can toughen up and learn to be truffle dogs."

"Yes, I can see, but they are cute; are they all boys?" I ask, smiling at the lovely images.

"One bitch, which Sara wants to keep; she 'as called it Penny. Ze dogs she 'as named, Patch, Pepper, and Freckles," he says, rolling his eyes, but I'm starting to see through his façade; he has a soft centre deep inside.

"How sweet – those are the puppies from One Hundred and One Dalmatians!" I gush.

Rolling his eyes skywards again, he adds, "I wanted to bring zem all back wiz me to grow up 'ere, but Sara wouldn't 'ear of it. I'll 'ave to wait eight weeks and 'ope zey 'aven't been too spoilt."

"Yes, I can see your dilemma," I add while fiddling with a screw that I've picked up off the floor.

Xavier puts his notebook in his pocket and walks towards me, cupping my hands in his. I freeze and look down; the contrast is striking. His large calloused hands swamp my small delicate ones. I try to pull back, but his grip tightens. "We need to talk, yes?" He says quietly.

I take a deep breath and look into his kind eyes while my brain tries to compile a proper response. "Xavier, I'm sorry. What happened between us was all my fault, but we need to get past it and move on. Please, can we pretend it never happened?"

"But it did 'appen. Didn't you like it?"

I desperately want the floor to open up and swallow me, or to be able to travel back in time and prevent it from happening, but I can't.

"Xavier, it doesn't matter whether we liked it or not, it wasn't appropriate; I'm your landlord and employer. We need to be able to put this behind us and carry on professionally."

He lets go of my hands and steps back, and I can see the confusion and hurt clouding his brown eyes.

"As you wish."

He turns abruptly and leaves. I knew it wasn't going to be easy, I've wounded his pride, but he'll get over it; like me, he's got no choice but to move on.

34

I see very little of Xavier over the coming days. He's clearly avoiding me, despite Alice's best efforts to bring us together. By the end of the week, the first bedroom is finished, and I'm desperate to get it painted and ready for my guest, Mr Miles-King. The new furniture and accessories have already arrived and are cluttering up the landing upstairs. I'm tempted to employ a local decorating company, but I realise that it would be costly, and I've already spent so much. No, I'll just have to do it myself. The workmen are busy refurbishing the next bedroom, and Adam is building the display cabinets in the library; one of them will help me if I get stuck. Entering the cavernous bedroom with a sense of trepidation, I know that it's too much for me to take on alone; the ceiling is lofty, and I can't reach it safely from the ladder. I'm going to need some help.

Deciding to behave like the grown-up that I've gradually become, I locate my phone and ring Xavier; it goes to voicemail. "Hello Xavier, I don't know what you have planned for the next couple of days, but I could do with some help painting the big bedroom. As you know, we have guests in a couple of weeks. Get back to me when you can. Thanks." Feeling optimistic, I say to myself, "There that wasn't too difficult, was it?" Pessimistic thoughts soon follow through, "Yes, Laura, but that was the easy bit." Being confined with him for a few days will be the hardest part. My ramblings are interrupted by my phone. "Hello Xavier, thank you for getting back to me," I say as professionally as possible.

"I am milking ze goats and will be zere soon, 'ave you got ze paint?"

"Yes, I've got everything we need, but I can't reach the ceiling."

"Don't even try, see you soon," he says as he ends the call.

Okay, now for the hard bit. I gather all the materials together, along with the radio from the kitchen, and change into a pair of old jeans and t-shirt, pulling my hair into a messy bun. My first task is to wipe down the surfaces, removing the new dust that has settled overnight. It's not long before I hear the rattling of a big ladder that Xavier is carrying up the stairs. "Let me help you," I say as he reaches the landing, but he shrugs and continues into the bedroom, setting up the ladder and going back for the boards to build a sturdy platform to work from. I turn the radio up, so there are no awkward silences to fill and hum along to the music as we work. Xavier quietly paints the ceiling while I undercoat the woodwork, trying to forget that he's there. At one-thirty, I suggest we break for lunch and head down to the kitchen, grateful to find Adam eating his sandwiches on the front steps. Good idea, we can join him outside. The two men chat about the progress of the cabinets and Adam informs me that he will have finished by the end of the day. "Fantastic, I'll be able to bring the items down to display," I say as I gather our dishes and head inside.

Back in the bedroom, Xavier begins painting the walls. "Phew, I'm getting warm," he says and pulls his shirt over his head.

"Yes, it must be at least twenty degrees today," I say looking away, trying not to stare at his solid torso; concentrating instead on the patch of the wall that I'm painting. A short while later, I stand up, stretch, and step back, trying to get some circulation back into my aching legs. "Ouch!" I begin to hop about on one leg.

"What is ze matter?" Xavier asks as he rushes over to my side, looking concerned.

Feeling a little foolish, I reply, "Oh, sorry to alarm you; it's only cramp, I think. I didn't know how painful it was; I've never had it before." I sit down on the floor.

"Straighten your legs, reach forwards and pull your toes back towards you," he instructs, bending down at my side, showing me what to do. He adds, "Is zat any better?" while watching me stretch. He sits down and takes my leg in his hands, then carefully removes my shoe. I look at him and nod mutely as he gently begins to massage my sore calf muscle. I try to get up and make my escape, but he gestures for me to remain seated while he continues his ministrations.

Reclining my head against the wall, I close my eyes and try unsuccessfully to erase his image from the inside of my eyelids. His unforgettable, musky aroma infiltrates my nostrils, despite the pungent smell of paint. I know he is close, but I refuse to open my eyes until he's backed off, or I might not be in control of my actions once more. What is wrong with me? He carefully places my leg back on the floor and stands up. I open my eyes to find him turning away with a smile on his face; he clearly knows what effect he's starting to have on me but doesn't seem in the least concerned. What am I going to do?

Neither of us speaks as he picks up his roller and continues painting. We persevere with our work for most of the afternoon in companionable silence, occasionally interrupted by calls and texts; one of them is from Alice informing us that she will come over later with Gus and prepare a meal for us all. Adam pops in at five-thirty to tell us he has finished the display cases and that they are now going home, and the old Chateau falls silent. "I'm going to look at the library," I say a short while later.

"Good idea," Xavier says, standing back and inspecting his work. "Zere's not much more we can do in 'ere until ze walls are dry; zen we can put ze topcoat on ze wood."

"Wow! This is amazing," I say as we enter the library, examining Adam's work. He has covered the back wall of the room with shelves and fitted glass doors onto the front of them and assembled several display cases down the centre of the room.

"Yes, it's better zan I imagined, now you can start ze museum," Xavier says, taking in the scene. "What are you going to put in ze ozer bedrooms?"

"Err, beds," I say, trying not to laugh.

"Yes, I know zat, but what about a family room wiz twin beds, or a cot?"

"Hmm, I hadn't thought about that; which room do you suggest?"

"Let's go and look," he says, gesturing towards the stairs. We wander through all the rooms and conclude that only the big front bedroom that we've just been painting would be able to accommodate a king-size bed, along with a pair of twins and a cot.

"But I wanted to keep that bedroom soft and romantic as the honeymoon suite, it would somewhat spoil the ambience if it were cluttered with beds," I grumble.

Back on the landing, he points to my bedroom door and says, "Your room is ze same size, you could put zem in zere."

I walk towards my bedroom, open the door and step inside but soon realise my mistake as Xavier follows behind me. I look around, trying to figure a way of getting out without having to get too close to him, but he stands in the doorway and doesn't move. I take a big breath and walk towards the window, turning my back on him, pretending to be interested in the view. I can feel his presence behind me as the hairs on the back of my neck stand on end, and a shiver travels down my spine when I hear the familiar tinkle of the piano below me in the drawing room. Trying to think of something to break the spell I whisper, "But I quite like my bedroom…" I don't get to finish my sentence because Xavier places the softest of kisses on the back of my neck, then onto my shoulder. "Please don't," I say quietly.

"Why are you trying to resist zis? Aunt Mary seems to approve," he says as his soft lips find mine. I am putty in his hands, and before long, I submit and return his kiss.

"Hello?" the sound of Alice's voice travels up the stairs, and I jump, drawing back and breathing hard. A lazy smile lights up his eyes as Xavier looks back at me. "Hello, where are you?" Alice's voice continues from the opposite side of the landing.

"Mama, we're in Laura's room," he shouts back as he turns and makes a show of lifting a hefty trunk from the top of my wardrobe.

Alice knocks and pops her head around the door, "What are you doing in here?"

"Oh, we were just discussing ze merits of transforming zis room into a family bedroom for guests," he says, "and Laura wanted a hand to get zis trunk down; it contains some of ze items for the museum."

Alice looks over to me and smiles, I know I'm letting the side down; I always was rubbish at telling lies. She has the good grace not to comment on my scarlet cheeks and asks, "But where will you sleep?"

"Err, one of the small back bedrooms I expect, but I will miss being able to look out down the drive."

"I could envisage you turning ze attic into a small private apartment. A penthouse wiz your own little balcony. You would need to improve ze stairs or better still, install a small lift." Xavier looks at my face for a reaction. My mouth opens and closes like a goldfish in a glass bowl. Will I ever be able to afford such a luxury? As though reading my mind, he adds, "but we're getting ahead of ourselves, zat can be phase two."

Having begun to regain my composure, I say, "I think it will be phase three, the campsite was phase one, and the bedroom and kitchen refurbishment is phase two. We need to concentrate on earning some money first. But it's a fabulous idea; one for the future, I think." Then add, "Come on, I'm starving." We head downstairs.

After supper, they leave me alone with my thoughts and memories. Not wanting to dwell on the kiss, I start to plan my museum and fall into bed, exhausted.

35

Adam and his colleagues arrive at eight-thirty, with Xavier following soon after. "Morning," I say as cheerfully as possible as he enters the kitchen. I place my breakfast dishes in the sink and continue, "I can probably manage to paint most of the woodwork myself, but I'd appreciate it if you could paint the window; then I don't need to climb the big ladder."

"I don't mind 'elping, zen we will finish sooner," he says.

"Yes, but you have other work to do on the estate, and I'm going to need your assistance tomorrow to hang the curtains, re-assemble the bed and put the furniture in. Then there will be the next bedroom to do; although it's much smaller."

"Hmm, you are right, I will paint ze window, zen get on wiz ze ozer work today," he says, looking a little disappointed. Result. I can't face spending another day in close contact, alone with him. Once upstairs, I begin painting the wood in the ensuite bathroom so I can't be tempted by his subtle advances. He finishes the window by late morning, and I make coffee for all the workmen before he reluctantly leaves to catch up with jobs on the estate. "Ring me if you 'ave ze problem," he calls as he hesitates by the door before climbing into his truck. I skip lunch and continue painting until the light begins to fade.

Exhausted, and aching from head to toe, I treat myself to the luxury of relaxing in the hot tub. I lie back and gaze at the star-studded sky, memories come flooding back of the fateful night that I sat here with Xavier; and the events that followed. Suddenly feeling queasy and lightheaded, I cautiously climb out, steadying myself on the wall and groping for the light-switch, while hugging the towel to my shaking body. Food, yes, that's it – I need food; I've hardly eaten since breakfast. I make it to a chair at the table and start to retch, but my stomach is empty. The biscuit tin is still out from earlier, and I slowly nibble at one of Alice's shortbread biscuits, then sip a glass of cold water and start to feel better. "Silly girl, you should have known better," I say, chastising myself, no one can run on empty all day and do as much as I have. I then make myself a light supper and take myself off to bed.

I'm relieved to see Alice climb out of Xavier's truck when he arrives the following morning. "I want to be here to see that he hangs the curtains properly," she says, getting a basket full of provisions from the back seat.

"What have you got there?"

"Only food, I thought I would cook here tonight; it will save you the trouble," she says casually and places the groceries into one of the fridges. "What's the first job this morning?"

"I've already scrubbed the floor; it should be dry now, so I suppose we could hang the curtains next," I reply. The day passes in a frenzy of activity, and by lunchtime, the curtains are up and the bed re-assembled. The workmen assist Xavier to move the big pieces of furniture, and by late afternoon the room is almost ready; I only have the finishing touches to add. "Thank you so much for your help guys; I'm going for a shower, then I'll help to prepare dinner," I say.

"You will do no such thing; you look exhausted. Go and have a leisurely shower. Xavier will do his rounds and dinner will be ready in an hour," Alice replies in her motherly tone. Grateful for an hour of tranquillity, I decide to have a soak in the bath, then flop onto my bed for a rest. I open my eyes, and I find Gus stood beside me.

"Nana says I have to tell you dinner is ready," he says, then turns and trots back downstairs. How long have I been asleep? Sitting up, I notice it's almost dark; it must be about seven o'clock.

"Sorry, I must have fallen asleep," I say, as I enter the kitchen to find the table covered with a small feast.

"I think you are doing too much. Both of you are. Why don't you take a day off; Gus and I can manage the essential tasks for a day," Alice says.

"Good idea, I will take you out for ze day on Saturday; Gus can care for ze animals and Mama can attend to ze campsite," Xavier says, looking over to me.

"Good, that's settled," Alice adds, obviously pleased with herself.

The rest of the week passes by in a blur; running the campsite, adding the finishing touches to the now finished bedroom, and collating the artefacts in the museum. Only five more bedrooms to go! No wonder I'm fatigued. A ping from my phone reminds me that I've arranged to Skype Jenny. A few minutes later, her auburn hair and bright eyes light up my screen.

"So, do tell! What's new?" She chimes.

"Hi, just the usual, work and more work. What about you?" I ask.

"Oh, dear, that sounds dull; you need to get out more. You do look tired."

"Well, as it happens, I'm taking tomorrow off."

"Ooh, its not your birthday – is it?" She frowns.

"No, don't worry; you haven't missed it. I'm being taken out for the day, but I'm not really looking forward to it."

"Don't tell me you've got back with Enzo, I did warn you; you've had your fling now move on."

"No. No, I haven't, and that's the problem. I did move on," I say, grimacing.

"What do you mean? Who did you move on to?"

"Anyway, what have you been up to?" I ask, trying desperately to divert the conversation.

"Woah, back up! What aren't you telling me?" She asks, cocking her head to the side. She then opens her mouth in shock and blurts, "You haven't!" Her wide eyes almost popping out of the screen, she continues, "You have, haven't you? Oh, my God! You've got down and dirty with Xavier!"

"I knew I shouldn't have told you," I say, as I feel the sting of tears welling up in my eyes.

Reaching her hand towards me, she says, "Oh, honey – don't cry; I wish I were there. Bloody Skype – I want to hug you!"

"It was a stupid mistake. I was tipsy…"

"Just wait 'til I see that shit-face; taking advantage of you like that," she interrupts.

"It wasn't like that… if anything, it was the other way around," I sniff. "He tried to leave, but I was rather persistent."

"Mm, awkward."

"You're not kidding. So, as I said, I'm not looking forward to spending a day alone with him," I say.

"Have you seen him since?"

"Oh, yes, several times. I tried to act as if nothing happened, but he keeps making subtle advances…" I say miserably. "…and on one such occasion, I caved in and kissed him."

"Oh, my God! You fancy him, don't you?" I lean back in my chair and decide not to answer, having incriminated myself enough already. "Well?" Jenny persists. I only nod, deciding I've said enough for one day. "You could do worse you know, you're already familiar with his history and his faults; it's obvious that he's nuts about you."

"That's one of the many things that concern me; he's always been keen, but I thought he was only looking for a mother for Gus, and security for their future."

She looks at me and pauses before saying, "That possibly was his original motive, but the last time I saw him, he was a changed man." She turns, distracted by something off-screen. "Sorry, got to go, I need to get ready for work; I'm on nights this week. Speak soon." Then her friendly face fades from the screen, leaving me with my thoughts once more. After letting Shadow out, I make a cup of tea and have an early night; I need to have my wits about me tomorrow.

36

"Okay Laura, you can do this," I say to myself as I look out of the window expecting his truck. I'm surprised by a knock on the kitchen door and turn to see Xavier letting himself in, "Have you walked?"

"Yes, don't look so shocked. We will be more comfortable in ze Yeti."

"So, I'm driving?"

"No, not unless you want to."

"Where are we going? Shall I make a picnic?"

"Do you 'ave any requests? And no, we'll get lunch out; my treat." He ushers me out of the door.

"Mm, I don't mind; somewhere new, please," I say as he opens the car door for me. Once inside, he taps a destination into his phone and pulls out onto the road. "So, where have you decided?"

"Zere are many small villages, some from ze medieval times zat still survive wiz ancient Chateaus. Let's be tourists for ze day."

Smiling, I put the radio on and sit back, looking out of the window and watching the vivid greens of the new spring growth go by, trying hard not to concentrate on his musky aroma that fills the car. Xavier remains quiet, apart from pointing out places of interest along the way. I notice I'm now on unfamiliar territory. "I haven't been this way before."

"It's a route I usually avoid, it gets 'ectic in ze tourist season; big traffic jams," he says. Gradually, the road gets narrower with twists and turns, and I get the occasional tantalising glimpse through the trees. Craning my neck, I try to see more. "In a few minutes we will stop to see ze view," he adds.

"Wow!" We come to a clearing in the trees. Xavier pulls into a parking area at the side of the road, removes his seatbelt and gets out. By the time he reaches my side of the car, I'm out of my seat and eager to see more.

"It's a long drive but worth it. Be very careful; it's quite a drop."

He takes my hand as I approach the edge of the cliff. "Woah! It's massive. Is this the Gorge Du Verdon? I've seen images of it on the internet, but they don't do it justice." I feel a little lightheaded as I look down.

"Yes, it's part of it; I believe it is seven hundred meters at its deepest point. Please don't get any closer," Xavier says as I cautiously inch myself nearer to the edge.

"I can't believe that It's not fenced off; it would be in England."

"It is vast; zere is way too much to fence off. Also, it would spoil ze view – yes?"

"Yes, and what a view," I reply as I try to take it all in, turning in a full circle. Aromatic pine forests give way to bottomless limestone cliffs, trapping a ribbon of sapphire blue water which snakes away into the distance. I take a big breath of the sweet-smelling air, "Thank you, Xavier, it's amazing."

"I'm glad you like it," he says, with a contented look on his face.

"It's a shame we didn't bring Gus – and Alice – they would love it here," I say.

Xavier steps closer and puts his arm around my waist, guiding me away from the edge, "Zey 'ave been before, it's our turn today." His warm body is too close for comfort, and I try to break the contact, but he holds me tight, "Come, zere is more to see."

We continue our drive, and I squeal with delight as we pass more amazing vistas, the road widens a little as we approach a small village. Xavier parks my car, and we get out to explore. Quaint and quirky houses nestle into the hillside as we wind our way through the narrow lanes, before stopping at a small café. "Hungry?" Xavier asks.

"Yes, I'm starving," I reply, "let's sit outside." Xavier pulls a chair out for me as we get comfortable underneath the stripy awning, gently rustling in the breeze. "It's beautiful here, I wish it were a bit closer to home; I'd love to bring Jenny."

"It is only a couple of hours away, we will all come again." Tilting his head to one side, his expression guarded, he asks, "Why do I get ze feeling zat you don't enjoy my company?"

I look about me for inspiration, but the only thing I notice is his big hands balling into fists at his side. What does he want from me? I sit back and close my eyes, thinking back to when we first met; it was pretty apparent that he thought I was a silly little girl, with little chance of succeeding. Perhaps I deserved his disapproval then. After all, I did make some stupid decisions. When did our relationship change? Was it after my accident in the snow? The court case with Gus and his grandfather certainly drew us closer, but in a platonic way; I saw him more like family after that. But what now? We've crossed the line, and it feels like there's no going back. I open my eyes to see him looking back at me in concern; is he scared of rejection? Leaning forwards and putting my hands on the table, I ask, "Xavier, what do you want from me?"

Now it's his turn. Not expecting my question, he slowly blinks his big brown eyes, then stares into my soul, "You, I want you; every piece of you." Slowly, he leans forward and covers my hands with his.

Frozen to the spot, I stare back at him. His face is so close. My lips are tingling with anticipation, but he doesn't move. He wants me to make the decision. So close, what should I do? I sigh, run my tongue across my top lip and pull back. "Xavier, I'm not sure what I want right now; I've recently ended one relationship. I'm not sure I'm ready for another just yet. And… I'm still your boss."

We are interrupted by the waitress arriving with our lunch. "Bon Appetit," she says, then leaves, taking my appetite with her. Xavier looks at his plate of mussels, and a lazy smile crosses his lips.

"When you are ready, I will still be 'ere."

37

Monday morning arrives, and the workmen return to refurbish the next bedroom. Xavier is coming over to continue painting, but thankfully I'm going over to meet Sylvie; it's her day off, and she's agreed to go with me to visit the local priest. He's a middle-aged man and originally from Northern France, so can't answer many of our questions.

"I do know of a nephew of Pere Flory, who was the priest here during the war; he's quite frail now but may be able to help you. Monsieur Armand is his name." The priest directs us to Monsieur Armand's address and apologises for not being more helpful. Sylvie and I thank him and say our goodbye's.

With renewed enthusiasm, we drive to Monsieur Armand's house; a modest cottage about thirty minutes away. I ring the doorbell but get no response, "Perhaps we should have rung in advance," I say, turning to leave, with Sylvie following. As we reach the garden gate, the door opens slowly, and a small grey-haired man with spectacles pops his head out. We turn back to the door. "Oh, sorry to bother you," I say, "I'm looking for Monsieur Armand."

"And you have found him," the elderly gentleman replies. "How may I help?"

I explain how we obtained his details, and he gestures for us to enter. We follow him into a small, cluttered sitting-room. "Sorry, it's quite untidy; I don't get many visitors," Monsieur Armand adds, pointing towards piles of books and journals haphazardly placed on every available surface. After sitting down on a small two-seater sofa with Sylvie, I explain about the artefacts that I've uncovered at the Chateau, the involvement of the local resistance, and the impending visit of Mr Miles-King and his mother. "I'm sorry, I have very little memory of that time; I was only a small boy, but my uncle, the priest, was heavily involved with the resistance. I didn't know at the time, but he wrote his memoirs down a few years before he passed away; they will be here somewhere in this disarray," he says, sweeping his bony arm towards the piles of books. "I'll ask my housekeeper to have a look for it when she next comes," he adds.

A short while later, after we say our goodbye's to Monsieur Armand, I punch the air with a fist once we reach the car, "Success at last! Where would you like to eat, Sylvie? My treat."

"Oh, I don't mind – pizza?"

"Pizza it is, lets hit the town and celebrate."

Later, I drop Sylvie back home after overindulging in the pizza and head back to inspect the progress at the Chateau. Everyone has left for the day. Xavier appears to have finished the second bedroom apart from the topcoat for the wood, which I can do myself. Result. I spend the evening finishing off in the library; printing labels to accompany the articles on display. Pleased with my efforts, I retire with a cup of tea.

In the morning, I open my eyes and roll over, burying my head under the duvet. Ugh, I feel dreadful. Sitting up slowly, I have a drink of water and take a deep breath. Pizza! That's it, I ate too much pizza – what did I expect. I slowly make my way to the bathroom and begin to retch, then empty the contents of my stomach. Yuk! I wonder if Sylvie is okay? We both ate the same type of pizza. After a refreshing shower, I pull on a pair of yoga pants and go down for coffee. As the fancy machine starts whirring my stomach lurches, mimicking its sounds. "Woah, that smells vile," I say, turning it off. I think I'll have tea instead. I'd better see how Sylvie is.

How are you feeling? I think my pizza may have been dodgy – I feel awful. x

I slowly sip my weak tea and await her reply.

Oh, dear; I'm fine. Perhaps you're coming down with something. I hope you feel better soon. X

Shadow wanders over and rests his head on my lap, looking at me with doleful eyes, sensing I'm not well.

Must be just me then. Perhaps it's a case of gluttony. X

Half an hour later, I force myself to eat a slice of toast and begin to feel human again just as the workmen arrive. I leave them to it and set about painting the woodwork that Xavier hadn't completed. It's quite therapeutic, apart from the smell, which does nothing for my headache. I hear Xavier talking outside to one of the builders, and it's not long before he knocks on the bedroom door and calls, "Laura, 'ow are you getting on?"

"Don't come in, I'm on the ladder painting behind the door," I shout, crossing my fingers.

"Okay, I'll drop by later; ring if you need me." He heads back downstairs. I feel a little guilty as I watch his truck pull away, but I don't want any company. By late afternoon I have finished my task and decide to take a walk. Shadow accompanies me to check on the campsite, all seems quiet; most of the guests are out enjoying the surrounding countryside. I walk back home, thinking of all the tasks I need to complete this week before my guests arrive. Tomorrow, the paint will be dry, and we can put the second bedroom back together; I will, of course, need Xavier to help me. I can scrub the floor this evening if I don't touch the paint.

I'm feeling snowed under with jobs for the rest of the week, printing breakfast and dinner menus and adding finishing touches to the Chateau. I arrive at the farmhouse to collect the stunning flower arrangements that Alice has been working on. "Alice, thank you, they're amazing."

Beaming with pride, she carries one out to my car, saying, "Let me help you. What time are the guests arriving?"

"I've had an e-mail this morning; they are hiring a car at the airport and should arrive early afternoon tomorrow."

"Well, good luck; ring if you need any help."

"Thank you, but I'm sure I can manage with two guests. I'm just going over to Monsieur Armand; he's rung to say that he's found his uncles journal."

"Brilliant," she says, adding, "take care," as I leave.

Half an hour later, and I've got the precious book in my hands. "Thank you so much; my guests will be thrilled to read about the heroic acts of the local people. I'll return it next week," I say.

Monsieur Armand shrugs. "Please keep it. Display it at your museum; I have no children to pass it down to. It belongs to the community."

Touched, I bend down at his side and look into his tired eyes, "Thank you so much, I will take great care of it. Would you like to visit the museum?"

He looks back at me with a resigned expression, "My health is failing fast, and I can't really get out anymore, but, thank you."

I drive back home with the book full of secrets sat burning a hole in the passenger seat. I can't wait to read it. I'm glad that all my chores are complete. I have an early night and settle down to read. I'm almost overcome with emotion as I open the pages; it's written in blue ink – in French, of course – but thanks to Sylvie, and months of experience, I can decipher most of it.

The journal begins in the summer of 1941; Pere Flory talks about his involvement rescuing and hiding Jewish children, whose parents have either been killed or captured. Apparently, he used to take them to local farmers who, at considerable personal risk, loaded them on their trucks; often hiding under piles of rotting vegetation or animal excrement. It seems that the Germans didn't often search through such cargos. The children, if they were lucky, were then deposited at convents where they were cared for by the nuns.

Another entry tells about his involvement with the dropping of supplies by allied forces. Pere Flory, along with several other brave locals, used to stand in the fields behind the Chateau in the middle of the night with torches; illuminating the area for planes to parachute in supplies. My mind wanders back to the metal chests that were recovered from the estate. One containing food and the other ammunition. I go on to read with interest as

Pere Flory tells us that one of the drops was a spy radio, which the resistance used to listen to and transmit, messages in code. He weaves an intriguing story as he enlightens me to the astounding lengths he went to, compromising his personal safety. He could only transmit for two minutes and then change location, as the Germans were also listening and could pinpoint his position; putting himself and others in danger.

My eyes start drooping, and I'm about to put the precious book down when I see the name of General De Ford. Abruptly, I'm wide awake and eager to learn more.

After dark, I walked down to the Chateau for a meagre supper with General De Ford; his housekeeper had prepared a thin vegetable stew, the best she could manage with the food shortages. Officially, that's why I was there; to organise the distribution of some of the crops grown on the estate, after the Germans had taken their quota, of course. But, unofficially, I went to help. We were continuing to hide some of the valuable items. If the Germans found them, they would be confiscated for the war effort. His farmhand, Pierre, and another local man helped as we barricaded the old car behind a wall in the carriage house. By dawn, we were frozen, and our hands were bleeding, but we had finished; all that remained to do was to pile manure up behind the wall to put them off.

His farmhand, Pierre; could he have been Pierre Besnard, Xavier's grandfather? This is amazing. Exhausted, I admit defeat and put the book down. If only I'd had this information sooner. I can't wait to learn more but reading in French takes more concentration than I have left right now. I need to sleep.

38

I awake the next morning, wanting to read more from the journal, but my guests are arriving this afternoon, and I need to be ready.

At two-twenty, I'm alerted to a vehicle entering the drive. A small black car pulls up outside, and a middle-aged man gets out. I step outside to greet him.

"Miss Mackley, I'm Harry," he says, extending his hand.

"Please call me Laura. Welcome; I hope you had a pleasant journey."

"Yes, thank you," he says, opening the passenger door for his mother to alight.

"Mrs Miles-King, hello," I say, as she stands beside me.

"Hello love, have we met before? Nice place," she says, looking at me.

"No, Mum; this is the Chateau where Dad hid in the war," Harry says, pasting a smile on his face.

"Do come on in; would you like tea?" I ask, showing them into the drawing room.

"Ooh, this is posh, do you live here?" Mrs Miles-King asks.

"Yes, I do. I'm afraid some of the rooms are still waiting to be refurbished; I've got some workmen on site, but hopefully, they shouldn't bother you." I say, adding, "Please excuse me while I make tea, then I'll show you to your rooms."

I busy myself in the kitchen and return a short while later to hear Harry saying, "Mother, put it down; it's probably valuable."

"Nice bit of China is this," she replies, holding up a vase.

Harry mouths "Sorry," in my direction as I place the tray on a small table in front of a sofa. "Come and have tea, Mother," he says, while gently removing the vase from her hands and putting it back, then steering his mother to a chair. Oh dear, poor Harry; he appears to have his hands full. I leave them to have their tea in peace while I put the finishing touches to their rooms.

I return half an hour later and show them to their rooms. "Your room is nicer than mine, and it's got a better view," Mrs Miles-King huffs like a stroppy child.

"Would you like to swap, Mother?" Harry says with a sigh, transferring the cases. As he passes me, he says, "I'm sorry, sometimes she gets a little muddled," adding with a grimace, "and tends to wander at night."

Oh, dear – this could be fun. Deciding to change the subject, I ask, "What time would you like dinner?"

Harry doesn't get a chance to answer. His mother promptly responds, "Sausage and mash with lots of gravy, at six o'clock."

Harry looks at me, apologetically, "Sorry, it seems to be all she wants at the moment. A couple of weeks ago, it was pie and peas; she seems to get fixated with things."

"No worries; what would you like?" I say.

"Oh, I can eat most things, but I'm not keen on fish," he replies.

"When you've settled in, I'll show you the museum I've put together in the library. Just shout if you need anything."

An hour later, Harry appears on his own.

"Mother has fallen asleep, so I thought I'd take this opportunity to look at the library if that's okay?"

"Absolutely, let me show you."

His wide eyes stare in fascination, "Those uniforms, did they belong to my father?"

"Quite possibly, I can't be sure; but this was definitely his," I say, pointing to the diary. Harry stands still, gazing at the small notebook behind glass. I carefully lift it out and give it to him. "Here, why don't you take it into the drawing room and read it at your leisure," I say.

"May I?"

"Of course, make yourself at home. If you need anything just ask, or ring my mobile if I'm not in," I say, then head back to the kitchen and prepare the vegetables for dinner; I do hope Mrs Miles-King doesn't object to wild boar sausage! Six o'clock arrives, and I seat my guests in the new dining area, "Here we are sausage and mash for you," I say to Mrs Miles-King.

"Ooh, my favourite; how did you know? Have we met before, love?"

"Mother, this is Laura; you met her earlier this afternoon," Harry scolds.

"Hello Laura, I'm Hilda, pleased to meet you; do you live here?" I only nod and smile while Harry apologetically looks at me. Poor man, it must be wearing for him.

"Did you read the diary?" I ask, trying to change the subject.

"Yes, thank you. May I take a copy of it?"

"Yes, of course, I can do that for you. Also, I've been fortunate enough to obtain the memoirs of the village priest from the war years; I haven't read it all yet. Hopefully, I'll finish it tonight then you can look at it if you wish."

"That would be lovely, thank you."

"There is a war memorial in the village which mentions your father's plane crash; you can't miss it, but I can show you if you prefer. Also, I know of a local goat farmer, Henri, who was involved with the resistance; I could invite him here if you would like to meet him."

"That's very kind, thank you. We only have a few days, with so much to fit in, I appreciate your help." He looks over to Hilda, who is chugging down her second glass of wine, "Mother! That's enough, you know you shouldn't be drinking with the tablets you're taking."

Oh dear!

"Good night sleep well; breakfast will be ready at eight-thirty," I say later, as Harry and Hilda retire for the night. I quickly tidy the drawing room and follow them up to bed to finish reading. There is quite a lot written about secret meetings with fellow priests from various towns and villages and the distribution of black-market goods, honey, cheese, wine, and crops. Also, an amusing tale of a large pig that is continuously on the move, to avoid detection. It seems Pepe the pig became quite famous, and when he was eventually slaughtered; he was shared secretly amongst the community, distributed by Pere Flory and a couple of volunteers.

At last, I get to 1943, and I'm transported back in time to the plane crash…

It was a hot summer evening, the sky awash with stars. I was woken in the small hours by a loud noise;

something was amiss. I rushed to the open window; the sound was now deafening. The dark shape of a stricken plane appeared; British, if I had to guess, flames coming out from one side, so low. Craning my neck to follow its path, I noticed one parachute, quickly followed by another. "They'll never make it, way too low to jump," I said to Sasha, my black cat. The plane carried on, staying remarkably level, still spewing fire, and just missing the top of the church spire. I held my breath and prayed that it would clear the village and spare the locals more misery. How much can humanity take? I counted to fourteen before I heard the sickening sound of metal colliding with the earth – followed by an explosion. God rest the poor souls.

I dressed quickly, all in black and hurried outside to see what could be done. I had to get there before the Germans; they would show no mercy. Several of the men from the village were out, and I could hear hushed voices nearby.

"Father, down by the school, there's two of them," came a man's voice.

"Henri, are they alive?" I asked.

"Yes, surprisingly; cuts and bruises, I believe – what are we to do?" He whispered.

When I got to the scene the parachutes had already been bundled up and hidden, nothing went to waste, and the two bewildered men were helped to their feet. It was established that they were fit to move, so we did just that; and very quickly. Bicycles arrived, and the two airmen followed me to the Chateau; we'd used that location previously with success, so it seemed like the obvious choice.

General De Ford and his housekeeper were expecting us, and the two allied airmen, Harry King and Norman Poirier, were safely stowed away in the attic. The brave pilot had perished in the crash. It could have been worse; far, far worse. The village was spared. The Germans were the first to reach the wreck but found no survivors. The villagers, including myself, were all interrogated at length, and all properties searched, not a pleasant experience. Thankfully, they didn't find them – not till later, anyway.

After a suitable length of time, it was deemed appropriate to move them north, it proved to be a mistake; their truck was stopped and searched, the driver was tortured then shot, and Harry and Norman were taken to a prisoner of war camp. To this day, I don't know what became of them. I hope they made it home.

Carefully, I put the book down and try to get some sleep, but I can't find the off button for my brain; it goes into free-fall as images of that fateful night are conjured up in my head. Adam, the joiner that built the cabinets for the museum was right; we can't let these stories die along with the few remaining people that remember those terrible events. I have the opportunity to keep the memories alive, in the vain hope that humanity can learn from its past mistakes.

I sit up abruptly, startling Shadow, who's asleep in the corner. "I need to document the story of this little village, and its heroic community, collating all the pieces of information. Yes. I'll build a website, and possibly have a small book printed; nothing fancy." I say to Shadow, who just yawns and goes back to sleep.

An hour later and I'm wide awake, jotting down ideas as they come into my head. "What was that?" I say as I sit still and listen. There it is again – a noise coming from downstairs. I pull my robe over me and creep out onto the landing. Nothing in view. I stand still and strain to hear – it sounds like a female voice coming from the drawing room. Of course, it will be Hilda; Harry said she wanders at night. I find her coming out of the drawing room. "Hello Hilda, can I get you a cup of tea?"

"Have we met before?"

"Yes, I'm Laura – come on, I'll put the kettle on," I say, leading her into the kitchen.

"Your other friend might want one," she says, picking up the teapot and pouring an extra cup.

"Which friend, Hilda?"

"You know… thingummy-bob. I've forgotten her name," she replies, pointing to the drawing room.

"Tell me, what does she look like?" I ask.

"Ooh, she's prim and proper, but I don't think she's very well," she says.

"What makes you think that, Hilda?"

"Well, you must have noticed – her face is the colour of candle wax."

The penny drops – Aunt Mary, but I didn't hear the piano. Hilda must be able to see her, which is quite strange; so far, she's only been visible to children. I suppose Hilda is very child-like. I stand and walk to the drawing room, with Hilda following behind me, but the place is empty. "Aww, she must have gone back to bed; she did look tired," Hilda says.

"Did she talk to you?"

"If she did, the words would have fallen through the holes in my head by now love."

"Come on, let's all go back to bed, Hilda," I say, taking her back to her room.

I awake to hear voices in the hall. What time is it? Damn, eight-twenty! I've slept through the alarm. After dressing quickly, I arrive downstairs to the smell of frying bacon. Ugh! My stomach lurches, and I turn tail and head for the toilet. After a few deep breaths, I paste a smile on my face and try again. Xavier is here and making breakfast for my guests. "Good morning," I say to Harry and Hilda as I pass them.

"Is he your bit of rough?" Hilda innocently asks, pointing through the hatch into the kitchen.

"Mother!" Harry barks.

"Well, I don't blame her; have you seen his muscles?" Hilda says, then looks at me and asks, "Is he the father of your baby?"

I stand still. Frozen. Entirely rooted to the spot. "What baby, Hilda?" I quietly ask, not really wanting to hear the answer.

"The one in your belly."

"That's enough, Mother, apologise to Laura," Harry orders.

"Why, it's the truth… I remember now; the old lady told me. And she does look green around the gills." Hilda says while dipping a slice of bread and jam into her cup of tea.

The world seems to be going in slow motion. I stand and stare. Harry is mortified and trying to shut his mother up. I peer through the hatch to see Xavier staring back at me, wide-eyed and open-mouthed. If only the floor would open up and swallow me this instant.

I'm brought back to the present by Hilda saying, "Go and put your feet up love, muscle man is doing a good job." Horrified, I take Hilda's advice and retreat to my bedroom in shock.

39

I flop onto my bed and stare at the cracks in the ceiling. How could I have been so stupid? I'm a trained nurse, Goddamnit! I should have known. I open the calendar on my phone and do the calculations. Yes – I'm late. Oh, shit! Who's the father – Enzo or Xavier? What a mess! I scroll back a month. It's Xavier. I had a period while Enzo was away on his jaunt. I let the phone slip out of my hand onto the bed while I process the information. Did we use a condom? I don't remember; I'd had too much to drink. What am I going to do? I allow myself to wallow in self-pity for a while then make myself decent and go back downstairs to face the consequences.

Thankfully, the coast is clear, and there's a note on the kitchen table from Xavier.

Your guests 'ave gone to ze village to see ze monument, and I've gone to collect Henri, ze goat farmer. I saw it in ze diary. Speak later.

I force myself to eat a slice of toast and try to formulate a plan, but nothing sensible comes to mind. "Okay Laura, pull yourself together and think!" I say to myself. First of all, I need to find out officially. Yes, I'll go and buy a pregnancy test. Hmm, I can't risk going into the village; everyone will know by lunchtime, and I don't want to bump into my guests. No, I'll drive to town. I can get there and back before midday when Henri arrives. After parking my car, I find myself wandering the streets, noticing so many young women with babies and toddlers; will that be me next year? I hope not. I'm way too young to become a mother, a single mother at that; that was never in my grand plan! Not that I had much of one. I suppose I expected to stay in Leeds, working as a nurse, possibly get married and have two point four children. Look at me now! I own a Chateau and business in the south of France. I can't look after a baby! I stand and look at my reflection in a shop window, I don't look any different. "Okay, you can't put this off any longer, Laura."

Taking a deep breath, I open the pharmacy door and walk in. It's surprisingly busy; more women with pushchairs blocking the isles. I slowly walk up and down, checking the shelves while making sure I don't recognise anyone in the shop, then find the pregnancy tests next to the condoms. Ironic. Now I'm confronted with my next obstacle; not just one test kit, no, that would be too simple. Several different types sit neatly in a row. Tests that you can use before you miss a period, ones that show lines, dots, or a plus and minus sign. Digital and non-digital, and one that gives you the result in writing. So confusing. I thought all you had to do was pee on a small stick and wait a few minutes! After much consideration, I choose the one that gives the result in writing, surely that must be the least confusing. With my selection placed in the bottom of my wire basket, I stride over to the till. Fantastic! It closes in front of me, and I'm asked to go and pay at the pharmacy counter, where there are three people before me. I make my way over and stand in the queue, anxiously waiting for my turn, so I can get home and do the deed. It might only be a tummy upset from the pizza, or I could be stressed out, which would mess with my body's natural rhythms. Fingers crossed.

"Hello, I thought it was you; how are you?" A voice behind me says; one with a distinct Scottish accent. Oh, shit! What am I going to do? I can't turn and let him see my now crimson face. Shall I make a dash for the door? Then what? Come back later? The next person in the queue is called to the counter. I'll pretend I didn't hear him; he might go away. "Hi, Laura," he says as he steps forward and stands beside me. "I don't blame you for ignoring me after the way I left you at the ice-cream parlour; I owe you an apology."

"Oh, erm, Enzo, hello, how are you?"

"I've just been bitten by a stray dog, that's the thanks you get for trying to help. I've picked up a prescription for some antibiotics – just in case. What about you?" He asks, then looks into my basket. "Oh…"

Why does this always happen to me? I could do with the floor swallowing me up, again! It's the second time today, and it's only eleven-fifteen.

"Don't worry – it can't be yours," I say curtly while turning away.

"Are you sure?" He asks, trying to look at my face.

"Positive," I respond, avoiding eye contact.

"Next," the pharmacist shouts. At last! I scurry forwards, pay for my purchase, and try to make my escape.

Enzo is quicker than me. As I turn away from the counter, he takes hold of my wrist and says, "I'm here if you need me."

I lift my head and reply, "Thanks, but I don't."

I make it back to my car and sit with my head in my hands. Why, oh why, did I have to meet him? Why didn't I think of an excuse? I could have said that it was for a guest or a friend. Because it was a common excuse – he wouldn't have believed me. Oh, my God! What if he tells someone? No, he wouldn't do that, would he? He's a professional. I sit back and try to imagine a baby with his ginger hair and piercing blue eyes. Cute. The next thing I see is the same baby with wavy brown hair and chocolate eyes. "Oh Laura, stop torturing yourself – go home and do the test; all of this agonising may well be for nothing. A storm in a teacup."

Harry's black hire car is parked at the front door. Damn, I'm not going to be able to escape for a while. How much longer do I have to suffer the torture of not knowing? "Hello, Harry," I say as I put my bags down in the hall. "Would you like some lunch?"

"No, thank you, we got something in the village," he says, presenting me with a bunch of roses. "Erm, sorry about earlier – Mum no longer seems to have a brain to mouth filter. Sorry if she embarrassed you."

"Think nothing of it, I understand; it must be difficult for you," I reply. Distracted by a noise outside, we both look up, "It's Xavier with Henri, I'll put the kettle on. Make yourselves comfortable in the drawing room." I head for the safety of the kitchen.

I carry a tray of tea and cake through to find Henri sat next to Hilda on the sofa several minutes later. Thankfully, Xavier seems to have left. "You stink, young man," Hilda says, holding her nose.

"Oh, Mother, I can't take you anywhere!" Harry says, striding over to his mother.

"Don't worry Harry, Henri can't speak a word of English," I say, as I hastily introduce Harry and Hilda to Henri. Slowly, I translate Henri's account of what he remembers of the war years, and then we move through to the library. Hilda loses interest after five minutes and sits on a tall stool in the corner, tapping her shoes together, gradually the tapping getting louder and louder.

"Mother, what are you doing?" Harry asks, his voice trailing off with a sigh.

"Look, Harry – my feet are having a fight," Hilda replies, looking pleased with herself. Harry turns and walks over to his mother.

"Would you like to take Shadow for a walk with me, Hilda?" I ask, just as Harry reaches his mother.

"Me and my shadow, strolling down the avenue…" she starts singing as she gets off the stool and follows me out of the library. I don't know how Henri and Harry are going to communicate, but they will just have to manage without me; I need some air. Hilda stands beside me in the hall and breaks wind. "Oh-ho! Let's get out of here, they usually stink!" She shouts, and trots off with Shadow in tow. I take Hilda on a tour of the farmyard and walled garden, finishing off at the orchard. "So, where's Mellor's now?" She asks, "Shall we go and find him?"

"His name is Xavier, and no Hilda, I'll see him soon enough."

"It's as much his problem as yours, you know; it takes two to tango."

"I think we should get back, what would you like for dinner this evening?"

"Ooh, sausage and mash with lots of gravy, at six o'clock," she responds, the distraction technique has worked. We arrive back as Xavier disappears down the drive with Henri. Good timing.

After dinner, I escape at last to examine this morning's purchase; the instructions suggest that its preferable to carry out the test first thing in the morning. Another sleepless night, no doubt.

40

After much tossing and turning, my alarm wrenches me from my nightmare at six-fifteen. Plenty of time. Bleary-eyed, I clamber out of bed and locate the test kit. After re-reading the instructions, I go into my shabby ensuite and pee on the device as directed, then place it on top of the toilet and walk away for the allotted time. Sitting on the side of the bed, my stomach heaves. It could just be nerves; I tell myself unconvincingly. The minutes pass by at a snail's pace as I sit and stare unmoving at the screen on my phone. One-minute left. This is it. The moment that has the potential to change the rest of my life. My phone buzzes in my hand and I look up and stare in the direction of the bathroom. I wish I could go back to bed and wake up again, pretend it was only a bad dream.

At last, my brain sends a signal to my legs, and I stand up and walk robotically into the mustard yellow bathroom; the colour alone is enough to make you feel nauseous. I can put it off no longer. I pick the offending item up and read the small word that has magically appeared. Enceinte. Oh, shit! I'm pregnant. I place it back down and wrap my arms around myself while looking in the scratched mirror. It brings little comfort. What now? My stomach decides my next action without delay, and I vomit down the toilet. This is not how I imagined my first pregnancy test; I was supposed to be in a bathroom, holding my husband's hand. He was to be the one to read the result, then sweep me up in his arms proclaiming his undying love for me. Well, at least I got one part of it right; I am in a bathroom – but the rest sucks!

Harry and Hilda seat themselves in the small dining area and read the menu, "I think we will only have cereal and toast this morning, please," Harry says, "it's not a good idea to fly after a full English."

"No problem," I reply, feeling somewhat relieved that I don't have to jostle with a pan full of dead pig.

Hilda sits playing with her napkin, remaining quiet. After a few minutes, she lifts her head and announces, "I don't want to go home."

Harry pours tea into her cup and without looking up, replies, "We don't have a choice. I'm back at work tomorrow, Mum."

"Well, I don't have to go to work, so you can collect me another day."

"You know I can't do that Mum; besides, what would you do all day here?"

"Ooh, lots of things, I can help thingamabob here," she says, pointing to me.

"It's Laura, Mum, and I think you'd be more of a hindrance than a help."

"No, I wouldn't! She told me she has a wedding booked soon – she'd be glad of the help in her condition."

"That's enough, Mum; finish your breakfast, we're leaving in an hour," Harry says sternly.

An hour later, and with my guests gone, I return to the tiny bathroom to examine the test kit in the vain hope that I read it wrong – it is in French after all. No such luck, the same unwelcome word stares back at me. I drop it into the bin, listening to the metallic clang as the lid closes. My phone, still on the bed where I left it joins in, alerting me to an incoming message. Wearily, I pad over and look at the screen. Enzo. Really?

Good morning. I hope you got the news that you wanted. I'm here if you need me. X

A kiss! How dare he? I don't think so.

None of your business sunshine!

There, that's told him! I scroll down through the other messages – nothing from Xavier. He may be a country bumpkin, but he's not stupid. I know he understood what Hilda blurted out at breakfast yesterday; his face said it all.

Slowly, I pull myself together and work my way through today's tasks; both guests rooms need to be serviced, I haven't got time to indulge in a pity-party. The workmen have now finished the third bedroom and have moved on to the next, so I need Xavier to come over to paint; not something I'm looking forward to. What am I going to say to him? "Hey Xavier, I'm going to have your baby!" Weird or what. I sit on the basket chair in the corner of the room and look out over the drive. Am I going to have this baby? I do have options; I'm only a few weeks pregnant. It's not even a baby yet – just a collection of cells. I could go to the doctor and get a small pill that would take care of my problem. Yes, that's what I'll do. I mean, no one else knows for sure – only me. I could tell Xavier that the test was negative, and he'd never know. If only I hadn't bumped into Enzo. It's none of his concern, if he persists, I can tell him it was negative too. Yes, that's what I'm going to do. Decision made. By the end of the day, I'm exhausted; the events of the last few days seem to sink in as I climb into bed and drift off into an uneasy sleep.

The next morning, Xavier arrives after tending the animals with a concerned look on his face, "Good Morning, 'ow are you feeling?"

"I'm much better now, thanks, think it was just a bug – nothing to worry about," I say.

His forehead momentarily creases into a frown as a look of confusion slowly turns into a smile; one that doesn't quite reach his brown eyes. "Zat's good. What do you need doing today?"

"I was hoping you would start painting the next bedroom, please."

"Sure," he responds, hesitating before turning to gather his tools. Was he about to say more? I don't give him a chance. I make a quick exit, not wanting to be alone with him longer than necessary. He affects me too much.

I spend the morning answering e-mails, the events company will be here next week to erect the marquee for the wedding. Thankfully, the bride, Anna, and groom, Willem, along with their small entourage are all arriving in caravans and motor homes from Holland. The campsite will be full; I do hope the weather is good. I send a quick message to Sylvie, reminding her about the wedding; she had said she would come with her mum, Rose to help. "Woah!" I say as I stand up and the room spins, I manage to grab the edge of my desk to steady myself. I take a couple of slow breaths and wait for the dizziness to pass; I really need to make an appointment with the doctor. Apart from registering when I arrived, I haven't had to visit the surgery. It's not a conversation I'm comfortable having but needs must. A short phone call later and I have my appointment booked for tomorrow morning. For some strange reason, Jenny's face pops into my head. I'll Skype her this evening, but I'm not going to tell her; it's not something I'm proud of.

"Laura, can you come up, please; we've found something," Adam shouts as his head appears over the top of the galleried landing.

"Yes, coming – what is it?"

"In here, come and have a look," Georges, his colleague calls.

I make my way into the bedroom, clambering over tools and boxes to get in, over to a hole in the floorboards. "Gosh, what is it?" I ask, peering down through it.

"It looks like an old wireless set," Georges replies.

"Wow! Pere Flory, the old priest, used to have one during the war – do you think this is it?"

"For sure, it certainly looks old enough. Adam, help me to lift it out." The two men grunt and groan as they gently retrieve the cumbersome object.

"It's much bigger than I imagined. Does it still work, I wonder?" I ask.

"I don't think so; the batteries and valves will have perished, and there will be nobody using that frequency now. It's outdated technology; fascinating though, and probably of some value," Georges says. "Where do you want it putting?"

"Oh, in the library please, if you can manage."

Adam and Georges carry it carefully down the stairs, stopping several times before reaching the safety of the museum in the library. "It will have to stay on the floor; the cabinets aren't sturdy enough to bear its weight," Adam says.

"How on earth did Pere Flory move it about?" I ask. "He didn't have a car."

"Perhaps ze General 'elped 'im, 'e 'ad transport," Xavier says from the doorway.

"Hello, I didn't see you there; Adam has found the old wireless set," I motion towards it.

"So I see, I didn't know it was still 'ere. I wonder 'ow many more secrets are 'iding in zis old building?" Xavier says, looking at me with an expression I find hard to read.

Once everyone has left for the day, and I have the Chateau to myself, I settle down to Skype Jenny. A short while later, her vibrant personality shines through her face on my screen.

"Hello, hello! How's it going up there in sunny Leeds?" I ask.

"Sunny it is not; wet and windy as usual. But you don't appear to have much of a suntan. You look a bit pasty, are you okay?"

"Sure, just overworked and stressed out; the builders unearthed a wireless set from the war, it's amazing."

"Ker-ching! Get it on eBay."

"No way, I've got it in the museum now; it will probably attract more guests – when I find the time to get a picture of it on my website, that is."

"You're working too hard; you should take a break."

"Too busy; the campsite is starting to fill up, I've got several functions booked, and the workmen working on the Chateau. I can't wait to show you the new bedrooms, they look amazing. When can you come again?"

"I'm taking a week off soon…"

"Please come down, I'll pay for your flight."

Jenny makes a sad face, "Sorry, Laura, Jacques is coming up to stay with me for a week – I'm going to show him the city life!" Wiggling her eyebrows and grinning, she continues, "Well, it will be an education for him; so different from here."

"It certainly is you never know, he might like it," I say with a grin.

"I hope so. I'm going to take Jacques to our old haunts. Talking of haunts, have you seen any more of your ghost?"

"Well, I haven't, but one of my guests did the other day; a lovely lady with Alzheimer's."

"Perhaps she was hallucinating."

"Mm, I don't think so; apparently, they had a conversation, and Aunt Mary told her things."

"What things?"

"Erm, personal things, things that no one else would know," I say, then instantly regret.

"Oh yes, what sort of personal things?"

"Erm, just things about the Chateau that Hilda couldn't possibly have known."

"Like what?"

"I can't remember exactly now." I quickly try to change the topic, "How's work?"

"Laura, what aren't you telling me?"

"Nothing! Erm, yes, the key; she knew where I'd found the key for the old bureau," I say hurriedly.

"I don't believe you," Jenny says, leaning forward in a sing-song voice. "You've got a secret; I've known you long enough to know when you're not telling me the whole truth."

"Rubbish; anyway, it's bedtime. I hope you have a fantastic time with Jacques. Miss you lots. Bye." I say, disconnecting as quickly as I can.

Oh dear, why did I think that was a good idea?

41

Hesitantly, I push open the shabby wooden door and step into the doctor's surgery; it's nothing like the health centre I'm used to in England. The first obstacle is an old, worn, stone step; how am I going to get a pushchair over that? I shake my head to get rid of the image; that is not going to be a problem. After all, that's why I'm here. Once inside, I take stock of my surroundings; a cramped, square room with an old desk placed in front of a window, which is supplying insufficient light to its dark interior.

"Hello, Mademoiselle Mackley, take a seat," a familiar lady behind the desk says. Where have I seen her before?

"Thank you," I mutter, my confidence beginning to falter.

I have no time to rehearse my prepared speech, as the doctor pokes his head out of a door in the corner, "Good morning, do come in." I glance about. There's no one else here. He must mean me. I somehow persuade my reluctant legs to move in the general direction and make it through the door, placing myself on the scratched wooden seat before me. The doctor's spectacled face looks at me in anticipation, "How may I help?"

"Erm, it's… kind of… personal," I stutter.

"Take your time," he replies.

After what feels like an eternity, I say, "I'm… erm, pregnant," while examining my hands in my lap.

A warm smile spreads across his face as he leans back in his creaking chair, "There; that wasn't too difficult, was it? Congratulations."

A surge of dismay pulses through my body and my gut convulses. The doctor doesn't understand. I should have gone to a clinic in the city. Anonymous. Efficient.

Like the sky on a windy day, his smiling face clouds over. He looks back at me in disapproval, "An accident?" My brain is currently having difficulty and is incapable of speech, so I only nod. "Okay, I don't have much experience with this situation. Give this to the receptionist on the way out, she will make an appropriate appointment for you at the hospital, is there anything else?" He grunts while scribbling a note on a piece of paper and waving it in my direction. I'm grateful that he doesn't articulate his thoughts, I'm capable of imagining them for myself: you should have known better, you are, after all a nurse. Or, how could you have been so stupid? I stand and stride the two steps to the door and leave, glad to be out of his pokey little consulting room.

My ordeal not yet over, I shuffle the few feet across to the receptionist and hand her the note. Her expression changes fleetingly, but she makes a rapid recovery. "No problem," she replies as she thumbs through a cardex on the side of her desk. "Here we are, I'll give them a ring; please take a seat." Five minutes later and I make my escape at last, with an appointment made at the hospital in four days. What am I going to do for four days? I'm met by Alice when I return.

"Where have you been?"

"Oh, I needed to pick up a few bits from the village," I say, discreetly slipping my appointment card into my trouser pocket.

"You've forgotten, haven't you?"

"Forgotten what, Alice?"

"You asked me to come and help you decorate the Chateau for the wedding; the bride and groom are spending their first night in the bridal-suite, aren't they? Then we were supposed to be icing the wedding cake that I've made for them."

"Sorry Alice; I'm here now, let's get started."

"Laura," she says, taking hold of my arm, "are you okay? You seem a little… distracted at the moment."

"Sorry, I'm fine; just too much going on at once. I'll feel much better when the workmen have finished; only one bedroom left to refurbish, then I'll have to decide what to do about mine." I say, trying to sound cheerful.

Despite keeping myself busy, the days appear to drag, but eventually, the time arrives and I'm in my Yeti driving to the city hospital. I've made the excuse that I'm going to a library to do some research for the book I intend to write about the war years. It landed on frosty ears, "Don't you think there's enough work for you here just now? Perhaps you could wait and do that in the winter when its quieter?" Alice suggested. But I told her I wanted to do it now while it was still fresh in my mind.

Eleven-twenty, it's a good job I'm early; the car park is heaving. After driving through its vast expanse several times, I sit in my car and wait in the hope that someone is bound to come out and move soon. My anxiety level increases with every passing minute; only seven more to go before my appointment, then I've got to find the correct department. Tapping my foot nervously on the floor of the car, I watch as a young couple emerges from the glass lobby with a new baby in a car seat. The woman is walking gingerly, carrying a pink balloon, while her doting partner gently places the infant into the back of a large estate car. He then waves at me, displaying an ear-splitting grin as he helps his partner into the car to sit next to their new daughter. This does nothing for my anxiety and sense of extreme guilt that seems to be creeping over me. The happy couple pulls out of the space, and I park the Yeti, trying to erase their perfect family image, with three minutes to spare.

Once inside, I locate a diagram on the wall and walk at a brisk pace, following the yellow painted line as directed. Then, out of breath, check-in on the computer screen and sit in waiting area B as instructed by the impersonal machine. Under better circumstances, I would have been eager to view my surroundings; interested in comparing this state-of-the-art new, French facility to the crumbling NHS hospital that I used to work in. But not today; I only want to get this over and done with so life can return to normal. A shiny, white door opens, and a young woman in a crisp uniform shouts my name and invites me in. This is it. No going back. Crunch time.

"Hello, Mademoiselle Mackley; first, let me check we have your correct details, then I'll do some general observations," she says. The cuff gets tighter around my arm, and the young technician looks at me with a concerned expression. "Do you usually suffer from raised blood pressure?"

"No. No, I don't – I'm feeling a little stressed. And I had to rush; parking was difficult."

"Yes, it does get busy. Just relax, and I'll try again shortly, can I get you a drink?" she says, as though this is an everyday occurrence.

Well, I suppose it is for her; I'm just another stupid young girl that behaved recklessly. A moment of passion, or was it insanity? With the absence of a response, she hurries across to the water dispenser and offers me the flimsy paper cup.

"I would drink it fast, they leak after a while," she says, before adding, "we're trying to cut down on single-use plastics," as the cuff once again strangles my arm. "That's a bit better," she continues while entering the result onto another screen.

After being weighed and measured and answering endless medical questions, I'm dispatched to the toilet to provide a sample; relieved to see that this is one single-use plastic they have retained. With the necessary tests completed, I'm asked to go and sit in waiting area C. Feeling a little numb with the whole process, I suddenly wonder why I didn't get to sit in waiting area A? What happens there that I've missed out on? I get to ponder no more, as another door opens, and this time a middle-aged lady greets me.

"Hello, I'm Amanda; I'll be doing your ultrasound scan."

"What?" I say somewhat alarmed, "I don't need a scan; that's not why I'm here."

"Don't worry, its routine procedure, we need to confirm your dates," Amanda calmly says while ushering me behind a rigid curtain. The cold gel hits my abdomen, causing a sharp intake of breath. "Sorry, it's cold," Amanda adds with a cheery smile. "It's a little early, I'm going to need to do an internal scan," she says, giving me little time to prepare for what comes next. Then I hear it. Fast and regular. A heartbeat.

I'm astonished by what my mouth says next, "Can I see it?"

"Oh, are you sure?"

"Yes."

Amanda turns the discreetly positioned screen as I hold my breath. My world stands still. A blob, only just visible, sits in the centre of the screen. "It looks like a pea," I whisper.

"About seven and a half weeks I'd say, that seems to fit in with your dates. Good," Amanda says, quickly withdrawing the probe without warning.

"Can I have a picture?" I ask sheepishly.

Amanda looks back at me, shocked, "Erm, it's not normal practice – I'll have to ask," she says, leaving me to clean myself behind the curtain. I hear the door open and close; I think she's gone.

Amanda returns as I fasten the button on my jeans, "Right, you need to go and sit in…"

"Waiting area D?" I say with as much mirth as I can conjure. But what about my picture? I decide not to ask. It was a rather ridiculous request; I'd only use it to torture myself in the future. No, not a good idea.

This time my wait is a little longer, giving me time to think. I try to concentrate on my clinical surroundings but its futile. An image of that little pea is burned forever into my retinas. My pea. Sweet Pea. Delicate, just like the flower.

"Mademoiselle Mackley." I don't respond. "Laura Mackley!" That's my name. I startle and look up to see a young man in a white coat standing at my side.

"Oh, sorry, that's me. I was miles away."

"After you," he says, gesturing towards yet another identical door. Once inside and seated, he looks into my eyes and gets straight to the point, "So, you're here requesting a termination?"

"Yes."

"Can I ask you why?" I don't answer immediately, so he continues, "You appear to be in good health…"

"I made an error – a one-night stand; I'd had too much to drink. I don't normally behave so stupidly…"

"I see. We all make mistakes at times. But now we must deal with the consequences. To be honest, Mademoiselle Mackley, I'm concerned with your request to first, look at the image of your embryo and then ask for a photograph. That's not the normal reaction of someone who wants a termination," he says, sitting forward in his chair.

"But… but I do."

"I realise this is not your home country, do you have any friends or family you could discuss this with? Is it a financial difficulty?"

"Are you a psychiatrist?" I snap.

"Yes, I work for the psychiatric team; its normal practice to be interviewed by a colleague or myself. We need to be certain that it's the best course of action, and in your case, I'm not convinced. You can't change your mind after the event."

"What, why?" I blurt out.

"For the reasons I've already explained. Here," the doctor says, handing me a small piece of card. The photograph. It's Sweet Pea. I take it from him and look at the grainy image. "Go away and come back in two weeks; if you haven't changed your mind, I will proceed."

42

I drive home with unseeing eyes, robotic, and arrive back at the Chateau on autopilot. Inside, Shadow greets me with his usual enthusiasm, a half-eaten rabbit carcass suggests that Xavier has recently left. Good, I don't feel much like speaking to him just now – or anybody for that matter. I'd assumed I would be halfway through the termination process by now; having taken the first of two tablets. That's how it was meant to go. Why did I open my mouth and ask to see it? I drop my bag and keys on the kitchen surface, where I see a note from him.

We need a meeting. Seven, here?

Oh, dear, what now? I've managed to avoid him recently. Xavier isn't usually enthusiastic about meetings; I wonder what he wants. If it were about us – personal – he would have waited until we were alone. Does Alice know?

As it happens, my fears are unfounded. Xavier sits back while Alice opens the informal meeting first, "I think I need some help with the production of chevre; we have more 'curd' than I can process on my own and it's going to waste. With another pair of hands, we could double the output."

I feel my body sag. Is that all? I was terrified that they knew where I'd been today. Unconsciously, I find myself putting a hand over my tummy in a protective gesture and remove it swiftly. Concentrate Laura, this is about work; not Sweet Pea. "Yes, I understand, I had an e-mail yesterday from a catering company asking if we would be interested in supplying cakes and pastries, I was going to decline; it would be too much work for you, Alice. Do you think Rose would be interested? She's an amazing cook."

"Xavier can't help with that side of the business, and I can't do it alone. You have too much on your hands with the camp-site and hotel side of things; can we afford to pay another member of staff?"

"I think so," I say, "if we sell more. It probably wouldn't be full-time. Rose would be perfect; do you think she'll be interested?"

"Possibly, would you like me to ask her?"

"Yes, please. You've known Rose for a long time; she might feel put on the spot if I approach her," I say. Xavier sits quietly, looking between his mother and me as we have our conversation. It dawns on me that he hasn't spoken since we began. "What do you think, Xavier?" I ask, looking into his big brown eyes that have been watching me all evening.

"Zis is not my area; I can do ze animals, vines and physical work, but not ze cooking. Rose is a good idea," he says, looking at me. With concern now etched on his face, he continues, "I am a little worried zat you are taking too much on, you 'aven't been well recently. 'Ave you been to ze doctor?"

How does he know? Has someone told him, or did he see me? What should I say now? "Actually, I have. There's nothing to worry about though, he thinks I'm possibly a bit run down; so yes, some help would be a great idea."

Xavier studies me carefully but decides to let the subject drop, "Ze workmen are on ze last bedroom, it will be better when zey 'ave gone. What 'ave you decided about your room?"

I sit and ponder for a moment; do I want to give up my big room – with a fantastic view? Like the bridal suite; we could charge more for it. "I suppose it makes economic sense to have it done while they are still here, get it out of the way. I'll ask them what they think. Any more questions or ideas?"

Xavier shakes his head and goes across to the drawing room to collect Gus, who had busied himself playing the piano while we were talking. I send an e-mail to the catering company, asking for precise details of their requirements, and the three of them head back to the farmhouse.

Once again alone, I wander aimlessly through the rooms of the Chateau, soul searching; but finding no answers. Later, sitting up in bed with a cup of weak tea, I take in the familiar, shabby surroundings. I've grown quite fond of my room. Yes, I'll be glad to see the back of the minuscule, mustard yellow shower room. I think I deserve a new ensuite if nothing else; I'll ask them to give me a quote in the morning. Not for the first time, my eyes are drawn to my bag sat on the basket chair in the corner; knowing what it contains. Sweet Pea. Should I destroy the image? What did the shrink say? *You can't change your mind after the event.* No, I'll keep it – just in case.

In the morning, Georges, the foreman, makes a call to his boss, and by lunchtime, I have my quote; it's very reasonable, and I request they place the order for my new shower room. At least I won't need to empty my room; I'll get Xavier to help me move the furniture to the side so they can get to the plumbing and electrics; it makes sense to have it re-wired at the same time. It can be decorated next winter when it's quiet. I can't stay in the bridal suite, as the wedding is looming, and it will be occupied. I'll move temporarily into one of the smaller bedrooms; it will only be for a few days. That's this afternoon's task. My phone rings just as I begin to make up the bed. "Hello Alice, what can I do for you?"

"I'm with Rose. She'd be delighted to accept your offer, but she can only work in the afternoons; does that fit in with you?"

"To be honest Alice, it's what fits in best with you, really; you'll be the one handling the orders."

"Hmm, I suppose we won't really know until we get going. When do the catering company want us to start?"

"They're sending a rep over to sample our products in two days. Can you and Rose manage that? I'll send you the list of their requirements."

"Sure – we're looking forward to it. Speak later."

Okay, on with my task. I manage to finish preparing my temporary room, just my personal items left to move when I hear Xavier shout up the stairs, "'ello, are you in?"

"Yes, in the back bedroom," I reply, meeting him on the landing. "What can I do for you?"

"I was passing and wondered if we could 'ave a tea-break togezer; in case zere was anything you wanted to discuss."

"I'm a bit busy, Xavier. I'm in the middle of moving rooms, they're starting on my bedroom tomorrow."

"I can 'elp," he says eagerly, "what is left to do?"

"Can you push the furniture to the side, so they can get the floor-boards up, please?"

"Sure," he replies, marching over to the basket chair. He picks up my bag and a pair of jeans draped over the back. "'ere," he says, handing them to me. "Oh, what's zis?" He asks, frowning. He picks up a white card off the floor. I know instantly what it is, my appointment card for the hospital. Oh, shit!

His eyes scan the object, and he hands it to me reluctantly, our fingers touching momentarily.

"Thank you," I say, tucking it into my pocket.

"You 'ave an 'ospital appointment. Why didn't you tell me?"

"Oh, it's nothing, just a check-up to be certain."

"What sort of check-up? Would you like Mama to go wiv you?"

"No thanks, I'll be fine; it's nothing. Alice will be too busy, anyway," I say, turning to carry some clothes through to my temporary room. Phew, that was too close for comfort. A moment later, I can feel him standing behind me, his steady breathing and spicy aroma filling the air. He gently puts his hands on my shoulders and turns me around.

"Don't."

"What is it, Laura? What aren't you telling me?"

He gazes into my soul. I can feel the solitary tear slip out of the corner of my eye and roll down my cheek, shortly followed by another. Calmly, he guides me towards the oversized bed, where I sit and put my head in my hands. Then the waterworks start. Quietly at first, but soon followed by sobs – big ugly ones. Xavier says nothing, only reaches over to the box of pink tissues placed artfully on the bedside cabinet; they weren't meant for me. A touch of luxury for paying guests. Patiently, he sits and waits for me to finish. It feels cathartic.

"Well?" He asks tentatively.

I blow my nose in a most un-ladylike fashion and look up at this kind man sat beside me. My breath catches in the back of my throat. I open my mouth, then close it again, making no sound. Once again, my eyes land on my bag; now on the floor in the corner of my new room.

"Xavier, please would you pass me my bag?"

He does as he's bid and places the bag on my lap, sitting back down next to me. I fumble with the clasp then put my hand inside to retrieve the photo of his child, Sweet Pea. With no words spoken, I glance at it before passing it to him. Bewildered, he takes it from me and examines the image, slowly running his finger over the surface. Several moments pass where neither of us speaks. Does he hate me now? I couldn't bear that. I know I love this big hunk of a man; I probably always have.

"Say something."

He places the photo on my knee and looks at me, "Is zis what I zink it is?"

I pick the picture back up and put it on the cabinet next to the tissues, and nod.

"Before you ask, yes, it is yours."

"I wasn't going to ask; it doesn't matter who ze fazer is. What matters is what are we going to do about it."

"I have a termination booked in two weeks," I whisper, hanging my head.

He picks up my hand and takes it to his lips, "Is zat what you want?"

"Yes… no. Oh, I don't know."

He shuffles closer and puts his protective arms around me, "I wish you could 'ave told me sooner; I would 'ave been zere for you. Do you find me so intolerable?"

"Not at all, Xavier. I would understand if you want me to get rid of it, but how am I going to run this business; a single mother with a baby?"

"You don't 'ave to be a single mozer. I asked you to marry me before; for ze wrong reasons, I know. But we 'ave both changed since zen. I said I would wait until you were ready; and when you are, I will ask again."

I take a deep breath and turn to look into his concerned face, "Yes, we have both come a long way; you were belligerent and self-opinionated, and I was clueless and naive. But I will not trap you into marriage…" He tries to interrupt me, but I continue, "It is very considerate of you, and I appreciate your offer; back in Aunt Mary's day I would have had no choice. It's like history repeating itself. But I genuinely don't know what I want now. I'm confused. When I went to the hospital, I was so sure that I wanted a termination; then I heard its heartbeat and saw its grainy image. It became real. Alive. I'm scared; what right have I to determine whether it gets a chance to live?"

"You're very tired and emotional, not in ze correct frame of mind to make ze big decision; you need ze rest. Come on, lie down and 'ave a sleep. I will bring dinner later." Bending down, he removes my shoes, before lifting me effortlessly up the bed and pulling a fleece throw over my legs. When he reaches the door, he turns and adds, "Zank you for telling me," then quietly slips away.

"What have I done?" I say out loud when I hear the front door close as my head flops against the pillow. Was it the right thing to do? Too late now. Will he tell Alice? It's her grandchild after all. No, I don't think he will. Oh, dear, what a mess!

The next thing I'm aware of is a gentle knock on the door. Where am I? This isn't my room. I stare around in confusion, the events from earlier come back into my head; yes, this is my temporary bedroom.

"Laura, are you decent?" Xavier asks from the other side of the door.

"Come in, what time is it?" I ask, leaning over to look at my phone.

"Seven, I've brought dinner."

"Gosh, I was out like a light."

"You needed ze rest; it did you good. Now you need food."

"Mm, this is really good, did you make it?"

"No, Mama," he replies between mouthfuls.

I put my knife and fork down and lean back, looking at him, "Did you tell her?"

"Absolutely not! I said you 'ad a nasty 'eadache. She wanted to come and see you, but I told 'er to wait until morning. You don't 'ave to tell 'er unless you want to, but I suggest you don't; it would break 'er 'eart if you… you know." He looks away.

"And what about you; how do you feel about it, Xavier?"

He puts his fork down and looks at me with a guarded expression, then runs his hand through his messy hair, "It is your choice, I will not put you under any pressure; but will support you, whatever you choose."

43

Xavier is incredible, as life continues at a fast pace. He hasn't once mentioned my condition, and Alice clearly isn't aware. He continues as if nothing has changed, but I can see he has; it's subtle, a glance here and a hand there. Attentive. The days are marching on, and I know crunch time is getting close. It helps to keep busy. Anna and Willem's wedding was beautiful; I didn't get much sleep that night, with the noise coming from the bridal suite on the other side of the landing! The meeting with the catering company went well; we've secured a contract for six months. Alice tells me that Rose's next-door neighbour, Madam Morel, is also interested in some extra work to fit alongside her part-time job as a receptionist. She's coming for an interview this afternoon.

The chimes of my newly installed doorbell echo in the hall and inform me of Madam Morel's arrival. My first ever interview. Wearing a sky-blue polo-shirt with our logo embroidered on the front, I answer the door with a cheerful smile on my face. It's swiftly replaced by shock; Madam Morel is the doctor's receptionist, the one that made my appointment for the termination. Shit!

"Mademoiselle Mackley, it's good of you to see me," she says confidently.

"Erm… ahh… Hello, you work at the doctor's," I stutter.

"Yes, and what happens in the doctor's surgery stays there. I'm not at liberty to discuss anything about our patients; I've signed non-disclosure documents. So, shall we start again?" She holds out her hand in a very English manner, "Hello, I'm Yvette Morel, I'm here about the part-time job. Thank you for seeing me."

"Hello, Yvette. Welcome. Do come in," I say, feeling slightly bemused.

The interview goes surprisingly well after the shaky start. I like Yvette; I'm sure she'll fit in well with Alice and Rose. And boy, can she bake! During her interview, she produced a small cake out of a tin, saying, "Here's one I prepared earlier." She has a sense of humour, too. And she can speak English. That's a bonus! Yvette agrees to a month's trial.

I move my possessions back into my newly refurbished bedroom now that the builders have finally finished. It's been a long haul, but worth it. It still needs painting. Xavier offered to do it for me this week, but under the circumstances, I've decided to leave it for now. There's no rush. It's almost like he's looking for every possible excuse to be at the Chateau; not that he says much when he is. No, I don't want his company this evening; or anybody else's either. Jenny has just text me and asked me to Skype, but I made up a suitable excuse. I want solitude.

Now I'm sat on my balcony, enjoying a glass of cold lemonade, watching the sun gradually dip below the horizon. This is it. Decision time. What am I going to do about Sweet Pea? I prevent myself from putting a protective hand on my still flat abdomen. I've purposefully managed to sweep it under the carpet until now; but not for much longer. My appointment is tomorrow. Where have the last two weeks gone? I expected them to be hell, a living nightmare, but I felt so much better after telling Xavier. He has a calming influence. I haven't trawled the internet for information like I would normally. It feels surreal; like it's not happening to me. I've found myself wondering about Aunt Mary; she wouldn't have had the option of termination, and I somehow doubt that she would have chosen that route if she had. No, she adored children; that much is evident from her brief but infrequent visits. Is she here now, looking down on me? I'm sure I'm a disappointment to her, sometimes I get the feeling that I'm not alone. I pick up my phone and re-read the text that Xavier sent earlier.

Would you like me to come with you tomorrow?

I haven't replied. Should I? He has been supportive, and it is his child. Yes, I ought to respond.

No, but thank you.

My phone pings as he replies immediately.

Ze offer still stands if you change your mind.

He's a great guy; I hope he finds someone special.

The next morning, I'm up in good time and stand under my new shower longer than necessary, enjoying the decadence of its rainforest head. Bliss. I then stand naked in front of my full-length mirror; do I look any different? My breasts are tender, and I still feel nauseous, but no other symptoms. I stand sideways, trying to detect a bump, but I can't see one. I torture myself and have one last peek at the photo. I know I should have destroyed it. I will when I get back. After weak tea and a slice of toast, I can procrastinate no longer and walk with lead boots to my Yeti.

I drive out of the village, down familiar roads but I don't notice the children walking to school, laughing with their friends, or holding tight to their mothers' hand. Nor do I see the grass verges, smothered with the blooms of wildflowers. The road works on the autoroute go unnoticed too; my head is otherwise engaged. It's busy watching the memories passing before my eyes; as though I'm in a trance or daydream of some type.

First, the letter, it's crisp white paper and sturdy envelope, informing me that I'd inherited a Chateau in France. The endless journey here. Being met by Monsieur Bertrand, followed by my first glimpse of the crumbling building. How could I forget that initial encounter with Xavier? That was something else, processing down my drive with Gus and a troop of goats and donkeys. I can laugh now, though I felt more like crying at the time. Yes, it's been a challenge; ups and downs. Would I swap what I have now for the life I used to live in England?

A beeping horn breaks my trance, and I look up to find myself once more in the busy hospital car park. I'm blocking in a car that's trying to reverse out of a tight spot. Can I get the Yeti into it? Only one way to find out. I make it on the third attempt, with little room to squeeze out of the door; it's a good job I'm thin. Once again, I'm transported in time – forwards this time; I try to imagine what it would feel like to be heavily pregnant. I close my eyes and conjure up an image: I'm wearing a pair of blue dungarees sporting a large bump. I quickly shake my head to rid myself of the picture and enter the hospital, following the same yellow line. The computer screen directs me to wait in area D; I should have known. I sit for a few minutes before the same door opens, and this time, an older lady pops her head out and calls my name. I try to stand, but my legs don't seem capable of movement.

"Miss Mackley?" She asks as she walks over to me, introducing herself, but I don't catch her name.

"Yes," I say, still sat in my seat.

"Would you like to come through?"

"I'm not sure?" I reply, my voice turning it into a question.

"You don't have to be sure, would you like to come in for a chat?" I nod. Eventually, my legs respond, and I follow her into her bright, white room. "Take a seat," she continues. "How have you been?"

"Busy."

"That's good," she says, hesitating before asking, "what have you been busy doing?"

"Refurbishing my home, which is also my business; just busy," I say shrugging, an image of Xavier performing the same shrug immediately pops into my mind and I smile; it's one of his many traits that I've come to know so well.

"You told me earlier that you weren't sure; what is it you're not sure about?"

"Erm – all of it really. I need more time," I whisper, looking over to the door that I've just come through.

"That's not a problem; you've got two more weeks, but after that, your options would be limited," she says, handing me a card with another date for two weeks hence, written neatly again in black ink.

"Thank you," I say, taking it from her then striding for the door. I need air; fresh air. I crave the verdant countryside, I want to feel the sun on my face in the walled garden, and watch the fruit swelling in the orchard, children having fun on the campsite. What am I doing here? Continuing to walk, with a sense of urgency quickening my pace, and keeping to the yellow line, I burst out into the sunshine. A feeling of relief floods through my veins. I take a lungful of the city air and the urge to get away intensifies. My legs, now feeling lighter, propel me to my car. I climb in and drive, no looking back this time.

With the city and its misery behind me, I pull into a village where I stop to buy an ice-cream. My taste buds seem to dance as the combination of flavours roll over my tongue. It's the best thing I've tasted for weeks. I sit on the bench a little longer and watch the few natives going about their business; an older couple tends their vegetable plot together, working in harmony. A young woman is pushing a giggling toddler on a swing in the small play area.

I reach into my pocket and take out my appointment card and examine the neat handwriting. A smile creeps slowly, first to the corner of my mouth. I place a protective hand over Sweet Pea as the smile spreads across the rest of my face. Decision made. I feel radiant. Standing, I rip the small card into four pieces, dropping it ceremoniously into the bin at the side of the bench. I know that I won't be going back.

It's only when I reach the safety of my Chateau – home, that I think about Xavier. What am I going to say to him? He has never once asked me not to go through with the termination; what if he doesn't want to be involved? What about Alice, will she hate me? Will she think I've tried to trap him? People will assume its Enzo's; he'll be back home in Scotland by the time I'm showing. It's none of their business anyway. It's between Xavier and me, and if he's not interested, I'll do it by myself. I know I can do this; I've come so far, conquered so much. Sweet Pea is mine.

The photo. I have a compelling urge to see the image. Upstairs, I open the bottom drawer and extract it from its sanctum; the only person I was hiding it from was me. I run my finger over its surface and hold it close to my chest, before propping it up against the lamp at the side of my bed. My eyes scan the room;

now seeing things differently, clearly, for the first time. I picture a small crib, gently rocking in the corner and smile. There's plenty of room in this Chateau for a family. My stomach grumbles, reminding me I need to eat; it's the first time I've felt hungry for ages.

After lunch, my phone pings. Xavier. My heart leaps, as I read the words.

I saw your car, 'ow are you feeling, would you like me to come over?

What's going through his mind, relief, or regret? He will assume that I've taken the first pill. What should I tell him? Nothing. Today is about me. I need space and time to come to terms with my decision. I'm going to take the rest of the day off. I'll take Shadow and have a leisurely walk through the estate, visiting all my favourite places, which change according to the time of year. In winter, I like the olive trees, old and wise, like sentinels in the snow and ice. It must be the orchard in spring, covered in frothy blossom, fringed with wildflower meadows – or the farmyard, bleating with new life. Summer, that's easy – the pond, it's surface like a mirror as the swifts and swallows dart across, catching insects for their young. Autumn, the season of mellow fruitfulness, winemaking time, and truffles. So, the answer to the question I asked myself earlier – would I swap what I have now for the life I used to live in England? Easy. No way!

No, thank you, can we talk tomorrow?

***

www.emma-sharp-author.com

ABOUT THE AUTHOR

Emma Sharp is the author of The Chateau Trilogy comprising of: The Letter, Sweet Pea and Secrets and Surprises. She is currently working on her latest novel, Innocence in Provence, which will be available in late 2020.

Emma, a former nurse was born and raised in Yorkshire. She has two grown up daughters, a grand-daughter and a much-loved French Bulldog, Nellie. She loves to travel and finds that she writes her best work when she's at her caravan amidst the stunning scenery of the Yorkshire Dales.

She has also appeared on local radio reading her short stories and is as a member of a writing group, who meet regularly to review and appraise each other's work.

I hope you enjoy reading her novels.

Printed in Dunstable, United Kingdom